Leaving FREEDOM

Also by Sharon L. Dean

The Deborah Strong Mysteries:

The Barn

The Wicked Bible

Calderwood Cove

Other novels:

Finding Freedom

Six Old Women and Other Stories

Leaving FREEDOM

SHARON L. DEAN

Encircle Publications
Farmington, Maine U.S.A.

Encircle editor: Cynthia Brackett-Vincent

Cover design by Deirdre Wait
Cover images © Getty Images

Published by:

Encircle Publications
PO Box 187
Farmington, ME 04938

info@encirclepub.com
http://encirclepub.com

For Sheila, who stayed,
and
Rod, who came back.

Contents

PART IV ~ RELEASE

PART V ~ THE JOURNEY FORWARD

PART I

Leaving the Dead Behind

Chapter 1

Early June 1973

Connie wiped her sweaty palm on a mini skirt that clung to her hips. The temperature was high for June in Massachusetts, as if the weather gods were preparing her for her move to Florida. Even the gravestone they stood in front of seemed to be sweating. Sarah, an inch taller and twenty pounds lighter than Connie. The mini skirt would have flattered her sister. Hannah, their mother, who held their arms while she cried for her dead husband.

Sarah's daughter Lizzie put a bouquet of dandelions on her grandfather's grave. Connie read the inscription. Samuel Mattson Lewis, March 4, 1912 – January 24, 1973. Dead just six months ago in an unseasonably warm January. Hannah's own name waited beneath it. Hannah Anderson Lewis, January 20, 1914 – .

"I miss Grandpa." Lizzie pointed with her free hand to graves that covered the cemetery's hill. "Are these all our relatives?" Lizzie's dandelions were already wilting on the newest stone.

"Just some of them." Connie took Lizzie's hand and squeezed it as if she could protect her niece. She read sorrow on the headstones in the family plot. Three baby girls dead a century ago in a scarlet fever epidemic that swept through Freedom, Massachusetts. Molly Davis Anderson, 1879 – 1939. Hannah's mother, whose husband disappeared shortly after Hannah was born. No stone marked a grave for Hannah's brother Charlie. Connie knew only that Uncle Charlie ran off when Hannah was twelve.

Charles Jarvis Anderson. The name shrouded in a secret Hannah refused to share.

Connie felt in her whole body the genes from her mother's family. Depression for Molly. Something unspoken for Charlie. Hannah battled her depression with so many pills, Connie worried that her mother didn't remember how much Valium she'd taken in a day.

She imagined a gravestone for herself. Constance Lewis. July 7, 1943. No middle name. No death date. Wherever she died, she wanted it to be away from the town she found too insulated.

Lizzie moved away from Connie and ran along the grass that separated the rows of gravestones. The robin she was chasing escaped with a worm into a maple tree.

Hannah, gray-haired, painfully thin, wearing a calf-length skirt that made her look a decade older than fifty-nine, reached for Lizzie's sad bouquet. She kissed it, knelt, and placed her forehead on Sam's stone.

Sarah paced behind her. Sarah's tragedy had a lining as gold as the artificial color of her hair. She was a widow with a young child, free of her husband George, who came back from the Vietnam War carrying memories as suffocating as the jungle he fought in.

Connie joined Lizzie, who was searching out letters of the alphabet on the tombstones. Lizzie began the litany of a five-year-old. "Why did they put Grampy's box in the ground?" "Isn't it dark?" "Isn't he scared?" "He's been there a long time."

"Just a few months. Your mummy and Granny are saying goodbye to him now. You're going on a long plane trip tomorrow, remember? All the way to Italy."

"Why aren't you and Granny coming? I want you to stay with me."

"You'll have a special tutor with you. James. We're going to Florida. You remember when you visited there last year."

"Can I visit again?"

"Of course. Your mummy will want to see us."

"But we won't see Grampy, right?"

"Right. He died."

"That's why he's in the ground. I hope he isn't scared of the dark."

"When a person dies, fear dies with him. So Grampy is resting peacefully. Like he's asleep."

This was enough for Lizzie. She pulled Connie back to the grave.

Sarah stopped pacing. "Mum, it's time. We want to plant flowers at George's plot, too, and we'll have just enough time for lunch before Elizabeth and I leave for Boston."

Hannah struggled to stand. "I don't know why you want to stay overnight in some hotel when you could stay with Connie and me."

Sarah steadied their mother. "You sold the house, cleaned most of it out. You're leaving next week. You don't need extra company."

Hannah's response surprised Connie. "I sold the house? Then I guess it's your last chance to sleep in your old bedroom."

"I have to leave my car at the dealership that's buying it. James and I need to use tomorrow before our flight to get books for Lizzie."

"Child should be in school, not wandering around Europe with a tutor."

Connie stopped them before one of their arguments began. "Europe will be good for Lizzie."

Lizzie started to cry. "I want to stay with Granny and Aunt Connie."

Connie bent to hug her. "You'll be seeing the whole world. When you come back, you can tell us about it."

They walked together to Sarah's Mercedes. Connie got in the back seat with Lizzie. She kept her arm around her.

The sun was marking noon when they drove into the newer cemetery where George's family was buried. The grass was green with the spring rains and each of the plots evenly mowed. Like George's, a few graves displayed American flags and most were shaded by oaks or maples. This was a park more than a cemetery, a place where the living were supposed to find the peace of the dead. Connie hated it. It reeked of tombstones announcing their cost and the importance of the deceased who lay beneath them. She preferred the simplicity of the graveyard they just left. Stones that were old, some dating to the seventeenth century, many covered with lichens, and none of them polished to an unnatural sheen.

Sarah handed her a geranium and a trowel. "Will you do the digging? I have to wear these pants tomorrow on the plane and I don't want to get them dirty."

Connie knelt to do the planting, feeling the still-wet grass on her knees. She pressed hard on the trowel to loosen the dirt. Hard like the cruelty that killed George after he survived a year fighting a meaningless war.

Connie murmured, "Goodbye, George." When she stood, she saw that Sarah was at the car with Lizzie. Hannah was looking at the grave through a brim of tears. "I miss George. So did your father. He was a good man. Sarah's lucky."

"Lucky?"

"She has a lifetime ahead of her. She'll find another George."

"I'm not sure she wants to. You're still young, Mum. Maybe there's romance in your future."

"I could never do that. Sarah's a different generation and I'm not like her."

Hannah would wear her sorrow as she'd been wearing it for the last six months. "Until death do us part" wasn't the right phrase for her. She'd pledged her troth until death reunited husband and wife.

"I'm sorry, Mum. We have to leave."

When they reached the car, Lizzie said she wanted to go to that diner place. Sarah opened the car door. "Zach's. That's where I met your father."

"He won't be there 'cause he's dead. Grampy's dead, too. I think they're not afraid 'cause they're together. When it's dark, they can hold hands."

"That's a beautiful idea. And eating at Zach's is also a great idea," said Connie. As they drove toward the diner, she watched memories streak by. The Congregational church where the Catholic kids couldn't attend the youth group dances. The park where she and her friend pushed their doll carriages and had tea parties in the grass. The wood-framed school that once housed eight grades and was now town offices. The high school where Connie worked with George on the school newspaper had been turned into a junior high a dozen years ago.

In high school, Connie had a crush on George. They dreamed of becoming journalists. George complained that every time he mentioned going away to school his father pressured him to stay local. In the end, George, entangled with Sarah whose blond hair and size 36C eclipsed Connie's brains, agreed. They married as soon as he graduated from the local college. When he was shipped to Vietnam in 1968, Sarah went to Zach's every

Friday and Saturday and played the role of worried spouse. Connie moved to Boston and joined the peace protests. She thought Sarah half-wanted George to be killed so she could play a new role. The grieving widow. She got that role four years later.

When they passed the road to Sarah and George's old house, she asked if Sarah wanted to drive by it.

"No, I never liked that house. That's why I sold it and moved into the mill condo."

Returning from Vietnam, George fought demons by overseeing the renovations to the cotton mill he inherited from his parents, turning the sturdy nineteenth-century construction into condos and shops and a restaurant. The renovations had just been completed when a train hit the truck he was driving and he was killed instantly. Connie suspected that he had driven his truck purposely into the oncoming train. The railroad company could have fought the insurance claim, but it preferred a quiet, non-public settlement out of court. Sarah exchanged a damaged husband for a generous liability settlement.

Sarah kept her eyes fixed on the road, not even glancing toward the house. "I think of George and me in high school much more than I think of being married to him. I wonder why."

"Remember the night you met him?" said Connie. "I had just gotten my driver's license and we finally talked Mum and Dad into letting us go to Zach's. Two hours, they said. One to get there and back and one to have something to eat."

"I remember. It was your senior year, I was a sophomore and we were late coming home because you introduced me to George. We kept ignoring the waitress when she came for our orders. English muffins. That's what we always had."

"You kept ignoring her. I kept looking at my watch. And I'm the one who couldn't take the car again for a whole month."

"I should say I'm sorry. I knew we'd be late. But I'm not sorry. I was already half in love with him."

"Half? You dated him because you knew I liked him."

"Don't go there, Connie. He was a good man, a great father. He just turned out to be rather boring. Until Vietnam. He came back crazy."

Connie checked the back seat. Hannah had fallen asleep. Lizzie was concentrating on her coloring, not listening. "But he loved you."

"I know. And I would have stayed with him. But now I'm free to go where I want to go. Do what I want to do."

"And Lizzie?"

"She'll be fine. Remember, she has a tutor. James will take care of her. She'll learn more than we ever did in the Freedom schools."

"Just watch out for her."

"What's that mean? Is there something wrong with wanting to leave this place?"

"Nothing at all." In exchange for Sarah's share of the money their father left them, Connie would wilt in the Florida heat, chained to a mother stalked by depression.

"You'll like Florida. I'll send you postcards. Florence. Paris. The Eiffel Tower. London. Is it Westminster Abbey?"

Connie added to the list. "St. Paul's. The British Museum. Canterbury. Oxford. Stratford."

"Stop, please. Stratford. Shakespeare. I know. God, how I hated English class."

They drove into Zach's almost full parking lot. Freedom's teenage gathering place had been around for forty years. When it was built, the land behind it pastured cows that provided the restaurant with milk and cheese and butter. The original metal diner had been transformed with a brick façade and a tasteless turquoise sign. It was surrounded by asphalt, a gas station on one side, an ice cream stand framed by more asphalt on the other. Across the street was a liquor store, a real estate office, a bank. There wasn't a tree in sight.

Sarah didn't wait, so Connie woke their mother and lifted Lizzie from the back seat. Lizzie hugged her. "I love you, Aunt Connie."

"And I love you, too, Lizzie. Here, give me your hand and we'll catch up to Mummy. Your hand, too, Mum."

Inside, Zach's hadn't changed since Connie graduated from high school twelve years ago. The same counter for solo diners. The same booths with the same miniature juke boxes. They used to crowd eight and ten people into booths built for four. They went to the back room where a mirror was supposed to make it seem bigger. Connie saw her reflection, her knees with grass stains on them, a body heavier than Sarah's. She wasn't beautiful like her sister, didn't have long hair, blond from a bottle that looked natural. But Connie's John Lennon glasses made her look more hip than bookish. Lizzie could be her daughter, the same dark hair cut short, the same solid build.

Sarah stood at a nearby table talking animatedly. Connie joined her while Hannah and Lizzie slid into a booth. She pretended to be interested as Sarah reminded her, "Connie, you remember Brenda and Susan. We were cheerleaders together. And this is Paul Gifford. They were in my class, but I'm sure you remember him. He played football. He works at Dad's old hardware store."

Connie said "of course" and asked the obligatory what-are-you-doing questions. They all lived in town. They all came to Zach's on Wednesdays for lunch together. The two women kept their hair blond with a bottle and wore tight sweaters and mini skirts that reminded Connie of their old cheerleading uniforms. A decade older now, they still looked good.

"Can't beat the corned beef sandwiches," Paul said. Connie felt better about her own extra pounds when she saw that he'd grown heavy, if not fat. He was drinking a lunchtime beer.

Susan said she was sorry about George. Brenda was more truthful. "How amazing that you're going to Europe. I'd love to go there but I can't get Andy to stop working long enough to take a vacation. Besides, whenever we have time, we go to the lake." Connie remembered that Brenda married Andy Therrien and his house on Lake Winnipesaukee. Not a bad trade for Europe if she could put up with Andy's ego.

Sarah touched Connie's arm. "My sister's going to Florida with my mother. Going to write a novel."

Brenda put on her cheerleader smile. "We always said you should be a writer. Just don't put us in your novel."

Connie was tempted to tell Brenda that whoever she meant by "us" wouldn't be interesting enough. Instead, she said, "I won't" and went to join her mother and Lizzie.

"I love Zach's," Sarah said when she sat down at their table. "There's always someone here who remembers me and George. Brenda even remembered the gown I wore to the senior prom. If George hadn't already graduated we would have been king and queen."

Connie drank from a glass of water. "You remember your prom dress? I can't even remember my date. Or maybe I didn't go at all."

"Stan Plummer, the nerdiest guy in your class."

"Ouch. Don't remind me. I had a horrible time. He was a lousy dancer and all he could talk about was how much he was going to miss his physics class."

Sarah glanced at the menu. "Did you like the class?"

"Never took it. The football coach taught it and even then I knew he hated women."

Lizzie had been squirming and finally interrupted. "Was your dress beautiful, Mummy?"

"It certainly was. Strapless. Pink with roses all along the skirt. I think I starched six petticoats to go under that dress. I still have it hanging with my wedding dress in the condo closet. I'll show it to you when we come back from Europe."

"I want to see it today."

"Sorry, Lizzie, no time. We'll buy even more beautiful dresses when we're in Europe."

A waitress saved Connie from saying something about the glory days. Hannah hadn't spoken since they sat down. She'd been staring out the window. When the waitress asked her a second time what she'd like to eat, she turned and said, "The fish chowder, please. It's always so good here."

The waitress looked puzzled.

"I'm sorry, ma'am. We don't have any chowder. How about a nice bowl of chili like your daughter's having?"

"Don't you always have fish chowder?"

Sarah grabbed Hannah's menu and handed it with the others to the waitress. "That's the Paramount Lounge, Mum. It closed a few years ago, remember?"

"Sometimes I get confused when it's been a hard day. Chili is fine."

Connie reached across the table and touched her mother's hand. "One more week, Mum, and we'll be driving to Florida. It'll be a whole new life. A whole new adventure." She wished she believed this.

Sarah continued to reminisce about Zach's and high school. The teacher they called Swish because her nylons swished together when she walked. The Latin teacher who cried every Ides of March over Caesar's death. The physics-teaching football coach who came to Zach's with the team after every home game. The waitress named Bertha who always snuck them an extra hit of syrup in their cherry Cokes. "I wonder what happened to Bertha," said Sarah. "She had a crush on George."

This was one of the rare bits of gossip Connie knew. "Rumor says she was fired for propositioning the football players."

Sarah turned her head so Lizzie couldn't hear her whisper, "I wonder if she ever slept with one of them. Not George. He would have told me."

"What would Daddy have told you?" Lizzie asked.

Sarah was saved from answering by the arrival of their food. Between bites she continued her monologue. She was interrupted several times by someone she knew in high school coming into the diner. Each time she climbed over Connie to hug a person trying to look eighteen instead of twenty-eight.

It was after one thirty when they paid the bill and Sarah hustled them into her car and back to the mill condo. James was waiting at the door with his suitcase. He looked Italian. Dark, dressed in a leather jacket, he reminded Connie of Al Pacino in *The Godfather*. He helped Sarah give a last minute check of the condo and wrestled half a dozen pieces of luggage into the trunk. Sarah hadn't mastered the art of packing lightly.

"I guess this is it," Sarah said. "Lizzie, give Granny and Aunt Connie a big hug and kiss. We won't be seeing them for a long time."

Lizzie started to cry. She hugged her grandmother then clung to Connie until Sarah pulled her away. "That's enough, Lizzie. Florence is waiting." Sarah motioned James into the Mercedes then sat Lizzie in the back seat. She turned to her mother, hugged her and said, "I'll send postcards from all over Europe."

Hannah gave Sarah an extra squeeze before getting into Connie's car.

Sarah pulled Connie to her, kissed her lightly on both cheeks. "You'll take good care of Mum. I don't need to worry." She got into the driver's seat of the Mercedes and closed the door. As she pulled away, Connie waved. Sarah didn't notice.

When Connie got into the Chevy that would get her and her mother to Florida, Hannah said, "I'm glad I have two daughters."

PART II

Secrets

Chapter 2
Late June 1973

Connie closed her suitcase and rolled up her sleeping bag. She loved the wood floor in her childhood bedroom but sleeping on it last night, she wished for plush carpeting. Only the wall light her father installed over her desk showed that she once lived in the now empty room. She touched the light as she left and looked into Sarah's room at the telephone jack next to where her sister's bed had been. Sam's gifts the Christmas when they were becoming teenagers marked how well he understood his daughters. A phone that would connect Sarah to the world. A desk and a light that would give Connie a place to retreat from it.

She stepped into her mother's bedroom. Hannah was pulling a T-shirt on over a gash on her stomach. Connie dropped her suitcase and sleeping bag. "Mum, what happened? What's that cut?"

"It's nothing."

"Let me look at it. We don't want it getting infected on our trip."

Hannah arranged her T-shirt with its printing that announced Freedom, Massachusetts. "I took care of it. Let's just go before I break down." She lifted her suitcase and pushed Connie aside.

Connie shook off the glimpse of her mother's injury. Hannah had taken care of enough of her daughters' cuts and bruises to be able to take care of her own. She balanced Hannah's sleeping bag with her own and with her suitcase, ignoring the banister as she descended the stairs. Every room held reminders of Sam's tinkering. Bookcases in the living room surrounding the fireplace, a shelf for photographs in the den, a hand-crafted cabinet over a porcelain sink in the bathroom. Once he made a mantle with a thick piece of pine, its bark still attached. A year later they heard sounds coming from within the wood. Eventually a bug burrowed its way out, leaving a perfectly round hole. Connie had been studying *Walden* in high school and told everyone who came into the house about Thoreau's description of a bug burrowing out of some apple wood.

Hannah stood sobbing next to the kitchen counter where she dropped her house keys. Connie took a tissue from the box that sat on top of their picnic cooler. She handed it to her mother. "You love Florida. You have more friends there now than you have in Freedom."

"Sam isn't there."

"He isn't here either."

Hannah blew her nose. Connie held out a plastic bag filled with their last bit of trash. Hannah dropped in the tissue. "Thank you, Sarah." Connie didn't correct her.

Outside the car waited in the shadow of the maple tree they nicknamed Molly for Hannah's mother. The 1970 Chevy Impala, white and multiple steps down from Sarah's black Mercedes, would get them to Florida. Connie unlocked it and set the cooler on the back seat next to a pot of lilac shoots Hannah insisted they needed to plant in Florida. The car smelled earthy and familiar. Hannah got in while Connie walked to the end of the driveway to deposit the trash bag in the can that would be emptied later in the day, their last disposable items hauled off to a smoldering pit. When she got into the car, Hannah's crying started with the start of the engine. Connie pushed the tissue box to her. It was going to be a long trip.

Hannah napped as they drove west through Massachusetts and south through Connecticut. She kept the cut on her stomach hidden. Connie watched for any sign of fever and reminded herself that her mother never bared her body in front of her children. When they crossed the border into New York, Hannah woke up. "I wonder if my brother Charlie came this way when he left Freedom."

All Connie knew about Charlie was that he ran off when Hannah was thirteen. Charles Anderson, the name shrouded in a secret Hannah refused to share.

"Do you think he went south? He might still be alive."

"He's not."

"What happened? You never talk about him."

"I loved him and he left. That's all you need to know." Hannah changed the subject as she always did if Connie asked about Charlie. "Your father and I honeymooned in Niagara Falls. I thought you'd marry George. Did you ever sleep with him?"

"No."

"When he married Sarah did you mind?"

"I got over it." Connie had no intention of talking to her mother about her sex life. She'd done some heavy petting with her college boyfriend, Solomon, but he always stopped before intercourse. He didn't want her to become pregnant, he said. In college, they directed their energy into the Civil Rights movement and the March on Washington in 1963. It awakened her to the power of social protest. She wasn't surprised when Solomon announced that he was joining the priesthood.

Her only lover had been David, the jazz musician she dated

when she lived in Boston. She never told Hannah or Sarah about him. He dodged the draft with a fake medical record, marched with her in protests against the Vietnam War, and smoked too much pot. In the end, Connie tired of him. He rejected pacifism and adopted a violent anti-war position that seemed illogical to her. He played music all night, slept all day, and never exercised.

Hannah mentioned Charlie again when they were in Hershey, Pennsylvania, overdosing on dark chocolate. "Charlie always gave me a chocolate Santa for Christmas."

"What did you give him?"

"I was young. I don't remember."

Hannah was still talking about Charlie when they drove into Harper's Ferry the next day. The weather was glorious, the hills carrying no scars from John Brown's raid and the bloody deaths of ten of his men. Hannah's knowledge of the raid surprised Connie until she remembered that her mother majored in history, even taught high school for a few years before Connie and Sarah were born.

In Savannah, they ate lunch at Mrs. Wilkes' Dining Room. Heavy, oily, and oh so southern. Family style platters of fried chicken and ribs and bowls of okra and collards and black-eyed peas. They ate so much they nearly fell asleep on their walking tour of the city.

"My brother Charlie was in the war," Hannah said to the guide.

"A Yankee?" said the guide. He'd been stopping at every monument to the Civil War.

Connie answered for her mother. "World War I." She wanted to tell the guide that the Civil War was over, he could stop celebrating the myth of the noble Confederacy.

When they left, Hannah told Connie that Savannah had been destroyed by General Sherman in his march through Georgia to the sea. "Charlie was in the Battle of the Somme. I think it was near the ocean."

"That must have been terrible for him. Did he ever talk about it?"

Hannah said what she had been saying whenever Connie probed. "I was too young. I don't remember."

After they crossed the border into Florida, Hannah never mentioned Charlie again. In St. Augustine, they walked the beach and swam in the warm ocean. They took a trolley tour of the ancient city, visited a coquina house, and the Indian prison at Castillo de San Marco. At the small and simple Fatio House, they learned about Florida's Minorcans and how a writer named Constance Fenimore Woolson used the boarding house in her travel narrative about St. Augustine. Just outside of town, they took a boat ride along the river where they watched alligators sun themselves on the roots of cypress trees. Connie loved it, especially when they branched into remote swamp areas, but Hannah, never comfortable on boats, worried her way through the whole ride. The humidity and the bugs wilted her. After a good dinner and a good sleep, they spent an obligatory day at Disney World, dodging frazzled parents and tired children wearing Mickey Mouse ears.

When they arrived at last at Dunhill, Connie felt closer to her mother than she had in years. She parked in the guest space next to the station wagon her parents left in Florida. She opened the car door for Hannah, who sat staring at the condo.

"You're home."

"It won't feel like home without Sam."

"We'll by okay." Connie led her mother to the front door. The musty odor inside announced that it had been closed up for over a year. Connie opened the sliding door at the back of the living room to let air begin to circulate and turned to Hannah, who stood in the kitchen wiping her eyes. "I thought you called a cleaning service. The place hasn't been opened since the last winter you were here with Dad."

"He was supposed to take care of it. That's his job. Let's just open everything up and go get dinner. We can make the Early Bird at Lobster Landing."

"If that's your choice." Connie hated The Lobster Landing. It wasn't on the ocean and Florida seafood didn't include lobster. She suspected the restaurant would expand into a national chain offering too much fake butter, too much salt, too many calories. She hated even more Florida's Early Bird specials. She said nothing. Time enough tomorrow to work out their living arrangements.

She moved around the condo opening its few windows. A cross breeze from the front and back doors was supposed to keep everything cool. The heat of summer had already arrived, but the condo needed air more than air conditioning. She opened the door to the bedroom her parents had shared, realizing that she would have to clean out her father's things. When she went into the room that she would call her own, she was shocked to remember its tiny size. She'd get rid of its oversized trundle bed and pick out the smallest single bed she could find. She'd move the dressing table under the window and use the full wall space for a desk and bookcases. With financial help from Sarah and her mother, she had a year to discover if she was the novelist she dreamed of becoming. She'd manage. She'd have to.

"Connie, can you help me in here?" Hannah called from the bathroom. "There's no water in the toilet and I can't get any out of the faucet."

She went into the bathroom, looked under the sink and turned two knobs. The toilet started to fill and rusty water ran out of the faucets in the sink and the bathtub. When she took off the plastic wrap that covered the toilet, she snapped. "Why in hell do you cover toilets with plastic wrap? This was festering in mildew."

"Don't get all snippy. That was Dad's job."

Before Hannah started to cry again, Connie kissed her cheek. "I'm sorry. We're both tired. Why don't you start to unload the car while I get this bathroom functioning."

"After I say hi to Jane."

Jane lived in the condo that shared a wall with Hannah's. Connie was glad for the friendship that would help her mother heal after Sam's death.

When she finished cleaning the bathroom, she went into the kitchen and turned on the water. While it was running, she looked in the refrigerator that hadn't been opened in more than a year. Not bad. A few staples like mustard and ketchup and a box of baking soda to keep it fresh. Some frozen pizzas and English muffins in the freezer, long past their expiration date. She'd toss everything in the morning and restock.

She finished and went outside to check the mailbox to see if anything had been forwarded. She punched in the code. Her birthday. 7743. Among the junk mail, she found an electric bill from her Boston apartment, her mother's *Ladies' Home Journal* and telephone bill. There was also a manila envelope addressed to Sarah from the Mercedes dealership where she sold her car. It would have to wait. Connie was in no mood to deal with whatever her sister left undone at the dealership. She joined her mother and Jane, who were outside talking. Jane was as small as Hannah. Joined together they would blow away in a Florida hurricane. Jane's size disguised a strength born of years of independent widowhood. Except for a head of gray hair and a face of wrinkles, she could have passed for a young boy.

"Connie, it's so good to see you. And to know you'll be living here." Jane hugged her. "I'm so sorry about your father. Sam was a good man. Your mother is lucky to have you."

Connie didn't say anything. Maybe her mother was lucky. Or maybe she was the lucky one, saved from a dull job and freed to write. Why, right now, did her luck feel like a looming prison?

"Sarah wishes she could be with us," said Hannah. "There wouldn't be room enough for her and Lizzie. She lost her husband, too, you know. She's off to Europe to distract Lizzie."

Connie wondered at the lie. Or was it self-deception. Sarah was off to Florence and then to Paris to flaunt her money and her high school French. She had no intention of coming to Florida.

"I do know that," said Jane. "You and Sam were here the winter after it happened. Such grief for your family."

Connie distracted her mother. "Jane, how about a hand with our things? The car is packed full and we just want to get everything inside so we can make the Early Bird at The Lobster Landing."

Jane opened the car door and started unloading. Connie went inside, dropped the pile of mail on the kitchen counter, the envelope from the Mercedes dealership peeking out from the bottom.

When the last box was unloaded, Hannah said to Jane, "Want to join us for dinner?"

Jane hesitated a moment. "Thanks, but I have leftover pad thai that I cooked last night. Why don't you plan on dinner with me tomorrow. That will give you time to settle in before you start having to cook."

"What do you think, Mum?" Connie remembered that Jane was an excellent cook.

"That will be nice."

The restaurant was crowded. The average age of the patrons hovered around seventy. A few tables held three generations. At least it wasn't February or April when every kid from New England seemed to head to Florida to see snowbirding grandparents before visiting the newly opened Disney World. Florida must have some permanent residents under the age of sixty but Connie wasn't hopeful that she'd find a circle of friends like the ones she made in Boston. Only once in Florida had she met someone interesting. A writer, a woman her own age whose first book became a best seller. Connie liked her. The woman knew she was lucky, that her idea about a returning Vietnam vet sold the books more than the quality of her writing. Connie thought the woman's writing adequate and the book, *Finding Home*, a feel-good page turner, refreshing amid the tumultuous years of protests.

Connie and Hannah both ordered lobster rolls and a bottle of wine. The lobster had once been frozen, but Connie agreed to it as an homage to New England. They talked through dinner about how they would manage living together. Connie was surprised at how perceptive her mother was. "This may be harder than you imagine," Hannah said. "The condo is small. My friends will be too old for you and your friends will be too young for me."

"What friends? I don't know anyone here except a few of the friends you and Dad made and the only one whose name I can remember is Jane."

"You'll make friends. Find a writer's group. Go over to the college and do your writing in the library. Have lunch where the faculty hang out."

"It's okay. If I don't publish enough to support myself, I'll move back to Boston and find a job."

"You'll make it. I don't want you to leave me alone down here."

Connie felt the prison door again. "You have lots of friends,

Mum. You'll be fine. If I make it big enough, I'll buy myself a place on the water and become a Floridian. Sarah will visit."

"Sarah won't visit. Oh, she might stay a day or two on her way to Disney World with Molly."

"Molly? You mean Lizzie?"

"Did I say the wrong name again? I don't know why I keep doing that."

Connie reached across the table for her mother's hands. "With us living together, you're just thinking of your own mother. Missing her, maybe."

"I do miss her. She was depressed a lot, but she always tried to hide it. When my father left, it was just the two of us. I was only twenty-five when she died."

"I'm not sure you ever told me how she died."

"She died of grief, I think. Depression isn't rational and she didn't have the medicine I have. In the end, she lost the will to live."

Connie released her mother's hands and leaned back in her chair. "You're not telling me she committed suicide."

"No, no. I wouldn't have kept that a secret from you. She caught pneumonia. I should have insisted she see a doctor sooner."

"It's not your fault."

"I know. But she was only sixty. My age. She never got to meet you and Sarah. It's a demon, depression."

"I know." Connie asked what she had never dared ask before. "Did your depression start after I was born? Postpartum? Is that why you quit teaching and started to work with Dad?"

"After Sarah, not you. It's not just childbirth. You have the curse. I saw it in you even as a child. You'd go through periods where you'd come home from school and close yourself in your room. I had to threaten you to get you to come to dinner. You're not like Sarah. She takes after your father. Maybe you should take pills like I do."

"No thanks. I'm careful. Writing helps and all those walks I take. Did your Uncle Charlie have depression? You've never told me what happened to him."

"Don't keep asking me about him. If I told you my mother would be furious."

"Your mother's dead."

Hannah poured more wine. "I know that. Charlie's secret dies with me."

Connie emptied the last of the wine into her glass, hoping it wouldn't give her a hangover. "You shouldn't have anymore wine. It's not good to mix so much with your pills."

A waitress who looked like she lived on the restaurant's calorie-laden food appeared at the table. She loaded dishes that had pools of fake butter on the bottom onto a standing tray and handed them dessert menus.

Hannah broke the silence. "Want to split something? The key lime pie?"

Connie scanned the menu. "How about the ice cream puff or the chocolate mousse. And coffee to counteract this wine."

"Ice cream puff, and we'll ask for chocolate ice cream instead of vanilla. No coffee for me. Won't you be awake all night?"

"Not likely. I drove from Orlando, remember. Right now I just want to eat dessert, drive home, hop into the shower and into bed." She motioned to the waitress and placed their order.

Two hours later Connie had her wish. She was propped on pillows reading a P.D. James novel, trying to gain some tips on plotting. The novel she'd started to write after she agreed to live with her mother would be a mystery. It wouldn't be hard boiled, no noir detective, no espionage, more like an intelligent cozy set on a lake in rural New Hampshire. Several town folk would be suspects in the murder of an older woman who had been keeping a secret about her brother, who had disappeared from town ten years earlier. She wasn't sure yet where the novel was headed, but she liked its simple title. *Secrets.*

She fell asleep in the middle of a P.D. James paragraph. She dreamed. She was in the Congregational church of her childhood, not sitting in a pew but kneeling in front of a priest giving her a communion wafer. She chewed the wafer and washed it down with a chalice of wine then began an undulating dance to the beat of a jazz riff. She woke, reaching for David until she remembered that she no longer had a lover. Her watch read 3:20. She picked up the book that had fallen to her side, placed it on the floor and turned out the light, remembering that she hadn't looked in the envelope addressed to Sarah. It would have to wait until morning.

Hannah was still asleep when Connie woke at her usual 6:00 a.m. She dressed quietly, left her mother a note, and picked up the envelope from the Mercedes dealership. She'd get coffee at Dunhill Pastries and open it before she did the grocery shopping at the Piggly Wiggly next to it. Outside, she glanced at her father's station wagon. Time enough to see if it started. Her mother would never drive it. They should sell both their cars and share something smaller. Connie felt the prison again. She feared she'd become her mother's chauffeur.

She got into her car and put the envelope on the seat. She turned on the radio and fiddled with the dials past stations broadcasting church services or religious music. There was no classical music, no jazz, only a single station playing "The

Twelfth of Never." She hated the song, so she turned off the radio and drove the three miles in silence. It was an easy drive. The intersections were all square angles, nothing like the labyrinthine roads of New England.

At Dunhill Pastries, she ordered coffee and an apple turnover that was dry. She forced herself through half of it before she opened the envelope. A note was clipped to a smaller envelope that looked like it might contain a greeting card. The message was scrawled in blue ink. "We found this tucked behind the driver's seat. Thought you'd need it." She recognized George's handwriting on the smaller envelope. "For Sarah." It had been opened. She wiped off the knife she used to cut her turnover and sliced through the taped flap.

The card was simple, a picture of a raven perched on a signpost that read Dead End. She opened the card and read. "You'll be better off without me. I'm going to the train. Love Lizzie for me. George."

She stabbed the knife into the turnover. A confirmation of the fear she'd nursed for a year about George's death by a train whose schedule he knew. She put the note back into the envelope, trying to understand why Sarah would hide it. Shame. She studied the tape. Maybe Sarah never saw it. Maybe the people at the Mercedes dealership opened it. She looked at their note again. "Thought you'd need it." "Need." Why? The car had been registered in George's name. They knew he died. Sarah wasn't one to hide the drama of how.

Her stomach screamed against the pastry and coffee. She tore up the manila envelope and put it into the trash. She went to her car and locked George's note into her glove compartment. The pig logo above the grocery store grinned at her. When she went into the store, she almost knocked over a cardboard cutout of the pig. In its white cap and apron, its red and white shirt and blue pants, it was an ironic patriot, a supporter of slaughterhouses. She rolled a cart through the aisles, picking up fruit, vegetables, milk, peanut butter, bread, all of the items Hannah would want. At the meat counter, she chose hamburger and chicken. A sign with another little pig in front of the pork announced "Freshness assured." Connie misread it as insured and knew what Sarah had done. Hidden a suicide note that would have denied her George's life insurance.

She wheeled her cart to the check-out counter. With each item she unloaded, she considered the few possibilities. "Need." Someone at the Mercedes dealership found the note and was blackmailing Sarah. Not likely. A blackmailer would have kept the note. Someone at the dealership opened a note that Sarah never saw. She watched the last of her groceries ring up. Behind her, a mother was telling her daughter that it was too early for the candy displayed at the checkout line. She looked at the child. A little younger than Lizzie. If she reported George's suicide, Lizzie would be the one to suffer. She loaded the bags into her cart. She wanted to believe that Sarah hadn't seen the note, but she couldn't. George would have left it visible. He wouldn't have been thinking about insurance money. He was desperate to be out of his pain.

The day George died, Connie came to Freedom immediately. It had just started to snow. Sarah answered the door and told her to wait, she'd pull the Mercedes into the garage so Connie could park in the driveway. Sarah stayed in the garage a long time. Their mother was in the house with their minister, already choosing hymns for the funeral service. They asked Connie to check on Sarah, but when Connie went into the kitchen to open the door into the garage, Sarah came inside. She was crying. Connie remembered being puzzled by what she said. "He never thought of us. So selfish."

She loaded the groceries into her car, unlocked the glove compartment, took out the note, and put it into her purse. She'd decide later if she should destroy it.

Hannah was in Jane's condo. Connie peeked in before she finished unloading the car. Jane opened the door. Her orange cat slipped outside. "Need coffee?"

"Thanks. I had some at Dunhill Pastries. Take your time, Mum. I'm going to put the food away and start unpacking my things. You can go through the cupboards later to see what I forgot at the grocery store. I'm tossing all the old stuff."

"I'm sure it's still okay. You don't need to toss good food." Hannah possessed the frugality of someone who grew up during the Depression. Connie would have to sneak out all the plastic grocery bags her mother had squirreled away along with the mold likely growing in them.

"Don't worry. I'm just getting rid of stuff past the due date. I'll leave the canned goods, the pasta, things like that." She rummaged through the kitchen for a trash bag and began to empty the refrigerator. She wiped down the shelves, unloaded the groceries that needed refrigeration, and started on the cabinets. When she finished, she tied up the trash bag. She thought about the note in her purse. She left it there and took the trash to the condo's dumpster. When she came back inside, she took the note from her purse, put it into the zipper compartment of her empty suitcase, and pushed the suitcase to the back of her closet. She didn't want to expose Sarah, but she wanted her sister to know what she found.

An hour later, Hannah came into her room. "How are you doing? I'm finished."

"Almost unpacked. I'm going to put the rest of the boxes in

the closet and look for a desk and bookcase. And a smaller bed. Do you mind?"

"Not at all. You need to make this your home. I never liked that bed, but it was a good guest bed. Not that we had many guests. I thought Sarah and George would visit often."

Connie eased into what they had to face. "How about we clear Dad's stuff for Goodwill."

"Can you can do it? I couldn't look at his side of the closet or in his drawers."

"I'll do it tomorrow. I'll call Goodwill now and arrange a pick-up. You can go out with Jane when they come."

"That would help. Let's quit for the day. Drive down to the beach and get a cup of chowder on the wharf."

"As long as we don't eat too much. I need to save room for Jane's cooking."

Half an hour later they were sitting on the deck of Gulfside eating chowder that was too thick with flour, but appreciating the breeze off the water. Connie watched in the distance as another high-rise hotel was intruding on what must once have been a pristine coast. Dunhill had escaped some of the encroachment, having zoned four miles of its shoreline to exclude high-rises. But like the rest of this area of Florida, its central arteries had been shaped by shopping plazas and traffic lights. Connie would have to navigate these to find her way to the college campus and its library. There was green on the campus. And flowers. And ocean. It should give her a good place to work.

They finished eating and Connie gave the car keys to Hannah. "Can you drive home? I'd like to walk. I just go along the Edgewater walkway until I hit Union, right?"

"It's about five miles and there's no beach to walk on. Do you have that long a walk in you?"

"No problem. I need to move around. As long as you don't mind driving."

"I mind a little, but I need to learn to do it. Your father did most of the driving here."

"Next week we'll sell Dad's car. Get one you and I will both like. You'll be fine with mine for now. You drove it through the mountains, remember. I'll see you at home in a couple of hours."

Connie walked her mother to the car, pointed her in the right direction and began her walk home. She focused on the horizon of water, trying to push away memories of George. The high school boy she partnered with on the school newspaper. The boy who saw Sarah and turned his back on Connie. The man who went to Vietnam full of confidence and returned so melancholic he could have been one of Connie's depressed ancestors. She wondered if Hannah's brother Charlie had been shell-shocked in World War I. She'd ask her.

Dunhill was on an inlet of the Gulf, so the water was calm. The sun made small flashes through the few trees that dotted the boarded walking path. It was still high in the sky and it would be hours before it set over the Gulf. Connie vowed to walk to the water evenings after dinner. A few people passed her and smiled. A mother pushing a stroller, the baby asleep to the rhythm of the mother's stride. An old couple holding each other up in a gesture that announced long years of marriage. Two women pausing in their animated conversation long enough to nod at Connie. A man walking his dog, another stopping to point a camera at the boats that sailed in the distance. Opposite the Gulf, Edgewater Road followed the path. The houses along it declared the wealth of owners who could afford the view. Some were large and showy with ornate doors more suitable for an Italian palazzo. Others were bungalows tastefully painted in blues or greens or yellows. All had gardens that looked like they were kept by chemicals and gardeners. The lovely, aromatic bougainvillea of a Florida June made Connie homesick for the lilacs of New England.

A man was standing in front of a car at the turn onto Union Street. He was looking at a map and Connie asked if she could help.

"I'm looking for the fastest way to Bayview College. I have an interview there in an hour and I seem to have gotten turned around."

Connie had enough of an idea of the directions that she could help. "I've just arrived myself but I can get you there. The directions are easy. Go back along Edgewater and you'll come to Dunhill's Main Street. Take it to Route 19 until you hit Pinellas. That will drop you right at the campus and you should see signs." Connie took the hand that wasn't holding the map and shook it. "Here's some good luck magic." She noticed strength in the hand and the intensity in the man's blue eyes. She said goodbye and turned onto Union, hoping that he'd get the job and that she'd meet him again at the library. He reminded her of David.

When she got back to the condo, Hannah was napping on the recliner in her bedroom. Connie went quietly into her room. Hot from her walk, she decided to put on her bathing suit and spend the rest of the afternoon reading by the condo complex's swimming pool.

No one was there. The snowbirds had left and the few full-time residents were at jobs or sleeping like Hannah. She swam a few laps in water that had become too hot. She wouldn't be distracted from her writing with the call of the pool. She sat in the shade of a pool umbrella and finished P.D. James in time to change for dinner at Jane's. Hannah was watching television when she returned.

"What's on, Mum?"

"I'm not paying much attention. Some kind of kid's show. *Open Sesame* or something."

"*Sesame Street*. Lizzie likes it."

"I knew it looked familiar." Hannah turned off the TV. "How was your walk? And your swim? You know I wasn't really sleeping when you came in."

"You should have come to the pool. It was nice out there. The walk was nice, too. Hot. I helped someone find his way to Bayview College for a job interview."

"Was he good looking?"

"Very. Don't get your hopes up. I didn't even learn his name. How was the drive home?"

"I got hopelessly turned around. Had to stop at a gas station to ask directions."

"How could you do that? I pointed you in the right direction."

"Don't harp. It happens."

"Sorry. It's almost five. I'll take a quick shower and we'll go to Jane's."

Connie went into the bathroom, telling herself that her mother was still tired from their long trip.

Chapter 3
July – September 1973

A week after their arrival, the moving van deposited more things than Hannah needed to transport to Florida. They unpacked her best cookware and dishes that Connie guessed they'd never use. They hung paintings of New England landscapes of winter and summer in Hannah's bedroom. Hannah put a photo of Connie and Sarah on top of the combination television/stereo cabinet. Connie hated it. Sarah was a cute, curly-headed five year old hugging Connie, a chubby seven year old wearing glasses. It was their future in miniature. Sarah traveling in Europe and Connie the dutiful daughter caring for their mother.

Connie avoided an argument over the photograph by going into her bedroom to unpack the few items she had put on the moving van. With a smaller bed she had bought, the room felt less claustrophobic. Her new bookcase didn't fit all her books, but she managed to stash some in boxes that she wedged into one side of the closet. She unwrapped a glass paperweight that David had given her. It enclosed a fern that reproduced asexually. A wave of desire invaded her. She willed it away as she set the paperweight next to her new, state-of-the-art Selectric typewriter. Extra ribbons and plenty of pens and legal pads promised something more in her future than the claustrophobia of the room and a relationship with a self-centered musician.

She finished arranging her bedroom and went into her mother's bedroom. Hannah was sitting on the bed looking through a box. She closed it quickly when Connie came in. The box was shallow and square, blue with a painting of a snowcapped mountain too peaked for New England.

"I don't remember that box. What's in it?" Connie said.

"I've had it since I was a girl. It just has junk from my childhood." Hannah got off the bed and put the box on the recliner that was squeezed into a corner. It made the room crowded, but during the winters they spent in Florida, Hannah liked to nap in it while Sam hung out by the pool flirting with the complex's gaggle of widows. They liked Sam, often called on him to fix a toilet or change an overhead light bulb they couldn't reach. The few times she visited, Connie teased him about his harem. It wasn't the women who interested him, it was the tinkering he missed after selling his hardware store.

Connie picked up the box. "Can I see?"

Before she had time to open it, Hannah grabbed it away. "Maybe later. We should unpack the kitchen boxes."

Connie looked around the room at the cartons Hannah hadn't opened. "I'll do it. You should finish in here." She went into the kitchen and sorted through the items Hannah had insisted on packing. She kept the best and set aside for Goodwill the ones that Hannah wouldn't miss.

It was noon when she finished, hungry and hot even with the air conditioning. She went into the bedroom to ask her mother if she wanted lunch. The moving cartons were open and empty and Hannah was asleep in the recliner, clutching the blue box. Connie let her sleep. She'd go to the Goodwill before she woke her for lunch.

When she got back, she was drenched from a humidity that made Massachusetts in July feel like the Arctic. Florida's climate would smother her. She found Hannah awake and standing at the bedroom window watching purple martins at the birdhouse Sam had made and hung on an oak tree that brought shade to the condo. He was as proud of luring the birds from the nearby golf course as he was of the house. "Charlie made birdhouses," Hannah said.

Connie put her arm around her. "You must have been thinking about your brother when you were looking through that box." Outside, a bird perched on its home. Inside, the box had disappeared.

"There was a photo of him in his uniform."

"I remember that photo. Army?"

"Yes. He fought in World War I."

"Did he come back traumatized like George? Is that why he left?"

"George would have been fine if that train hadn't hit him."

"What about Charlie?"

"Time for lunch." Hannah, as always, refused to talk about her brother.

By September, they had planted the lilac bush near the backyard oak tree and watched it die in the Florida heat. New England memories wouldn't come from familiar shrubbery. They settled for a red dwarf azalea and planted variegated coleus under the front windows. They traded Sam's station wagon and Connie's Impala for a Volkswagen Beetle. Connie chose a canary yellow one with the best price and named it The Yellow Submarine. Hannah hated the color and The Beatles. That it annoyed her mother gave Connie a touch of satisfaction. Hannah never drove the car further than the grocery store. Only once did she get lost.

Connie settled into a routine. She got up at seven o'clock, walked until nine, then ate breakfast and drove to the Bayview College library. In the evenings, she typed what she had written. Her resentment decreased in proportion to the accumulating pages.

On Sunday evenings, they watched *Columbo*. Connie loved the show and the way Peter Falk developed a character whose rumpled trench coat and battered Peugeot convertible belied his intelligence. "I love Sunday night," Hannah would say. "So nice to watch television with my daughter instead of listening to her bang on a typewriter. Sarah should be here."

Connie would answer, "Too bad you fall asleep and can't remember who got murdered." Hannah was becoming increasingly forgetful, sometimes buying half of what they needed at the grocery store and more of what they already had. Connie liked peanut butter, but eight jars of Skippy were more than she'd use through the fall.

The pages of her novel were adding up, well over two hundred by the end of the summer. The setting in New Hampshire on Newfound Lake helped her capture the tension between the permanent residents, the summer people, and a group of environmentalists. Her reluctant sleuth was female, young and aggressive rather than spinsterish like Agatha Christie's Miss Marple. She liked how the character was developing. Dr. Maura Appleton, a smart botanist with a PhD from the University of New Hampshire, discovers a murdered woman among the wild blueberries of Mount Major.

One Sunday before they turned on *Columbo*, Hannah asked about it. "Tell me your novel's plot."

Connie described the setting and Maura.

Hannah wanted more. "What's the plot? Does she find the murderer?"

"I haven't gotten that far, but she will. The murdered woman has a brother who disappeared. There's a diary with a long description of a place in the woods where the woman describes saying goodbye to her brother. Maura identifies the location. She remembers the place and the brother of the murdered woman. He used to walk in the woods and talk to the trees."

Hannah was knitting and dropped a stitch. She started to pull out a row. "Sounds like my brother Charlie."

The connection surprised Connie. She was using a picture of Grandmother Molly with Charlie as a way of imagining her characters.

"Want to tell me about him? Maybe it would help me develop the mystery."

Hannah stopped listening and concentrated on getting her stitches back on the needle. "Sarah would never ask that."

Connie slammed out of the room. "I'm going for a walk. You can watch *Columbo* alone." It was always Sarah this, Sarah that. She wanted to smash the picture of her and Sarah that never let her forget that her sister was exploring Europe while she was cooped up with their mother. They'd had only three letters, all meeting with Hannah's praise for how well Sarah was coping with George's death. Connie would think about George's suicide note and how easily Sarah had hired a good-looking tutor for Lizzie. If she was having an affair with James, it was short-lived. Sarah's last letter said that James had quit and Sarah and Lizzie were leaving for Paris where an American they knew had found them an apartment overlooking the Seine. She gave a forwarding address. The American she kept nameless and genderless.

One Friday afternoon in the waning days of September, Connie returned to the condo to find the door open but no Hannah. Jane's door was locked so she assumed the two had gone out together. She put on her swimsuit and walked to the pool where she found Eva Swenson, the one person she considered more a friend than an acquaintance. Eva had a grown son and an ex-husband she divorced in the early days of the women's rights movement when she realized all he expected of her was a clean house, a good meal, and sexy negligees. Eva graduated from Florida's Rollins College where she majored in history. After she graduated, she became a teacher. Even before Connie moved in, Eva often visited with Hannah. She told Connie she was fascinated with how New England history seemed to have been born into Hannah's bones. Connie would tell Eva about their interminable visits to historical sites when she was a kid. Sarah would whine through every tour until she got a bag of penny candy or a trinket from a gift shop. She imagined Sarah now, buying truffles and high-end jewelry in Paris.

Eva opened her eyes. "Okay, you caught me napping. I left school as soon as the kids did."

"They give you trouble?"

"They wouldn't dare."

"You look like one of them. Is that why they like you?" At five feet tall and a hundred pounds, with natural blond hair that framed her face like a halo, Eva looked closer to thirty than forty-five.

"They respect me. I'm not sure they like me. I have an eye-bending stack attack of papers to grade this weekend and decided to relax until tomorrow when I'll hit them with a vengeance."

"Wish I could help. Can I forge your handwriting?"

"If wishes could come true."

"Since you're taking the night off, how about we go to a movie and grab something to eat after."

Eva got off her lounge chair and dangled her feet in the water. "Better than an Early Bird with the blue hairs."

Connie let herself into the water and hung on the pool's edge next to Eva. "Do you hate those specials as much as I do?"

"My wallet doesn't, but, then again, I don't qualify for the senior discount. What movie is playing?"

"Your choice, *American Graffiti* or *Jesus Christ Superstar.*"

"Let's go with Jesus Christ. It will perk me up."

"Not sure about that. Jesus gets crucified, remember."

"But the music is good."

"J.C. it is, then." Connie pushed off the pool's edge. She swam a few laps, trying to imagine herself in the Newfound Lake of her novel. She needed to write in a good swimming scene, capture the tingling cold that reddened a swimmer's skin, and describe the clear view of glacial boulders in all but the deepest parts of the lake.

"God, I miss New England," she said as she pulled herself out of the too warm water and sat next to Eva, who was still dangling her feet.

Eva confessed that the one time she visited Maine, she ran into the ocean in Maine and nearly died of shock.

"Didn't someone warn you how cold the Atlantic is in the state of Maine?"

"It was August. My friends said the annual summer current had warmed the water."

"It probably had, all the way up to the low sixties. It's bracing, as we like to say. I'm off. I need to round up my mother and Jane. Meet me at my unit at five-thirty. I'll drive." Connie stood up and reached for the towel she had draped over a chair.

"I saw your mother a couple of hours ago walking by herself," said Eva.

"Where? She never walks alone. Can't find her way around

here except to go to the grocery store. She confuses the Dunhill streets with the Freedom ones."

"She was heading down Union toward Edgewater. I figured she was going to walk the ocean pathway. She's in great shape. How old is she?"

"Almost sixty. She and Jane are both in great shape. Helps prevent hardening of the arteries, Jane says."

"Your mother has symptoms?"

"Goodness, no. Though she has been pretty forgetful lately. Speaking of which, I just remembered that the show starts at six-thirty not six o'clock, so don't rush." Connie dried herself as she walked back to the condo. Hannah hadn't returned. Maybe she shouldn't dismiss Hannah's forgetfulness. She knocked on Jane's door. The cat escaped when Jane opened it. "Have you seen my mother?"

"Not since this morning."

"That's strange. She left the door open and Eva says she saw her walking alone toward Edgewater."

"She never walks alone. You get dressed and I'll just take a drive down the road to look for her."

Connie was getting out of the shower when she heard Jane and Hannah in the living room. Jane was asking Hannah how she got so turned around that she ended up on Citrus. Connie didn't hear the answer. When she came into the living room, she pretended not to worry.

"Hi, Mum. I wondered where you were. You left the door unlocked."

Hannah slammed down the purse she insisted on carrying. "Don't get all huffy. It was so nice I decided to go feed the seals."

"Seals? In the Gulf?" said Jane.

"Don't you start on me, too. I mean the seagulls."

"I thought you hated seagulls," said Connie.

Hannah sat down on the couch. Hard. "I just wanted to take a walk, okay?"

"Okay, okay. You'd better get dressed if you and Jane are going to make the Early Bird. I'm going to a movie with Eva."

"Eva? I like her. We talk about history. I'm not so senile I can't remember history." Hannah disappeared into her room.

Connie looked at Jane. "Do you think she's okay? It's not like her to get so angry."

"She's gone off like this a few times while you've been at Bayview. But she's always found her way back so I didn't say anything. She was really confused when I picked her up."

"Let me know if it happens again. You can call the college library and they'll page me. Monday I'll call to make her a doctor's appointment. She's overdue."

Hannah showed no more signs of distress through the weekend. On Monday, they asked Jane to recommend a doctor they both could see. Jane suggested her own, Dr. Francis Wilberforce. When they called his office, they discovered they would have to wait until after Halloween to schedule back to back appointments. For the rest of the month Connie watched her mother carefully. If she wandered during the day, Jane never said. She still confused the grocery lists and still couldn't follow *Columbo*. That seemed normal enough. Connie wasn't so good at *Columbo* herself.

Chapter 4

October – November 1973

At the beginning of October, well into the revisions of *Secrets*, Connie looked up from the library desk she claimed as her own and saw the man she met on her first Edgewater walk. She recognized his athletic build and the sandy hair that curled at his neck. He was checking out a book. She walked over to say hello, wondering if he'd remember her. "You must have gotten the job," she said. His face was a blank, then broke into a smile that radiated to eyes that were deep and bright and blue. Yes, extremely handsome, she thought.

"I remember you. You directed me to Bayview back in the spring."

"I wondered how it worked out."

"I got the job. In the English Department. Now I have a stack attack of freshmen papers."

"That's the same expression my friend Eva uses. She teaches high school history."

"The two hardest subjects to teach, English and history. The paper load never ends. But I love it. The students here are great. The freshmen are overwhelmed and getting sick as they always do a couple of weeks into the semester."

"Oh?" Connie remembered her own first semester and how sick she felt most of the time. She blamed it on the cigarettes she tried learning to smoke.

"They stay up too late. They drink too much. They eat all the wrong stuff in the cafeteria. But they make it to my class. Most of them are even awake when it starts at ten o'clock."

"Don't remind me. I didn't settle into college life until sophomore year."

"No sophomore slump?"

"Short-lived. I discovered the campus newspaper and dreamed of becoming the next Martha Gellhorn."

"Hemingway's wife?"

"The third of four. But the attraction was her journalism, not her man."

He looked at his watch. "It's noon and I was about to have a quick lunch before my two o'clock class. Want to join me?"

Connie tried not to seem too eager as she accepted. "I'm Connie Lewis."

"Will Baldwin." They walked out into the Florida sun, past a statue of Confederate General William Wing Loring. Connie hated the reminder of The Civil War.

"I hoped I'd see you again," said Will. "I'm still getting used to Florida and want to find friends beyond Bayview College. Not that I don't like my colleagues."

They reached a string of restaurants and went into one called The Groaning Board. They ordered from a table on a deck with a view of the Gulf.

"What a life these Bayview students have. How do they get any work done?"

"They seem to manage."

"What courses do you teach?"

"Freshman writing core and upper level classes in American

literature. I grew up in New England where American literature started. It seemed like a natural fit to concentrate on when I got to the U. of Minnesota for my graduate work."

"Where in New England? I grew up in Freedom, Massachusetts."

"Close. I'm a New Hampshire boy. Born and bred in Littleton. I went to UNH as an undergrad. And you? What's a nice girl from Massachusetts doing in Florida?"

"Living with my mother."

"Do I detect resentment?"

"Sometimes I feel trapped. We came here because my father died and they owned a condo in Dunhill. My mother needed to live more simply than she could in Massachusetts. She sold her house and here we are."

"What do you do besides hang out with your mother?"

"It's not what it sounds like. We have a deal. I live with her and help her acclimate to living full-time in Florida. In return I get to live free and see if I can make it as a novelist."

"You must have left a life back home."

"That wasn't hard. I was working for MIT Press. It sounds glamorous, but I was really just a glorified typist. I haven't lived in Freedom since I graduated from college. My only real ties there were my mother and my sister."

"Is your sister still there?"

"No. Her husband died. She's taken her daughter to Europe to try her wings."

"While you get to stay with your mother. Doesn't sound like you got the best end of that bargain."

"You're right. My sister inherited a boatload of money from her husband. She's in Paris right now. So far her letters mostly complain about how the French treat Americans."

"Do I detect a conflict with your sister?" said Will.

"She has a little girl. Lizzie. I miss her."

"Lizzie or your sister?"

"Mostly Lizzie." Connie took a spoonful of the chowder that arrived and changed the subject. "This is delicious."

"I'm a New Hampshire boy, remember. I know how to find the places that don't thicken chowder so much it tastes more like flour than fish. Is the writing going well?"

"I think so. I could use some feedback."

"How about if I read what you have? Return the favor for your role in getting me this job."

Connie hadn't meant to hint for Will's help. She studied his face. Clean-shaven, soft more than sharp-edged, his sandy hair curling on his forehead and around his ears. His eyes held hers, their blue irises large and unencumbered by glasses.

"Hardly a fair exchange. But if you really want to." Connie hoped for more than a reading. If not a relationship, at least a friendship. They walked together back to the library. Connie gave Will her first chapter with the revisions she had typed the night before. They agreed to meet at The Groaning Board on Thursday. When he left for his class, she wondered if she'd really get it back. She was grateful for her carbon paper so she had an extra copy.

When she arrived on Thursday at The Groaning Board, Will was waiting for her at the same table. A bowl of chowder steamed next to the manuscript.

"I knew you'd be on time and I knew you'd like the chowder. This is to celebrate. Your novel is off to a terrific start. I hope you brought me the next chapter. Or two or three."

Connie sat down, as relieved that he showed up as she was that he liked the chapter. "I've been worrying all week."

"Why? You should know it's good."

"I wondered if you'd like it. After all, you're used to the best literature. I even wondered if you'd show up."

"That's not very flattering."

"Well, I've only known you for about two hours."

"I'm glad you trusted me. I grew up on mysteries. Hardy Boys to Agatha Christie to P.D. James."

"Me too. Even the Hardy Boys."

"No Nancy Drew?"

"Too girly. I hated how she called her father 'Father.' She was a rich bitch. Just like Honey in the Trixie Belden series. I always liked Trixie the best."

"Sorry. Never read those series. No sisters."

"Brothers?"

"One. He's older. Lives in Portsmouth and coaches high school football."

"Married? Kids?" Connie watched a sailboat struggling in a wind that had come up. She waited for Will's answer and a clue to his relationship status.

He took a long time before he said, "Me or my brother?"

"Both."

"My brother has a little girl around two years old, I think, and a new baby boy that I haven't seen." He didn't volunteer more.

"Do you still read mysteries? Or just mine?"

"Lots of classic literature has an element of mystery. What's *The Scarlet Letter* if it's not a mystery. *Jane Eyre*? *Wuthering Heights*? *Crime and Punishment*?"

"I'd sure like to be in that club. I'll settle for the C list."

"Aim higher. You know how to develop a character. How to create a scene. How to pace the narrative. It doesn't hurt that you have a terrific writing style."

"What's the 'but'? I need criticism."

"I wrote down a few things. Mostly I'd like more of a back story on Maura Appleton. I trust her and her knowledge of botany. But what prompted her to study it? A charismatic professor? A crush on a guy in her botany class? Give her some history."

"I get it. Some comes out in the next few chapters but I can do more. I like the idea of a crush. How many women her age, which is my age, shaped their lives by these early crushes? My sister is a perfect example."

"Was your sister's crush the husband who died?"

"Yes. The same guy I had a crush on. But this was high school. I was long over it before they got married."

"Good. I suppose there were crushes in college. And after. Probably real relationships." He was testing her sexual history.

"One boyfriend in college. One after. The college boyfriend ended up becoming a priest."

"No future with a priest. And the other?"

"A jazz musician. He's a terrific pianist, but after a while I hated the lifestyle. Late nights. Lots of drinking. Drugs. That I never took," she quickly added. "We parted friends. How about yourself? Girlfriend? Fiancée?"

He lowered his eyes, finished his chowder, murmured "Nope." He looked at his watch. "Sorry. I have to get to class. If you can give me more to read, let's meet again next Thursday. It's a good day for me. Is it for you?"

"Any day is okay," she answered, reaching into her bag for more manuscript pages. She gave him the next two chapters and took back the pages he read, anxious to see his comments.

They walked back to the campus in a wind that had become stronger. On the horizon over the Gulf, Connie saw the rain that was heading toward shore. Will left her at the building that housed the literature and writing faculty. She continued to the library and spent the afternoon reading his comments, making notes for more revisions, and wondering if she was heading toward anything beyond friendship.

By November, Connie was meeting Will every Thursday. He pushed her writing hard. She liked him so much that when she and Hannah kept their appointments with Dr. Wilberforce, she asked for a prescription for birth control pills even though Will had made no sexual advance. She was surprised when he said he only prescribed birth control to married women. She resolved to find another doctor for herself.

When he finished examining her he left the room to see Hannah, who insisted that Connie not stay with her. It seemed a long time before he found Connie in the waiting room and called her into his office. He was honest but gentle. "I suspect your mother may have hardening of the arteries."

"How can that be? She's not quite sixty. Why would you even be looking for it?"

"You mentioned her memory to my secretary when you made the appointment. We're becoming more aware of the different aspects of brain deterioration. In a few more years, we'll be calling what your mother might have Alzheimer's. I ran through a series of memory questions researchers developed five years ago. She didn't do well. She had trouble remembering a name and address and she thought this is the month of August."

"That's easy. Last week it was like August in Massachusetts." Connie defended her mother.

"Your mother couldn't remember how she got that nasty scar from her breast to her navel."

"A scar?"

"You haven't see it?"

Connie remembered when they first left Massachusetts and she saw a gash her mother wouldn't let her look at. "She cut herself a few months ago. The cut should be healed by now."

"It's much older than that. It's bad enough that she should remember what happened."

"She's never let me see her naked. I have no idea where she could have gotten it."

Dr. Wilberforce wrote a note on what looked like Hannah's medical chart. "Sometimes what I'll call Alzheimer's is early onset. Is there a history of mental decline in the family?"

"My grandfather left the family when my mother was twelve. My grandmother died before I was born. I never knew either of them. There was mental illness in some ancestors."

"Mental illness might have been Alzheimer's. We didn't have any diagnoses until recently. Diagnoses still aren't very good."

The idea of caring for a mother with whatever this disease was called terrified Connie. "So maybe you're wrong?"

"I hope so. But watch her. Keep her active. Exercise seems to help. She's functioning well right now so I wouldn't tell her anything. Being told a diagnosis can increase anxiety and the symptoms. I'll put her on a six-month check-up list."

"On what excuse? She knows she doesn't need check-ups more than once a year."

"She takes those anti-depressants. I'll tell her a six month check-up is required to keep her prescription filled." He left the room. Connie realized that she had been shivering in the examination gown. She dressed quickly and joined her mother in the waiting room.

They stepped out of Dr. Wilberforce's office onto pavement. No stairs, an entry designed for an office that catered to elderly retirees. Connie began to think of Florida as a place where old people came to die. It had started to rain, the steamy, slick rain of Florida that was so unlike the raw November rain in Massachusetts. She was glad she had taken an umbrella when she saw the threatening clouds. She opened it, held onto her mother's arm, and steered them to the parking lot.

"He was a nice man. Dr. Wilber. Said I have the heartbeat of an athlete." Hannah had been using that phrase since Connie was in high school. Dr. Wilberforce told Connie just the opposite. Her mother's heart was good, but it would weaken if she didn't exercise and if she got any thinner. She had started losing weight after Sam died and even with Florida's Early Bird specials, she wasn't gaining it back.

"If you want to keep it that way, you need to take more walks with me. We can walk along Edgewater after dinner." Connie kicked a rock out of the parking lot. Another bit of freedom lost.

"It's raining. Your car is a stand in for the sun." Hannah patted it and called it sunshine. Her gesture made Connie feel guilty. Hannah was her mother and she was facing something dreadful. They both were facing it.

She unlocked the passenger side door. "Do you have any family health records? Dr. Wilberforce likes to have them. Maybe in that box with the mountain painting on it."

Without answering, Hannah got into the car and began knitting the blanket she had started in July when the days reached a hundred degrees and ninety percent humidity. They drove home to Hannah's undertone of "knit four, purl two, knit four." When she got to the reverse side, she'd say, "reverse, purl four, knit two, purl four."

They ran from the carport to the condo. Hannah carried her knitting bag inside. Connie stayed outside under the umbrella. She needed to talk with someone. She dodged puddles that had formed in sunken parts of the walkway.

Eva opened her door before Connie had time to knock. "I saw you from my side window. What's up?"

"I need company. Someone besides my mother and the way her knitting needles click together while she chants the stitches. I'm glad you're home."

"Not only am I home. It's Friday and I have no papers to grade over the weekend. How about a beer? I've got your favorite. Corona."

"That would be great." Connie sank into Eva's sofa. White. A risky choice for someone who dug in the dirt at a community garden. The room was a replica of Hannah's living room, but instead of the clutter of two women living together, it was almost too stark. A stereo cabinet with a television opposite the sofa. Stored inside it were a few classical records Eva had once showed her. She never played them. Connie liked to tease her about her limited repertoire. Eva teased back about how Connie's collection of music overflowed the top of her cabinet, her coffee table, sometimes even the floor. Eva's cabinet displayed a photograph of her son taken the last time he visited and a vase that she kept filled with seasonal flowers, today an arrangement of yellow and bronze spider mums. Scattered on her walls were reproduction prints commemorating events in American history.

Eva carried in a tray loaded with cheese and crackers and two bottles of Corona, each with a lime in the mouth. "Your mom going to The Early Bird in this rain?"

"I don't know. We just came from our doctor appointments. She's probably asleep in the recliner already."

"The doctor give you bad news? Is that why you need to talk?" Eva handed a beer to Connie, who took more of a swallow than a sip.

"She might have Alzheimer's."

"What's that?"

"The new name for hardening of the arteries."

"She's only sixty."

"Not until January. It's early onset."

"That explains why she keeps getting lost. You need to write your sister. Tell her to take some responsibility."

"I will." Connie drank again. She could blackmail Sarah with

George's suicide note. "She won't rush back until she's tired of this Arthur guy. Did I tell you about him?"

"Just that they celebrated Lizzie's birthday doing things no six-year-old would like. Visiting the Louvre and the Eiffel Tower."

"And letting Lizzie eat so many marrons glacé she went to bed sick with her birthday present, a stuffed kitten she named Arthur."

"Is Arthur the new tutor?"

"Something like that. I told Sarah she should hire a woman."

"Do I detect some hostility?"

"Always."

"At least convince Sarah to visit your mother. She and this Arthur guy can take Lizzie to Disney World."

"I'll think about it." Connie wanted a Lizzie hug. She needed someone to touch her.

"Want another beer?" said Eva.

"Thanks, but I should go home. Check on my mother."

"She'll be fine. She's not senile. Yet. Stay and have dinner with me. I've got a pot of chili on the stove. Finally it's cool enough for soups."

"At least it's not chowder," said Connie. She and Will hadn't varied their lunch since they met.

"What's that mean?"

"Nothing. Chili sounds good. I'll come back in an hour. I'll do what you said. Write to Sarah."

Connie opened the door and picked up her umbrella. She ran to her condo in rain that had moderated only a little. Hannah was in her bedroom, holding the blue box on her lap.

Connie got a pen, some stationary and an envelope from a kitchen drawer. She sat on the couch. When her mother woke, she'd ask about the box. She began the letter to Sarah, deciding to be blunt and to use the label Sarah would understand. *Mum and I had doctor appointments today. The news isn't good. She has hardening of the arteries. It isn't just names that Mum confuses. She's been doing that for years. She gets lost. She gets angry. She's losing weight. You need to drop this Arthur guy and get your ass here for a visit soon.* She crossed out *your ass* so Sarah wouldn't be able to read it. That would make her resist. She toned down her plea. *Maybe for Christmas. Or Easter. See Mum as much as you can while she still knows you.* She ended with a carrot. *We could take Lizzie to Disney World. She's a perfect age to enjoy it.*

As she folded and sealed the letter in its envelope, she heard Hannah push the recliner upright. When she started toward her, Hannah closed the bedroom door, calling through it in a voice too loud, "I'll be right out."

Connie went into her own room and left the letter with her purse. Hannah called from her bedroom. "Come help me." Connie rushed to her mother. All she needed was help with a garnet necklace. Connie recognized the red teardrop on a silver chain as one that Hannah said had belonged to her mother. A symbol of happiness, wealth, and health, none given to a woman abandoned by both her husband and her son. None promised for Hannah's future.

Connie fastened the clasp. The box was nowhere in sight.

Chapter 5

November 1973

Connie stood in front of her closet deciding what to wear to Will's. After six weeks of lunch discussions about *Secrets*, he finally invited her to dinner. She looked through dresses she hadn't worn since she stopped working at MIT Press. They weren't lawyer suits, but they were boring, subdued prints with Nehru collars or crew necks and straight or slightly flared skirts that fell to her knees. She should give them to Goodwill. The pants hanging next to them were either heavy corduroy or too summery for a November evening in Florida. In her bottom drawer, she found a pair of bell-bottom jeans she hadn't worn since she left Massachusetts. She put them on over underpants that weren't sexy but were at least fake silk rather than cotton. Struggling to button the jeans, she vowed to lose weight and did some crouches to stretch them. She looked in her T-shirt drawer and through the shirts in her closet. Her white peasant blouse would work with the jeans. She put it on and loosened the cord that laced at the neckline then went into the bathroom to look at herself in the full-length mirror. The peasant blouse hid that her breasts were too small for her muscular hundred and forty pounds. Sarah might be glamorous with her Barbie doll figure, her styled blond hair, and her perfect make-up, but Connie preferred a natural look, short hair, no make-up, clothes that looked like she'd go for a hike if anyone asked her. Will seemed to like how she looked. He once told her about hiking all the four thousand footers in the New Hampshire mountains. Maybe they'd find a place to hike together in the Florida flatlands. Maybe they'd make love under the trees.

When she came out of the bathroom, Hannah was sitting in the dining room fingering her garnet necklace with one hand and with the other jiggling something that sounded metallic on the table. She stood up and showed Connie a string of gold beads. "Your father gave me these the day we were married. He gave me my necklace, too. I can't remember when."

"Dad didn't give you the necklace. It was your mother's."

"Never mind. Just take the beads. They'll bring you good luck."

"He's just a friend, Mum. Don't get your hopes up." She let her mother fasten the beads around her neck. Hippie style love beads would have looked better. Or crystal beads that carried magic.

"You look beautiful." Hannah sat at the table again.

Connie felt a tenderness toward her mother that she hadn't felt since they drove to Florida. She bent and kissed the top of her hair. It was thinner and grayer than even a few months ago. "Goodnight, Mum. Don't wait up."

"You can tell me all about it in the morning."

Whatever happened, Connie wasn't likely to share it. She got into her car, unhooked the beads and put them in the glove compartment. When she drove into Will's neighborhood, she admired the craftsmen style houses. If she could get her novel published, make her own money, this was the kind of neighborhood she'd live in. She parked The Yellow Sub in front of his house, checked herself in the rearview mirror, and walked to the door. She could smell spices that announced they'd eat something Asian.

Will opened the door and gestured her directly into the kitchen. He wore jeans and a white shirt that was almost a twin to Connie's except for its short sleeves. He kissed her lightly on the cheek. His hair smelled of lavender. It wisped above eyes as blue as Paul Newman's. She handed him the two bottles of wine she brought. "I didn't know what we'd eat, so I brought a red and a white."

"You didn't need to bring anything." He glanced at the labels. "Good choices."

They went into the kitchen where something was simmering in a large pot. "It smells delicious," she said.

"I decided it was time to get you off The Groaning Board's menu. I hope you like spinach and lamb and Indian spices."

"Yes to spinach and lamb. The spices smell so good I'm sure I'll like them."

"My friend Siddha is Indian." He pointed to a photo on the counter. Will and another man were sitting together on a beach somewhere, their backs to the camera, the ocean opening up in front of them. The beach looked deserted.

"Whoever took this picture is a terrific photographer."

"Just one of our artistic friends." Will stirred whatever was in the pot and took two wine glasses out of his cabinet. He opened the bottle of white, poured, and raised a toast. "To someone who gives me something better to read than student papers."

Connie clicked his glass. "To a perfect reader." She needed him for feedback as much as she wanted him for a lover.

"And to friendship." Will picked up a tray of something and steered her through one of two doors that opened from the kitchen. The rooms were laid out in a circular pattern like the ones her best elementary school friend had lived in. As kids, they would march from kitchen to living room to dining room, playing parade. In the living room, she glanced at a closed door that must be Will's bedroom.

They sat in front of a glass coffee table on an off-white sofa that looked like Eva's. The room was neater than Connie expected of a bachelor pad. An armchair matched the sofa. A high bookcase held books neatly arranged and a few photos of what looked like family members. Four paintings hung on the only available wall. They were abstract, colors bleeding into swirls that resembled trees or water or mountains.

She picked up something that looked like a fried vegetable. She bit into it. Cauliflower. "This is delicious."

"Sid's recipe. Also broccoli and carrots." Will traced the rim of his glass with his finger. He seemed nervous.

Connie strained a little to make conversation. "These paintings are beautiful. They look like originals."

"They are."

"An artist friend? The one who took the photo?"

"Kenny's the photographer. Brian's the painter. They'll make it some day. Right now they live in Minneapolis and sell their work in some of the parks."

They talked for a half hour about natural parks versus the kitsch of Florida's theme parks. When they finished the bottle of wine, Will picked up the hors d'oeuvre tray and walked toward the kitchen. "Time for the real stuff. You'll see what a good cook Sid is."

"I thought you made it."

"Confession. Sid made it. I just warmed it up."

Connie's stomach clenched. "Is he on the Bayview faculty?"

"I knew him in Minneapolis." He didn't elaborate.

They carried rice and curry and what Will identified as sag

paneer, naan, and mango chutney into the dining room. The walls held several black and white photos, all of men posed against backdrops of natural landscapes that were muted so the figures stood out. One was of Sid dressed in jeans and a flannel shirt, his dark skin shining against the light trunk of a half-fallen birch tree. The trunk angled to one side and Sid, his eyes hidden behind sunglasses, angled his head to the opposite side. The image took up so much of the photo that only hints of a forest behind the tree showed.

"Photos by your photographer friend?" said Connie.

"Kenny. Like I said, he's good."

"I recognize Sid. Are all these others your friends?"

"Only Sid. The others are just photos I like." Will opened the bottle of red wine before he said, "Kenny's gay. One day he hopes he'll have enough for an exhibit that says 'Here we are. Gay men in all our variations.' White, Black, brown. Fat, skinny. Flamey and effeminate. Muscular and athletic."

When Connie heard the "our," a wave coursed through her pelvis, the kind she felt whenever she saw an open wound. "Oh." She was afraid to say anything more. Accepting the bowl of rice Will handed her, she looked at his hand. Strong. She spooned rice onto her plate and topped it with curry. Will passed the rest of the dishes, poured the wine, and toasted again. "To us. Writer and editor."

Connie relaxed. They talked about *Secrets* as they ate. Will helped her to see why a chapter where Maura Appleton talks with the old woman whose brother disappeared wasn't working. The scene needed more background. Will suggested that Connie describe the objects of her house in more detail. They told something about the woman. Connie closed her eyes for a moment and pictured her mother in her rocking chair holding the box she guarded so well. She opened her eyes and across the table saw the photograph of Sid. She looked down at her plate, her stomach clenching.

"Are you with me?" said Will. "Does any of this help?"

"It does. I know what to do now."

Will stood up. "Let's go outside. Digest a bit before dessert." He led Connie through the living room onto his back deck. She heard him breath in. "I suppose you've guessed by now."

She didn't want to name it.

"You know, don't you?" He leaned against the deck's railing, his fingers drumming nervously along it.

"Sid is your partner."

"Say it, Connie. Too many people avoid the word."

Connie stifled a sob and said, "You're gay."

"I've wanted to tell you for some time. I'm sorry."

"Don't be sorry." Sorry was for her. And embarrassment at her naiveté. The rejection hurt, as if he were saying she wasn't attractive, was too heavy, too small breasted, whatever.

"I'm not sorry I'm gay. Just that I didn't tell you sooner." He moved from the railing and tried to hug her. "Friends."

She stiffened.

He stepped back to the railing. "I thought you'd understand."

Behind him the full moon was veiled by a wisp of cloud. "I'll try."

"Let's sit." He motioned her to a wicker love seat.

She hoped he wouldn't sit next to her and waken her desire. She looked up and saw that the cloud had passed beyond the moon, leaving a clear night sky with myriad stars.

Will continued to lean against the railing. "I trust you."

"Trust me? How?"

"This is Florida, not the liberal north. Not that New Hampshire is a hotbed of liberalism. Nobody at the college knows."

Angry now that he wanted her as an alibi, she spat out, "In

other words, you're closeted at the college. If I ever meet anyone there, I'm your disguise. A pretend girlfriend."

"Not quite so crass as that."

Beyond a magnolia tree and a fence covered in star jasmine, she heard laughter. If she spoke above the neighbors' joy, she'd cry.

Will broke the silence. "I have another problem besides Bayview."

Connie forced herself to listen.

"My family. I haven't been able to tell them. They wouldn't understand."

"I won't be your disguise there as well." She jumped up, went into the house, grabbed her purse, and slammed out the front door.

Will caught her by the arm as she was unlocking her car. "Please don't leave. I want you for a friend, not a pretend girlfriend. A friend I don't keep secrets from."

She jerked her arm away. "So if I meet your parents I just let them think we're lovers. They've probably figured out what you are."

"I'm not a what. I'm a who. A gay man who wishes he lived in a world where he doesn't have to keep secrets. If my parents wanted to know, they'd ask. It's not like I ever brought any girlfriends home."

Connie breathed slowly to control her anger. Will was more hurt than she was. She let him lead her back to his deck. He stood in front of her. "I cried about it for years. Not any more. Things are better than they used to be, but not so good that we can live openly without fear."

"How did they used to be?" Connie's voice cracked.

"People like me weren't allowed in bars or restaurants unless they disguised themselves. Weren't allowed to be teachers or work for the government. We still can't serve in the military, though I'm sure many of us do. Until this year, we were labeled pathological in the *Manual of Mental Disorders* and sent off to clinics to be cured. Now we just have sexual orientation disturbance."

Connie remembered the debates over what qualified as a mental disorder. Those opposed to the new designation wanted to send homosexuals to camps where they'd be cured. Young men were telling stories about the horrors of conversion therapy, about shocks to the genitals, electroshock to the brain, nausea-producing drugs, religious indoctrination. "Would your parents have sent you to conversion therapy?"

"Maybe when I was a teenager."

"Would Bayview fire you if they knew?"

"It's not a Catholic or Evangelical school, so probably not. Many students wouldn't like it."

"When did you realize you're gay?" She still had trouble pronouncing the word. Being attracted to a gay man was as foreign to her as the Indian food roiling in her stomach.

"Early, even though I did what boys do. Had pissing contests. Compared penises."

Connie had no brothers. She'd never thought about prepubescent boys.

Will continued. "It got bad in high school when all my friends started to like girls. I tried having sex with a girl. I was afraid she'd tell someone what a disaster I was." He sat next to Connie on the loveseat.

She wanted to move away. "Did anyone suspect?"

"No. It helped that I'm athletic. I don't look gay, right?"

Connie had seen photos of Oscar Wilde, had read Truman Capote, had listened to news reports about the Stonewall Riots in New York City. She had been horrified at pictures of gay men in drag being clubbed by police and having bottles and stones thrown at them.

"When did you first--" She couldn't finish the question.

"Have sex with a man?" Will tugged at his hair. "In college. A discreet affair. In grad school I found some gay bars. I was uncomfortable in them. So I vowed to be celibate. I was jealous when you told me about your college boyfriend who became a priest."

Connie reached for his hand to stop him pulling his hair.

Will held it tight. "I'm happier now than I've ever been. I love Sid. He followed me here. Lives with me. He's taught me to be comfortable. Brian and Kenny run with an artist crowd. They don't need to be closeted."

"What's that joke? Why did God make homosexuals?" Her voice cracked again.

"Without them, who would be the artists? I've heard it a million times. Seriously, hiding what I am at Bayview is minor compared to the fear I used to have in high school. Are you okay with this?"

She squeezed his hand and choked out a "yes."

"I've talked more than I want. Come inside and we'll have Sid's extraordinary flan."

She followed Will into the kitchen. The photo of Sid stared at her from the counter. She wanted to throw the flan in his sunglassed face. Part of her wanted to leave Will to the secret he kept even from his family, drive home and out of his life forever. Instead, she accepted the dish Will held out to her. She needed his friendship. They sat this time at his kitchen table. She ate the flan she barely tasted, drank coffee, and after an agonized hour agreed to meet him on their usual Thursday.

He walked her to her car. When she started it, he leaned his head in the window and kissed her cheek. "Thank you," he said above the strains of some music she didn't recognize on her radio.

She drove to the nearest beach and got out of her car. She sat in the sand, her knees pulled to her chest, her head bowed over them. Her body shaking with sobs, she released the feelings she had been disguising as much as Will disguised his sexuality. Finally spent, she straightened herself and blew her nose on her blouse. It would wash more easily than her feelings. She kicked off her sandals and walked to the water. It wasn't cold enough to numb her. She cupped water into her hands and splashed it onto her face. The salt couldn't heal her wounds. She started to walk deeper into the water, wanting to wash away her loneliness. When she heard voices, she turned back to the beach. A couple was walking, hand in hand. They stopped and the woman pointed toward the sky. Connie looked up. A million stars floated around a moon rising above a cloud. It looked like the sun rising at dawn.

She wiped her nose on her blouse again, slipped her feet into her sandals, and went back to her car. The radio came on when she turned the key. She recognized the jazz piece from listening to David play in one bar or another. A priest, a jazz musician who took too many drugs, a gay man. She had lousy taste in men. George had been the best of them and he chose Sarah.

She turned off the radio and found her way home.

Chapter 6
November 1973

She woke to the smell of bacon and the voices of Hannah and Jane. She fumbled for her glasses and looked at her watch. 8:30. She put the glasses back on the table, rolled onto her stomach, and hugged the pillow.

Hannah knocked on her door. "Ready for breakfast? Jane's in the kitchen. We want to hear about your date before we go to church."

She turned onto her back and breathed to find enough energy to answer. "I'm awake." She'd shower before she faced them. Quiet her head and have time to think about how to describe the evening. She opened the blinds and looked outside. Sun. She cracked the window. Warm enough for jeans and a T-shirt. The peasant blouse she draped over her desk chair was covered in tears. She threw it and the underwear she had chosen so carefully into the laundry basket she kept in her closet.

She grabbed clean underwear, a T-shirt, and her jeans from last night. The jeans smelled of Indian spices. She moved fast from her bedroom into the bathroom. The mirror greeted her with a reflection blurred by her nearsightedness. She pulled aside a shower curtain designed to look like a forest and stepped into the bathtub. She closed the curtain as if it could shelter her in a stand of trees. Cool water helped with her headache. Finished, she dressed, brushed her teeth, and ran a comb through her hair. Maybe she'd grow it longer, learn to style it, lose a few pounds. Tomorrow is another day, she told herself.

She opened the bathroom door to the monotony of the present where Hannah and Jane were talking about the latest episode of *General Hospital*. This was their lives. Soap operas. Early Bird dinners. People sitting around a pool asking if the mail came yet. She went into her bedroom and opened her window wide. At least the weather was good. She threw her pajamas in the basket, retrieved her glasses, and went into the kitchen to face a barrage of questions.

Hannah wasted no time. "How was your date? Are you seeing him again?"

Connie poured a mug of coffee. "Will's just a friend. Call him my writing coach."

Hannah touched the garnet necklace she had started to wear every day. "Didn't my gold beads help?"

Connie shrugged without answering. She'd left them in the glove compartment. They were gold-plated, as fake as the veneer she'd put on her evening.

"Scrambled eggs and toast okay?" said Jane.

"Not too much," said Connie. "We ate Indian food last night. My stomach isn't used to it."

"Indian food?" said Hannah. "Don't they eat the same things we do now that they can't hunt buffalo and wild game? Don't know what they ate in Florida. Probably alligator."

"Indian from India," said Connie. Hannah's palate hadn't expanded beyond chili. She still preferred New England's familiar meals of chowder or meat, potatoes, and vegetables.

"What kind of food is that?" said Hannah. "Who knows

how to cook it? Or did you send out?"

Jane shook something into the eggs, held up the jar to Connie, and smiled. Connie smelled curry powder. Jane must have brought it from her condo to spice up the bland eggs. It would disguise the blandness of her life. "Will's friend cooked. Lamb curry. Naan. That's a kind of bread."

"There was an Indian with you? I never met an Indian before," said Hannah.

Hannah was right. Her Freedom had been a hundred percent white. It was slowly changing, but even when Connie was in high school there were no Blacks, no Asians, not even any Jews. It wasn't Hannah's fault. Maybe she'd introduce her to Will. Maybe she'd show her that homosexuals lived and breathed in places like Freedom and Dunhill. Not today. She was too tired. "It was just Will and me. His friend left the food for him to warm up. It was wonderful." She managed to add, "So was the evening."

Jane began filling their plates. "You can tell us more while we eat."

At the table, Connie listened to Hannah's and Jane's plans for the day. After church, they'd drive to Pinellas Park for a walk. "You should come with us," said Jane. "Meet some of our church friends. There's a whole group of young people who come every Sunday. After church they go some place for lunch and a walk. They meet every Wednesday for Bible study. You'd like them."

Connie doubted it. "Maybe another day. I'm going to see Eva." She needed to peel away her gold-plated shell before she plunged into a depression that nearly led her into last night's beckoning water.

Eva was still in her bathrobe reading, a cup of coffee on the table beside her. She held the cover toward Connie. *The Peaceable Kingdom.*

"It's light, but the Quaker history is interesting."

"I need something light right now."

Eva sipped coffee. "Want some? It's strong. I drank too much wine at the party I went to last night."

"So did I. But I had breakfast with my mother and Jane. If I drink more coffee, I'll float down to the ocean."

"Sit. Tell me about your date."

Connie took hold of the blanket that rested across the top of the couch like Will's. She spread it along the seat.

"You don't need to do that," said Eva.

"Jeans that I wore outside last night. They're sandy. Your white couch might not like them." She kicked off her sneakers, sat so she could face Eva, her back against the arm, her legs spread out in front of her. She pulled her knees up and wrapped her arms around them.

"Did the jeans stay on?"

"You're not exactly subtle."

"You don't have to tell me details. I just want to know if I'm going to lose a friend to a boyfriend."

"You're not."

"You're about to cry. Was it that bad?"

"Not at all. We ate Indian food."

"You're avoiding the question. Is there something I should know?"

Connie hugged her knees tighter. "I'm pledged to secrecy."

"Then let me guess. You ate Indian food. Who cooked it?"

"Will's friend Sid."

"So there were three of you for dinner?"

Connie swallowed the eggs that were rising into her throat. "I don't know where Sid was, but he lives with Will. He's Indian.

Will just warmed up the food."

Eva got out of her chair, moved Connie into an upright position, and sat next to her. "I get it."

"Get what?"

"No sex. Male friend who cooks and lives with him. Will's gay."

"You figured that out fast."

"At least he's not married."

Connie stifled a sob. "If he were, I might not feel so rejected."

"It's always too complicated if you have an affair with a married man. Go ahead and cry. Don't bury your feelings."

She didn't cry easily. Never cried in front of others except at George's and her father's funerals. With Eva holding her, she let herself go and sobbed out all her frustration with life.

Eva got up, brought her a box of tissues, and sat next to her again. "You don't need to worry about me. I can keep a secret."

Connie needed five tissues to finish blowing her nose. "I shouldn't be so upset. It's not like he led me on."

"It's not just about Will."

"I know. I've only met him half-a-dozen times."

"Doesn't matter. What's that song? 'The First Time Ever I Saw Your Face.'"

"David used to play it in jazz clubs."

"Maybe it's David you want, not Will."

"No. David's history. Will was the future."

"He's still in your future. You shouldn't leave him because you can't have him."

"I won't. He helps my writing."

"Is that using him?"

Connie didn't answer. Using him as an editor would be as bad as Will using her as a pretend girlfriend. Their meetings had been helpful. It was sometimes hard to hear a harsh critique, but he was honest. The honesty had been drawing her more deeply into their relationship. It would have to be enough.

Eva broke the silence. "What else is bothering you?"

"Everything. I take care of my mother while my sister wanders around Europe. I miss Boston and my friends there. I miss sex. I'm afraid of becoming a boring old spinster. "

"You don't need sex as much as you need something in your life besides your mother and Jane and your writing."

"Spoken by someone who swore off sex when she divorced. I'm glad I have you."

"I'm not enough. Find a hobby."

Connie hated hobbies. "Like knitting with my mother?"

"Something active, then. Volunteer work."

"I can't tie myself to someone else's schedule."

"You're athletic. Take up running or bicycling. Florida's a great place for that."

"A distraction from the crappy life I have."

"Don't hoard your depression. Florida's not such a bad place. If you were in Massachusetts today, you'd be wearing a winter coat and a hat. Sloshing through snow in boots."

Connie laughed. "My wardrobe's cheaper here." She wanted to say she hated Eva's home state. She feared she'd never find a place to call home.

"Isn't that why all the snowbirds invade us in winter? Move out of the high tax states when they retire?"

"I'm thirty years old. A long way from retiring."

"So use your time. Get that book finished. It's your future."

"If I'm lucky."

"I have faith in you. Write secrets into your novels. Too many people keep them. Think about all those gay people who hide who they are. They marry. They have children. They lead miserable lives."

"Do you know people like that?"

"One of our teachers. He finally left his marriage."

"Is he still teaching? Have people accepted him?"

"He was fired. A year later he committed suicide."

Connie couldn't tell Eva about George's suicide note tucked away in her closet. But she could talk about her mother. "Maybe that's my mother's secret."

"Your mother has a secret? She always seems so open."

"She has a blue box with the image of a mountain on it. She won't let anyone see it. Says it's filled with memories that don't matter. Every time she holds it, she says something about Charlie."

"Who's he?"

"Her brother. He left home when she was fifteen. She never talked about him much until we moved here. Now she talks about him every day. Out of context."

"It's the disease. What are they calling it now?"

"Alzheimer's. I know. But she's hiding something."

Eva swallowed some of her coffee and made a face. "Yuck. It's cold. So what's the secret? He was gay or he committed suicide?"

"Maybe both."

"Things are getting better for gay people now. Not so many suicides. You should be glad Will shared his condition with you."

Connie flinched. "Condition? You think it's some kind of mental disorder?"

"Sorry. Habit."

"I shouldn't have told you."

Connie bent to put on her sneakers. I'm going for a walk. Clear my head. Figure out my life."

Eva walked her to the door. "We're still friends."

"You're the only one I have here."

"And Will."

"Right. Maybe the first line of my next novel can be "They were friends, not lovers."

Chapter 7
Christmas 1973

On Christmas Eve, Connie went to church with her mother and Jane. She squirmed as the minister narrated the Christmas story, describing the star of Bethlehem, the manger, the wise men, the virgin birth. His literalness troubled her, but she enjoyed singing the old carols.

After they said goodnight to Jane, Connie and Hannah filled stockings with secrets and put gifts to each other and Jane under an artificial tree set up in a corner. A box from Sarah still in its brown mail wrapping lay under the tree. A zillion stamps and *Par Avion* stickers displayed its foreignness. Hannah wanted to leave cookies and milk for Santa. "Did we make your grandmother's recipe? The ones with the sour cream?"

"This morning."

"I forgot. I remember the Christmas you stopped believing in Santa. You still wanted to leave cookies."

"Believing in Santa is like believing in a virgin birth."

"Don't spoil it." Hannah banged through the kitchen. "Where are the cookies?"

Connie went to help her. They were visible in a plastic container on the counter. She arranged a few on a plate while

Hannah poured a glass of milk.

As they placed the futile offering on the coffee table, Hannah said, "Charlie loved these cookies." She kissed Connie lightly on the cheek and whispered, "Goodnight."

Connie sat alone in the room staring at a Christmas tree so fake even Charlie Brown's would have been better. The ornaments carried memories of happier Christmases. The miniature animals her father had made. The knitted Santa Clauses from her mother. Connie's and Sarah's baby handprints pressed into clay and hardened. The top of the tree held an angel, always Sarah's choice while Connie would argue for a star. She stood up, reached to the top of the tree and took it down, leaving the spot empty. She ate a cookie shaped like a Santa, drank the milk, took the angel into her room, and went to bed.

In the morning, she woke to a sadness she felt too often. It would pass as it did every morning if she forced herself out of bed. When she joined her mother in the kitchen for coffee, Hannah was washing the cookie and milk dishes. "Did we have cookies last night?"

"We left them for Santa. I ate them."

"Why do I keep forgetting?"

Connie squeezed her hand tenderly. "We're still adjusting. This is our first Christmas in Florida. We'll be okay."

"We still have the stockings. You and Sarah loved that part."

"I did." Sarah had always been impatient to get to what she called the real presents. They went into the living room and sat on the couch facing the pretend tree. The stockings looked out of place lying under the tree instead of hanging from a fireplace mantel. At least they were real, knitted by Hannah years ago. Connie picked up the one with her name knitted into the top and gave Hannah the other. Hannah read Sarah's name. "She should be here."

A bitter aftertaste of coffee rose in Connie's throat. "Well, she's not."

"I wonder if Lizzie has a stocking."

Connie doubted it. "I'm sure she does."

They rummaged through their stockings. Typewriter ribbons, pens, toiletries for Connie. More toiletries, mini-crossword puzzles, and socks for Hannah. An orange in the toe of each stocking. Connie felt more cheerful. "Florida oranges. Juicier than weeks old shipments we'd get up north."

They cut up oranges and grapefruit, brewed more coffee, and called Jane over for omelets. After they ate, they sat on pillows in front of the tree for a gift exchange. Connie gave Jane an apron with a quote from the gospel of Matthew, "Give us this day our daily bread." She also gave her a serious set of knives to replace her dull ones.

Hannah gave Jane a sweater in a lightweight cotton suitable for Florida. "I don't dare knit sweaters, but I'm knitting a blanket for you."

Jane held the sweater against her chest. "Yellow, my favorite color. I love it. I'll love the blanket, too."

Jane handed Connie a gift that was obviously a book. "I don't know anything about this, but the title is good."

Connie opened the package. *The Optimist's Daughter.* "I like Eudora Welty. Maybe she'll help me become an optimist."

Jane pointed to the Bible quote on her apron. "God's not finished with you yet. And we're not finished with the presents." She took a package from under the scraggly tree and gave it to Hannah. From me to you."

Hannah opened a boxed array of yarn and a pattern book for the dishcloths she favored. She paged through the book. "I hope I can follow the patterns."

Jane glanced at Connie before she said, "Mostly you just count knit/purl stitches to create the design. Knitting a new pattern is good for the brain."

They opened the last of their presents to each other. A monogrammed canvas bag for Connie from her mother. Connie presented Hannah with a pair of good walking shoes and a framed photo of the last Christmas George was alive. He and Sarah were crouched down holding Lizzie, who wore a Santa hat. Behind them, Hannah and Sam had their arms around each other.

"What a lovely photo," said Jane.

Hannah put her finger on Sam's image. "Charlie was handsome, wasn't he?"

"Who's Charlie?" said Jane.

Hannah looked at the photo again. "I mean Sam. Charlie was my brother. He's just a memory."

"Oh," said Jane. She took the photo from Hannah. "Where were you, Connie?"

"I'm the invisible photographer. Like the ghosts of Christmas past."

Hannah passed the photo to Connie. "We always had wonderful Christmases."

Connie put it under the tree and picked up Sarah's gift box. "Open Sarah's package. It will make you feel like she's with us." She tore off the brown paper with all its stickers. Notes from Sarah and Lizzie lay on top of a box of wrapped gifts. She handed Sarah's note to her mother.

Hannah waved it back. "Read it out loud. Jane will be interested. Sarah must be missing us today."

Connie began to read.

Dear Mum and Connie,
Merry Christmas from Paris. We've been here only

*a few months and Lizzie is talking like a six-year-
old native. Art's been helping me review my high
school French, but I'm hopeless.*

"Who's Art?" said Hannah.

Connie wondered when Arthur had become Art. She imagined him and Sarah drinking champagne while Lizzie played on the floor of an apartment Sarah hadn't bothered to decorate. She gave Hannah the package labeled *Mum*. "You remember. He found them an apartment in Paris."

Hannah tore at the ribbon. "I remember. The tutor left. Forgot his name. Is Art a new tutor?"

"James was the tutor. I don't know what Art is." A lover, Connie assumed. She continued to read.

*I haven't written because we've been busy shopping
while we're still in Paris.*

Hannah pulled the ribbon off her package. "Sarah loves clothes. Every Christmas I'd buy her something nice. Connie liked books better. Remember the Christmas you got those cute mattress shirts?"

Connie hated the shirt that made her look like a patchwork bag of potatoes. "It was bleeding madras. You washed them and they bled all over my favorite yellow sweater."

"I remember madras," said Jane. "It used to bleed onto my bras."

"Keep reading," said Hannah. "What else does Sarah say."

Connie skimmed the rest of the letter and summarized. "She's tired of visiting museums and tired of French people who treat her like a tourist. After the holidays, they'll fill their suitcases with her Paris designer clothes and take a six-city tour through

Brussels, Amsterdam, and Zurich."

"They?" said Hannah.

"Sarah and Lizzie." Connie omitted Art.

"Will she come home then?" Hannah started to untape the paper on her present.

"Doesn't sound like it. They'll go south through Madrid and back to Italy, this time through Venice and Rome." Connie read the last few sentences.

> *When the Italian summer arrives, we'll rent rooms*
> *in London. Maybe an English city will be more*
> *hospitable than a French.*

Hannah looked at Jane. "Sarah will come as soon as she can. I know she misses us." The note didn't sound like Sarah missed them. Connie gave it to her mother. "You can read it over later. There's a card from Lizzie." Connie smiled at the drawing Lizzie had done of the Eiffel Tower. She read, *I wish you koed taak me to the parck. I mis you and I love you." XXXOOO, Lizzie.*

Hannah took the note. She read it and started to cry. Above her teary eyes, she had lost all her eyebrows. She looked shriveled and old.

"Don't," said Connie. "Open your gift. It will make you feel better."

Hannah opened a small bottle of French perfume. Sarah had forgotten that perfume triggered their mother's headaches. Jane opened the gift Sarah had included for her. A cookbook, translated but with measurements in grams and liters. Sarah never paid attention to details.

When Connie opened her gift of Camus' *L'Etranger*, she read a note Sarah had tucked inside.

I received your letter and know our mother is in good hands. If I must return, I trust you will inform me. Meanwhile, enjoy your Christmas together.

—Sarah

Connie folded the note and brought it into her bedroom. She took the Christmas angel off her desk, tore up the note, and stuffed them both into her wastebasket. "Fuck you, Sarah. I'm not our mother's nursemaid." She tossed the book into her closet and went back into the living room.

"I just needed a minute. Sarah remembers how much I liked Camus in college," she lied. She tolerated Camus, but she'd hated Sartre, hated the whole idea of existentialism. She wanted more than the absurdity of Sisyphus rolling a boulder up a mountain, watching it roll down, and rolling it up again, forever and ever. When Jane suggested a walk along the beach, she vowed to let her writing move her beyond the futility of walks on the sand.

Hannah turned in a circle, looking for a door. "I'll just get my hat and scarf and gloves."

Connie moved beside her. "It's okay. We're not in frigid Massachusetts."

Hannah regained her sense of place and joked that with her new shoes she might take up running.

Chapter 8

June 1974 – August 9, 1974

Connie wrapped one of her mother's afghans around her legs. She was listening, huddled in the middle of the living room with her mother, Eva, and Jane, listening to the violence of a tropical storm. "This is the worst storm since we moved here."

"I've lived here all my life and never seen one this bad," said Jane.

Eva lay on her back looking at the tree outside the sliding door as it bent in the wind. "Imagine if we had an actual hurricane."

Hannah held her arms as if a self-hug could protect her. "I remember the one in Massachusetts when I was a kid. 1938. The Merrimack River flooded and destroyed blocks of houses close to it."

The wind toppled something outside. The lights flickered and went out. Jane started to pray. Hannah joined her in the Lord's Prayer. Connie got up and pulled the drape across the sliding door. She couldn't see as far as the swimming pool. It must have overflowed. She checked the bedrooms and the kitchen. The wind shook the blinds but no water leaked onto the sills. The rain drummed on the roof, but no spots of water showed on the ceilings. When she came back to the living room, she could feel the house vibrating. She sat down and pulled the afghan over her legs. "Everything's tight. These condos are well-built."

Hannah moved closer to her so they could share the afghan. "Your father tightened everything up when we bought this place."

Eva looked at Jane. "Don't worry. Ours will be okay."

"I hope so," said Jane. "I shouldn't have left my cat alone."

Connie leaned back against the sofa. "Rusty's a survivor. He'll be fine."

They stopped talking and waited beneath the fury of nature. When the storm ended at last, they walked outside to survey the damage. Their feet sank into the saturated grass. The pool was flooded, the azalea Connie had planted was demolished, and the bird feeder her father had built was blown to the ground and smashed. The worst of New England blizzards never left this much damage.

Jane tried to open the back door of her condo. It was locked. "I need to check on Rusty. He'll be terrified."

"And I need to see if any rain got into my place." Eva followed Jane through Hannah's unit.

Connie picked up pieces of the bird feeder and piled them next to the door. Hannah stood motionless beside her until Connie brought her inside. "I need to call Will. See if he's okay. He lives closer to the water than we do." She tried the phone. Dead.

She led Hannah to Jane's door. When Jane opened it, the cat rushed out. Connie watched him scratch in the spot near the dumpster that he used as a litter box. "Rusty survived the storm just fine. Everything okay inside?"

"Thank God," said Jane. "Come inside."

"Go in with Jane, Mum."

"Where are you going?" said Jane.

"The phones are down. I want to see if my friend Will is okay."

As she walked away, she heard Hannah say, "I think he's her boyfriend."

The car radio came on along with the engine. This was the worst storm to hit Tampa since Hurricane Easy in 1950. Twenty inches of rain had fallen, power was cut all over the city, and neighborhoods near the water were flooded. Three people were confirmed drowned. Connie drove slowly, stopping at jammed traffic where streetlights were out. A fallen tree forced her to detour to Clearwater harbor. Boats were smashed against each other and into the pier. Steam rose from the asphalt like ocean fog. The twenty-minute drive to Will's turned into forty.

She got out of the car and stepped around leaves and twigs that littered his yard. Sid appeared at the door. Connie liked him. He was smart, funny, handsome in a slightly effeminate way, and it was obvious that he loved Will. Months ago she had pushed away her jealousy and learned to embrace the friendship these two men offered her.

"Your place must be okay or you wouldn't be driving here in that yellow submarine of yours. Have any trouble?"

"Lots of trees and wires to dodge. Tampa got hit the hardest."

"Come out back. Will's picking up debris and figuring out what to do with the magnolia limb decorating our deck. I told him we should be singing 'deck the deck with boughs of flowers.'"

They walked through the living room onto the deck where a tree limb had smashed the wicker furniture into a pile of sticks. Connie stepped over it onto grass that was saturated into the consistency of a sponge.

Will pointed to the magnolia branch. "Got any ideas?"

Connie began picking up debris. "My dad would have gotten out his chain saw."

Will pushed the trash barrel to her. "So would mine. I'm just the gay guy who can't do anything manly."

Sid grabbed the twigs Will was holding and tossed them into the barrel. "You know better than to say that. You're an athlete. I'm the one who cooks and disguises the high register of my voice behind my accent."

A face appeared over the fence that separated Will from his neighbor. "You guys okay?"

"Except for the forest on our deck." Sid emphasized his Indian accent. Connie wondered how he and Will kept their secret from their neighbors. She suspected they knew.

"I've got a chain saw. I'll come over and cut it up for you." The neighbor disappeared behind the fence. The rattle of the saw started.

Will began picking up debris again. "Glad he didn't say he'd loan it to us."

Connie deposited another pile of twigs into the barrel. "Let him be neighborly. People like to help. I'll come back later. Right now I need to go back with my mother. She'll be worrying." If she remembers, she thought. She hadn't shared the fact of Hannah's Alzheimer's with Will and Sid. They weren't the only ones keeping secrets.

"Why's that man saluting? Was he a soldier like Charlie?" Hannah spoke from Jane's recliner to the television more than to Connie and Jane.

Connie glanced at Jane stroking Rusty who was sitting on her lap. He drooled so much Jane joked that his hormones were out of whack. "That's Nixon. Remember he resigned." She couldn't cover her mother's Alzheimer's much longer.

Hannah moved to the edge of the recliner. "I know it's Nixon. Never liked the man. He has shifty eyes. I just want to know if he was a soldier like Charlie."

Walter Cronkite continued to talk about the drama of Nixon's downfall and American democracy at work. There were crowds cheering the disgraced Nixon where a month earlier others had demonstrated for his impeachment.

Connie thought Nixon's wave looked more like a Heil Hitler than an American soldier salute.

Jane defended Nixon. "He was in the navy. He did some good things as president. Got us out of Vietnam."

Connie wanted to say "not soon enough." Maybe Ford would bungle his way through a more honest presidency.

Hannah got out of the recliner. "Charlie was in the army. I'm going home to check on him." She left before Jane or Connie could stop her. Connie got up to check that she went into their condo. She came back, turned off the television, and sat next to Jane.

Jane set Rusty on the floor. Her pants had a spot of drool that she wiped with the cloth she always kept on her sofa. "She talks about Charlie a lot, but she's never been this confused. She must have been close to him."

Connie bent down and grabbed Rusty before he escaped the room. "Something happened. Has she ever told you why he left?"

"No. It's only since you both moved here that she talks about him so much. Last week she called the mailman Charlie. Something's wrong."

Connie fingered Rusty's neck, calming herself with his purr. "She has hardening of the arteries."

Jane reached for Connie's hand. Startled, Rusty jumped away. "I thought it might be from that medicine she takes for depression. Nasty stuff."

"She's been taking that for years. Dr. Wilberforce diagnosed it. He says they've started to label it Alzheimer's. I've kept it a secret from her and from everyone except Eva. The doctor says it's best not to name it, so people won't treat her differently. He thinks the decline will be slow."

"She's my best friend." Jane started to cry.

Connie got off the sofa to find a tissue. She gave the whole box to Jane and sat down again. "Please don't act differently. My mother needs routine, she needs friends, she needs you."

"So do you. I'm sorry you didn't tell me sooner. I could have helped."

"There's nothing to help with." Yet, thought Connie.

Jane blew her nose and controlled her crying. "Have you told Sarah? Will she come to help?"

"She's not through with Europe yet."

Connie knew she could blackmail Sarah with George's suicide note. It wasn't time, but she'd do it if she had to.

"You'd better go check on your mother."

"She went inside. She'll be fine. She's probably looking through a box she keeps hidden. I think it has to do with Charlie. Has she ever said anything to you?"

"No. What does it matter?"

"It doesn't." If she discovered whatever secret her mother was hiding, she wondered if she'd have to hide it the way she was hiding George's note. "For now, just treat my mother the way you always have. Take her to The Lobster Landing later. I'm supposed to be at Will's."

"That man you keep hiding from us? Your mother has you married to him."

"He's just a friend." Connie patted Rusty, the cat she thought of as gay, and left Jane alone with the box of tissues beside her.

Sid greeted her at the door with hand waves imitating Nixon's farewell. "Champagne's waiting. Tricky Dick is history." He modulated his voice to sound like Nixon's. "'I leave with deep humility and gratefulness in my heart.' Hallelujah. The mighty has fallen."

Will appeared behind Sid. "How'd that neighbor of yours take it? Didn't you tell me she likes Nixon?"

"We had other things to talk about."

Will handed her a glass of champagne. "Come sit. I know that look. Something's wrong."

They sat on Will's white furniture. Will and Sid listened while Connie told them about Hannah's Alzheimer's and her obsession with Charlie.

"You don't deserve this," said Will. "Life's not fair."

"No one ever said it was." Connie lifted her glass to Will and Sid. She swallowed the champagne along with the secret of George's suicide.

Chapter 9

February – March 1975

Connie's writing propelled her until the beginning of 1975 when she landed a publishing contract with Random House for *Secrets*. She ran to Eva's, waving the contract, then drove to Bayview where she found Will on his way to class. He caught her hands and they did a dance on the steps of the English Department until the college chimes told Will he had to leave. The euphoria dwindled as she drove home and began to worry about the nine months until the release date. There'd be editing to do, acknowledgments to write, a cover to approve. She dreaded the idea of an author photo and resolved to lose a few pounds before Random House sent a photographer.

Hannah kept calling the novel *Whispers* instead of *Secrets*. Connie feared she wouldn't hang on to her memory until October.

Will threw a party to celebrate and invited everyone from Bayview's English Department. He removed the photos of gay men that decorated his walls and scheduled the party when Sid was out of town. Connie was surprised that she missed the photos. The walls looked bare and she worried that someone would ask about the nail holes. Without Sid's humor and his cooking, the house felt empty despite the dozen guests.

After dinner, they gathered in the living room for a game of charades. *Light in August* stumped her team, but she guessed Will's acting of "Smoke Gets in Your Eyes" the moment he pretend-smoked a cigarette and wiped his eyes. Her years with David had been good for something. She drew "Beware the Ides of March" to act out. Tough. "March" was easy. "Ides" rhymed with "tides," but imitating the ocean would be hard. Maybe she could do rhymes with "brides." She'd try "Beware" by pretending to wear clothes and add a stinging bee to it.

Her team started the timer. She used her fingers to signal a quotation then five fingers for five words. She held up five fingers a second time.

""Fifth word," someone called.

She nodded and began to march in place.

Annette, the lone woman in the English Department guessed "March" easily.

She signaled first word, second syllable and pretended to strip off her shirt.

The calls came fast. "Strip." "Blouse." "Shirt." "Naked."

She gave up on that approach and tried for the first syllable, her hands imitating a bee stinging her arm. They got that and began calling out "become," "betrothed," "because" until the department chair's wife guessed "beware." From there it was easy. Third word, little word. "a," "an," she nodded at "the." Annette got it just as the hourglass ran out. "Beware the Ides of March." Everyone congratulated her.

"You're as good at charades as you are at writing," said Will, putting his arm around her when the game ended.

"I haven't had this much fun since I came to Florida."

When Will's colleagues began talking about the revision of the freshman curriculum, she went outside. She stood alone on the deck where Will had first told her he was gay. It was repaired after the fallen tree and he had bought new wicker furniture. The moon floated above her, waning just above the clouds.

Annette joined her. She destroyed Connie's image of what the first wave of women hired by English Departments would look like. Instead of cropped hair and big glasses, she had dark wavy hair and sea green eyes highlighted with eye shadow. Inside playing charades, Connie had watched how the soft folds of her green dress accented her eyes. She wore an emerald ring on her right hand, the left bare, the nails of both unbroken and polished in a pale green.

"We've all been waiting to meet you," said Annette with the hint of a southern accent.

Connie read her innuendo, that she and Will were a couple. "Will's been a wonderful friend. Besides helping me with my writing, he's helped me adjust to living in Florida."

"You're from the Northeast, aren't you?" said Annette.

"Massachusetts. Near Boston. Will's from New Hampshire so we have New England in common."

"You should come teach with us. If we listed a new class and called it Creative Writing, I'm sure you'd get an enrollment."

"I watch how Will reads papers. I'm afraid I haven't the patience."

"You learn to skim."

"Will doesn't skim what I write. I'd be like him. Zero in on every word."

"I guess you're close. The college would look the other way if you moved in together."

"We're not lovers." Connie turned her back and left Annette on the deck, remembering her fear a year ago that Will was using her as a cover.

After the euphoria of having her novel accepted, Connie felt the letdown that came to many writers when they finished a first novel. She imagined it was like birthing a baby, the excitement of becoming pregnant to the exhaustion of the delivery and the fear of releasing a child into a judging world. She struggled to start a new novel and to fight off the depression. She'd wake, pull the covers over her head, and go over what she had to do that day. Watch her mother for signs of decline or walk along Edgewater listening to the sound of a dull Gulf. Drive to the Bayview campus where she'd sit in the library forcing herself to work on a novel that was going badly. On the weekends, she'd go to a movie when Eva insisted. She lied about her progress on the new novel. At night, she'd sit with Hannah through a television show she ignored until nine o'clock when she pretended she was going to bed to read. Sometimes she managed a few pages. Most nights she simply fell asleep until morning came and she dragged herself from bed again.

Her meetings with Will continued sporadically. Twice he was away at conferences. Once she canceled, too embarrassed to show him the little writing she had done. One Thursday in March, she forgot their meeting at The Groaning Board. He found her in the library, a blank paper in front of her, staring at the pale yellow of the wall.

He picked up her legal pad and saw nothing but doodles of faces with downturned mouths and figures with hunched shoulders. He put the papers in her briefcase and, taking hold of her arm, nudged her out of the chair. "Come with me. You need to get outside. We need to talk."

Two students stood arguing next to the statue of General Loring. "It's a good thing," said the young woman whose dark hair was permed into an Afro. "The war's over. There'll be an airlift to rescue people."

"And boatloads of refugees," said the male, his blond hair a badge of his Anglo heritage. "Florida will be overrun with Vietnamese fishermen."

"So?'

"What about our jobs?"

Will steered Connie away. "Ignore that guy. I've had him in class. He's a racist."

They walked away from campus along a path that bordered the Gulf, mixing the salt smell with the smell of freshly mowed grass. "You're not writing," he said.

"I have no ideas."

"A slump after the first book is finished?"

"Maybe. I have no energy. Can hardly get out of bed in the morning."

"You should be loaded with energy. You've got a great contract. It's spring. Look at that ocean. There must be a hundred sailboats out there. Students are already sunbathing on the quad."

She kicked away a clump of grass the mower had shot onto the path. "It's March. They should be sunbathing on the last of the snow banks."

"Something's going on besides writer's block."

"I should have heeded that charade. 'Beware the Ides of March.'"

"I thought you were starting to like Florida."

"I was adjusting. Getting used to losing my father, George, my roots in Massachusetts. That statue of General what's-his-name reminds me that they're still fighting The Civil War down here."

Will stopped at a path that led to the beach. They walked down it and he pointed to a place on the sand. "Sit. Unload on me."

"I'm from New England. We don't talk about our feelings."

"I know that for sure. Try it anyway."

She sat on sand whose warmth she could feel through her

jeans. She took off her sneakers and dug small ditches with her feet. Underneath the top layer, the sand turned cold. "My brain feels like its been invaded by cobwebs. I'm as fuzzy as my mother. I walk, I eat, I write letters to Lizzie that I'm afraid my sister never reads to her."

"How old is she? Can't she read?"

Connie calculated. "Seven last birthday. Sarah's been dragging her all over Europe. Showing her things no kid cares about. At least when they come back to Massachusetts, Lizzie will find friends her own age."

"They're coming back?" Will put a hand on Connie's foot to stop her from digging.

"I thought I told you. They're coming in July. Apparently Sarah doesn't like Europe. She's not enough of a big fish there."

"Does that make you want to go back to Freedom?"

"Never. I need a city like Boston. Sarah wants to be a townie. Join some country club. Have lunch with high school friends who never left."

"What's wrong with that?"

"Nothing, I suppose. All Sarah wants out of life is for people to admire her."

"And you? What do you want?"

She pulled her knees to her chest, tempted to tell Will about George's suicide. Some secrets she couldn't share. "I want something besides Early Bird specials and a mother who confuses me with her mother and keeps talking about her brother Charlie."

"Are you incapable of joy?"

Connie thought a moment. She knew that her moods sank when she faced transitions, lifted when she began to feel more settled. "I'd be okay if I could start writing again."

"Maybe you're afraid to."

"I'm afraid *Secrets* will be a flop. If it's a success, I'm afraid the next one won't fulfill its promise."

"*Secrets*. Maybe you can use Charlie's secret for the new novel."

"If my mother would ever tell me about him. I don't even know where he went."

Will touched the hand she had begun burying in the sand. "Make it up. Isn't that what fiction does?"

"Give me an idea."

"Start with the setting. You're good at that. Imagine someone coming to Florida from New England."

"To do what?"

"I don't know. Start an orange plantation or something."

She brushed the sand off her feet and put her sneakers on. "If I can get started on this new novel, I'll be okay."

"Your book release trip will help."

"It should. When they send me from New York to Boston, I'll spend some time with Sarah and Lizzie."

"You've got six months before then. You need to stop being depressed. Find the energy that got you to write such a good first novel."

"I'm working on it."

"The novel or the depression?"

"Both."

Will turned toward the English building and Connie walked toward the library, an idea about a character who leaves Massachusetts to start an orange plantation in Florida slowly forming. Except her Uncle Charlie was turning into Aunt Charlotte and an orange plantation that comes with a charlatan who strips her of her money and leaves her to find her way, a stranger in a strange land.

PART III

Success

Chapter 10

October 1975

Connie's flight arrived late the night before the launch of *Secrets* in New York City. Dazed from the sound of honking taxis and so many flashing lights she couldn't see the stars, she fell into a restless sleep. She ate breakfast in her hotel, then went outside planning to explore. The frenzy of the city seemed an assault. In Boston, she had lived on Boylston Street, surrounded by restaurants and high end stores. The new Prudential Building was directly across from her apartment, but even with its shops and convention center, Boston was an oasis of calm compared to New York City.

She was warned not to go into Central Park at night. It seemed safe enough, if a little dirty, in the morning. Frederick Law Olmsted's vision of a park where people connected with nature and with the diversity of the city hadn't fulfilled its promise. People all over the United States still lived as walled off from each other as enemy tribes. As she wandered through areas segregated into groups with nannies, joggers, vagrants, she began thinking of ways to fit the tension into *The Orange Grove* where plantation owners, Minorcans, field workers, whites and Blacks, never mixed.

At the hotel, she rehearsed her remarks and the section of *Secrets* she planned to read. She showered and put on a black dress that fell just above her knees. The room's mirror told her the little black dress that was supposed to work for most occasions made her look more like a small town spinster than a New York sophisticate. She was tall enough, but too heavy with hair too short to be stylish. She wished she had kept her John Lennon glasses. The new ones she wore were too large for her face. Their frames screamed tortoise.

She arrived at The Eighth Street Bookshop in Greenwich Village a few minutes early. Instead of going inside to look at books whose quality would intimidate her, she walked up and down the street, assaulted by smells that drifted out of Italian trattorias. A young man with a guitar nodded as he stepped into a café. She followed two women with long hair and ankle-length hippie skirts, listening to their conversation about all the places that were closed for renovations. Change was coming to The Village and they didn't like it. She passed several openly gay couples and tried to imagine Will and Sid walking here, their secret lives freed by Greenwich Village's acceptance.

A two-year-old poster advertising the Village's first Halloween parade hung in the window of an art supply store. Inside a pumpkin shaped figure, phrases announced "The Two-Headed Pig Beast," "Demons of Hell," "The Lobster Man," "The Golden Lion from the Crypt." At the bottom, an image of a skeleton lurked. It felt like an omen that her novel would decay in a crypt of dead letters.

She turned from the poster and walked back to the bookstore that occupied a renovated townhouse. Her editor, Naomi Rhinebeck, told her it lacked the ambience it once had when its dark green wrought iron facade triangled between Eighth and MacDougal Streets. But it was still the best place in New York to launch a book.

At the bookstore, she met Naomi in person for the first time. She expected an older woman dressed in a sedate business suit. Instead, she found a woman her own age, tall, thin, and as hippie-like as the women she had followed on the street. Naomi scanned Connie before she said, "You look lovely." She escorted her around the room, introducing her to people whose names she couldn't remember.

She got through the reading and answered a few questions without making any egregious mistakes. When it was over, Naomi brought her to the café where the young man with the guitar was playing and singing to a small audience who drank coffee and smoked cigarettes. Connie thought the young man's fame was as unlikely as her own until Naomi said, "You were wonderful. I didn't want to intimidate you, but there were reviewers there from *The Village Voice*, *The New Yorker*, and *The New York Times*. *The Village Voice* asked you how you made metaphors sound so natural and *The New York Times* said you captured the feel of the New Hampshire lakes."

"He was the one who had a summer home there?"

"Yes. When we were leaving, he told me you had a future."

"The woman with the fly-away hair didn't seem impressed."

"Mostly a film critic. From *The New Yorker*."

"Why was she listening to me?"

"When a Random House author reads at Eighth Street, she comes. She likes the bookstore and she's friends with one of our senior editors. Don't worry about her. *The New Yorker* only likes urban novels. They won't review *Secrets*."

Over coffee, they talked about Connie's new novel. Naomi suggested that she immerse herself in Florida's botany so she could do for it what she had done for New Hampshire's. "Make the landscape a character. You do that so well."

Connie left the café elated, planning ways to make Florida

feel like a home that would come alive in her writing.

In Boston, Connie checked into the Lenox Hotel on the corner of Exeter and Boylston Streets. She felt almost at home. When she lived in Boston, the hotel's rectangular windows framed in red brick would draw her eyes upward and she'd imagine scenes of wedding nights, illicit liaisons, or solitary escapes for women overwhelmed by the obligations of family life. She rested until it was time to put on her black dress and walk to the Boston Public Library for her reading. How many hours had she spent sheltered behind its granite walls and arched windows? Climbing its few steps, she looked across at the rough-stoned browns and tans of Trinity Church's towers. She remembered how one evening in winter, she watched a bride and groom embracing under the front archway while snow fell on the world around them. She hoped their marriage was as idyllic as the scene.

Inside the library, her host, another beautiful woman, met her. She was relieved that they didn't go to the reading room whose vaulted ceilings and vast length would have swallowed her into its history. They went to a smaller room in the new Johnson addition where she was greeted by an array of familiar faces. People she knew from when she worked as a glorified typist at MIT Press had come to listen.

Linda, who started to work at the press the same time as Connie, asked the first question. "Is there a lot of autobiography in your writing? Maura seems a lot like you. Tough. A survivor."

Connie wasn't sure if that was a compliment or an insult. "I'm not sure I'm a survivor, but I suppose I put my view of the world onto Maura."

"What about your other characters?" said a woman Connie

hadn't liked and whose name she couldn't remember. "Any of us? Others you know?"

She glanced at her old boss, Leroy, who was standing at the back of the room. She had used his hair, a red so bright it bordered on orange. She answered carefully. "I need to see what people look like, so I get an image of someone and then manipulate it. I might use a comment from someone, but everything is reimagined. It's all fiction."

Leroy raised a hand. She nodded at him to ask his question. "I couldn't miss my hair. It's okay, though. I'd never do the things that character does. I like what you do with the setting. I feel like I'm right there."

"I start with a sense of place," said Connie.

"Will you do that in your next novel? What place?" said Linda.

"It's mostly set in Florida. I'm still working on feeling at home there." She answered a few more questions before signing a dozen books, some for friends, some for strangers. After, she went with four of her unmarried women friends to the Eliot Lounge. She sank into one of the plush leather seats. They all told stories about their first years living in Boston. Linda reminded them of the Christmas party when they went back to someone's house in Cambridge. She flirted all night with a man who had known Dylan Thomas. On Monday, Leroy called her into his office and asked if she'd ever date a married man. Linda still claimed she hadn't invited the man into her apartment. Connie told them about the time her first roommate had come home late from a date. She didn't want to wake Connie and in the morning she found her roommate sleeping in front of the door, holding her purse. There were stories about guys picked up at The Eliot Lounge and dumped when they expected sex for dinner, stories about stolen groceries replaced by the grocery store manager who also wanted sex, about the guitar Linda bought only to find out later the man who sold it to her had stolen it. They had all been naïve and they had all been burned by some man or another. But they all still knew how to laugh and to have a good time.

When the conversation turned to office politics, Connie said goodnight. She walked alone down Boylston Street, trying to sober up. She stopped at the steps of her old apartment. The Chinese restaurant below was still open, the smells of its spices drifting into the night air, reminding her of the night Will came out to her. In the two years since then, she had birthed a book and cut the cord that tied her to the people she had just been drinking with. Boston was a pleasant memory but no longer home.

She woke to a throbbing headache. A shower and a double dose of aspirin helped only a little. The idea of an expensive breakfast at The Lenox turned her stomach so she checked out and locked her suitcase in the rental car she had left in the parking garage. She walked again to her old apartment and found her favorite bagel shop a few doors down from the Chinese restaurant. The shop hadn't changed. Strictly Bagels. Choices of cream cheese doctored with olives or chives or topped with lox. She ordered a plain bagel with plain cream cheese and a large coffee, no cream. She found a spot in front of the window. Outside, the Prudential Building loomed.

Someone had left a copy of *The Boston Globe* on the table. A photo of her at the library stared from the Arts page. The headline read, 'A SECRET SUCCESS'. She wiped her forehead with a napkin, blaming the sweat on the hot coffee and her hangover. She scanned the review. It looked okay, so she read more carefully. Constance Lewis was a Massachusetts native who set her novel on a lake in New Hampshire familiar to any Bay Stater who ventured north. The town was as full of secrets as Grace Metalious's *Peyton Place*. Her protagonist, Maura Appleton, was as tough as the weather. The reviewer coaxed readers into buying a debut novel that represented a promising start for its author. Her heart quieted. She sipped at her coffee as if it were champagne. When she left the bagel shop, she carried the Arts section folded so it showed an author looking confident in a black dress.

She walked left onto Exeter Street past the theater where she had watched *Deliverance*, alone, forced to move her seat when a man who smelled of tobacco and booze sat next to her. At Commonwealth Avenue, she crossed onto the pathway that was part of Boston's Emerald Necklace, a design that linked eleven of Boston's parks. Traffic was light, most people avoiding an area that a few weeks earlier would have been jammed with cars moving students into rental apartments in the once elegant private residences. The trees canopying the walkway showed hints of fall color. She passed students walking in groups on their way to subway stations that would take them to BU or MIT or Northeastern. The ones walking, like her, toward The Public Garden and Emerson College wore multi-colored or beaded shirts that looked like theater costumes.

A young woman passed her, whispering lines of a Shakespeare sonnet. Connie thought about writing a play, casting the young woman as part of a group of friends gathered together in one of the galleries on Marlborough Street. They could reminisce about their friendships, brag about the homes they found after college, disguise the sadness of their lives. It was a silly idea. Holding the newspaper walking along the Emerald Necklace on a glorious fall morning, she couldn't conjure up sadness. She wanted to call Will and tell him she was still capable of joy.

She crossed Arlington Street into The Garden. The masses of tulips that bloomed in the spring had been cut back. Daisies, lupine, and dahlias were giving way to chrysanthemums that would weather the fall. She turned left onto the path that led her to the boats and thought of Robert McCloskey's *Make Way for Ducklings*. She should publish a book for children. Something that would become iconic. Something that would give her a steady income. The line at the swan boats was short, mostly adults with preschoolers or couples whose intimacy marked them as lovers. She accepted the hand of a young man who helped each person onto the boat. He'd hide himself behind the fiberglass swan, paddle the boat through the lagoon, and tell the tourists seated on the red benches about how the rides began in the nineteenth century. Connie knew the spiel. She and David used to ride the boats so they could laugh at the tourists. She folded the newspaper into the canvas bag her mother had given her for Christmas. She'd call her from Sarah's and pretend she missed Florida.

She sat on one of the uncomfortable wooden benches. Two young women carrying baskets of flowers made it onto the boat just before it left the dock. They scanned the benches, nodded at each other, and walked toward Connie.

The taller one spoke to her. "Will you sit in the middle? We like to be close to the water. The flowers like it better."

Connie moved to the middle of the seat as they settled beside her with their baskets. They smelled of incense.

"It's like a fairy tale," said the taller one, pointing to the island where families of ducks made their home. "We're the ugly ducklings grown into swans." Dressed in long, worn skirts, they looked more like "The Little Match Girl."

The shorter one, who wore her hair in braids with a flower fastened above her ear, spoke over the paddler who was giving his spiel about the history of the boats. "We're selling flowers. Will you give us a dollar?"

"That's not the way to ask, Talia." The taller one lifted her basket toward Connie. "Talia's new. We sell these flowers for the Unification Church. Do you know about our mission?"

Before she left for Florida two years ago, Connie had read about Sun Myung Moon and how his group of converts had begun to appear in Boston selling flowers. Girls like these, kidnapped and brainwashed into believing Sun Myung Moon was the Second Coming of Christ. "Moonies," she said.

The taller girl moved closer to the edge of the boat. "That's an insult. We aren't creatures howling at the moon. We worship a God who is both male and female. Equality. Surely you care about that."

Connie put her finger to her lips and pretended to listen to the paddler, who was telling them about the island where the ducks lived and the habitat the island provided in the middle of the city. He did his job, directing the tourists to the souvenir shop that sold copies of *Make Way for Ducklings.*

The two converts kept silent until the swan boat approached the dock. Talia gave Connie a flower from her basket. "One dollar will support our mission."

Connie stepped onto the dock alongside the girls. She handed the tall one a five dollar bill. "Use it for yourselves. Call your parents. Tell them where you are."

"We share all we have," said Talia.

The tall girl pocketed the money. "Come to our meeting tonight. It's at six o'clock. Two-fifty-six Newbury Street. Bottom floor. We'll tell you how we fight communism, how we worked to get Nixon impeached. Our efforts helped to get him to resign."

Connie put the flower back into the basket. "Call your parents. You'll be more help to society if you go to college."

"The Unification Church is our home," Talia said.

Connie wanted to take Talia's hand as she would Lizzie's. Lead her away from the false home of a cult. It was futile. She left the girls and their baskets of flowers and walked out of The Public Garden into The Boston Common. She went to the old burial ground next to the Park Street Church. When she saw the grave of Judge Samuel Sewall, notorious during the Salem Witchcraft Trials, she thought of the two girls. Their belief in Sun Myung Moon was as misguided as the notion that inconvenient women were witches.

She walked down Tremont Street back into the park to look at Saint-Gaudens' bronze relief of Colonel Shaw and his 54th regiment of Black soldiers. Carved into the memorial were the words OMNIA RELINQVIT SERVARE REMPVBLICAM. She knew the translation. "He forsook all to preserve the public weal." Where was today's Robert Gould Shaw who could rescue the girls from a false home that was enslaving them?

Chapter 11

October 1975

Connie stood for a moment in the hallway of the Freedom mill condos. The ceiling was high and windows at each end helped to light a space encased in brick. It felt like her life, a window into the past at one end, a window into the future at the other, the present trapped between the two. She wasn't like Sarah, who could seize the day without regard for what would be best for Lizzie. Or best for Hannah. Connie pushed aside her resentment. Maybe Europe had softened her sister. She knocked on a door that had been crafted from one of the mill's originals.

Lizzie opened it and lunged before Connie could see what she looked like. She felt the difference. The hug was stronger than two years ago, the top of Lizzie's head nestling higher on her breast. She took Lizzie's hands and moved backwards from her. "I think you grew five inches. What was in that European water?"

"I'm seven."

"I can see that. Strong enough to carry my suitcase inside?"

Lizzie lifted the overnight bag. "It's not heavy. We had lots more suitcases in Europe."

Connie remembered the full trunk of Sarah's Mercedes. "I have a bigger one in my car."

"Can I help carry it?"

"I won't need it. Didn't Mummy tell you I'm only staying two nights?"

"That's not long enough. You and Granny need to come home. Freedom's nicer than anywhere in the world. Except I want a yard to play in."

Sarah came out of the bedroom. "You'll have one soon." She moved to Connie, her hug half as strong as Lizzie's. She stepped back and studied her. "You look good. A little heavier. Florida must suit you."

Connie wished she could say Sarah looked anorectic. But her sister was beautiful as always. The bottled blond of her hair looked natural as it fell to shoulders covered in a scoop necked sweater. A strand of colored beads accented the sweater's blue. "Do I see a hint of Paris in your necklace?"

"Just a trinket we found in a glass blowing shop on the Champs-Élysées."

"We?"

"Arthur and me. The necklace is all I want of him."

Lizzie clung to Connie's arm. "I liked Art. Better than James."

Sarah put her hand on Lizzie's shoulder. "James made her study. Arthur just played games with her. Bought her presents every time we left her with a babysitter. With my money."

"Mummy said Arthur was bleeding her dry. That means taking her money."

Sarah picked up Connie's overnight bag. "Enough talk of Arthur. Freshen up. We're going to the mill's restaurant for dinner."

Connie liked the restaurant and how George used the beams and the duct work in its design. Its walls were original brick. The transformation of the mill's interior had been so remarkable it was given a cover story in *AIA Journal*. Now Sarah owned it all.

She could live the rest of her life on its profits. She hadn't needed to hide George's suicide.

Connie would have to wait until they were alone to confront her with the suicide note. She picked up her bag. "Cotton to Cocktails. It's a great name. A little history and a lot of class. It'll be like going to Paris after all the meals I eat with Mum and Jane at The Lobster Landing's Early Bird Special."

"Not quite Paris. Get settled while I open some wine. I'll tell you all about Europe."

Lizzie sat down on a gold brocade sofa Connie recognized as one Sarah and George had bought when they first married.

"I didn't like Europe," said Lizzie. "No yards to play in. Mummy says we're getting a new house with a huge yard. And a swing set."

Connie bent and kissed the top of Lizzie's head. Her hair smelled the clean floral of Prell shampoo. Lizzie must like its emerald green as much as she had when she was seven. "You're lucky."

The window in front of the sofa faced a small garden plot whose chrysanthemums needed deadheading and a brick wall that housed another section of the complex. The interior of the renovated mill was a designer's dream, but even a landscape architect couldn't transform parking lots and tiny islands of grass into something natural. No child would like it here.

Connie carried her overnight bag into the room she'd share with Lizzie. It had one brick wall and three of wallboard painted a pale yellow where Lizzie had hung drawings. They didn't suggest a future artist. One could have been the Eiffel Tower, another showed trees Lizzie drew with brown trunks and squirly lines that were supposed to be leaves. The leaves' shape was the same as the lines that outlined clouds. A yellow ball at the corner with straight lines jutting out represented the sun. Butterflies and fish filled other sheets of paper. Lizzie was better at those.

A child's desk was centered between the two beds, both overflowing with dolls and stuffed animals. The desk was cluttered with paper, crayons, scissors, and scraps where Lizzie had cut pictures out of magazines. Apparently she spent more time with arts and crafts than Lego bricks or Lincoln Logs. The room had everything a little girl might want, but something was uncomfortable about it. Connie picked up the only photo on a bookcase against one wall. It showed Lizzie with her and Hannah. Lizzie was sitting on a rope swing George had hung from a tree. Connie was behind her so she wouldn't fall backwards. Hannah stood beside the swing, smiling beneath a straw sun hat. Connie remembered when George took the photo. He had enjoyed the day. Only after he barbecued hamburgers did he say something about blood oozing from just-killed soldiers. A few months later he drove his car in front of the train.

The photo told Connie what was wrong with Lizzie's room. There were no windows. A house with light and a yard hadn't been enough for George, but it might help Lizzie to grow without plunging into the depression that stalked Connie's family. She put the photo back on a bookcase she wished was filled with books and went into the living room. Lizzie was drinking a Coke and munching on potato chips. Beside her, Sarah was holding a glass of wine. She placed it on the table and poured some for Connie, who snuggled on the other side of Lizzie.

Lizzie tapped on her Coke can. "When I asked for tonic in England, they didn't understand. I learned to say fizzy drink or ask for a Coke. Everyone understands that."

Connie understood the problem. She grew up in the only pocket of the world that called a soft drink tonic. She still got tripped up in Florida. "What do you call it now?"

"Tonic, silly. I love being home."

Connie toasted Lizzie and tasted her wine. It was smoother than any she had ever had. "Sarah, this is wonderful."

Sarah handed her the bottle. Connie looked at the label. Tan with a coat of arms and the name Chateau Musar. "It looks terribly expensive."

"It is. That's why I had only one case shipped. Savor it. Whatever else I might say about the country, the French do have the best wines."

"Europe didn't turn out so well?"

"There were moments. The Paris boulevards are beautiful. You'd love the gardens in England and the mountains in Switzerland. I found the Alps threatening."

"That's because Art left us there alone," said Lizzie.

Sarah corrected her. "I left him. The Swiss watch he bought with my money was one charge too many."

"Art was so fun," said Lizzie. "He took me on the gondolas every day."

"Up those threatening mountains?" said Connie.

"Silly. The ones in Venice. That was my favorite place. When we weren't stuck in some stinky hotel."

"Lizzie got tired of hotels and castles and cathedrals. So did I." Sarah swirled the wine and drank. "Like I said, the best thing about Europe is the French wine."

Connie took a handful of potato chips. She needed something to eat or the wine would make her drunk. No matter how French it was. "You were there for two years. Mum missed you."

"She had you and I needed to figure out how Lizzie and I would manage without George or Dad. It was James's idea."

"You stayed even after he left."

Sarah corrected her the way she had corrected Lizzie. "I left. There were good things."

Like Arthur, Connie thought. "What were the best ones?"

"The Louvre is overwhelming. I preferred Florence's Galleria dell'Accademia except that Lizzie couldn't stop asking about all the penises she was seeing on statues."

Lizzie interrupted. "I know all about men now. I liked the Boboli Gardens better. I chased birds there."

Sarah described the Ponte Vecchio where she bought a leather jacket and some designer boots. Paris's dress shops were fashionable but carried little that she'd wear unless she cracked into the elite French society. That was impossible. Even the waiters at all the best restaurants ignored her unless she was with Arthur.

Lizzie reached for a handful of potato chips. "I liked when we were in Florence and those teenagers bought us ices so we'd help them with their English. We were with James then. He loved them."

"Too much," said Sarah. "I knew then he was more interested in flirting with the multitude than staying with Lizzie and me. That's why I found Arthur and France."

"The cafés in Paris were nice," said Lizzie. "They have the best pastries. English pastries weren't as good, but I got to climb on the rocks at Stonehenge. In London we saw bushes shaped into animals and weird designs. What did you call them, Mum?"

"Topiaries. Kew Gardens. The gardens were lovely, but London traffic is horrible and in the Underground, there's the danger of IRA bombings."

"They took away all the trash cans so no one could put in bombs," said Lizzie.

Sarah put down her wine glass. "Arthur wanted to stay in London. It was too dirty for me. So we went to Venice."

"I'm glad we saw Venice with him instead of James," Lizzie said through a mouthful of chips.

"Not such a good thing," said Sarah. She described an afternoon on a bridge that spanned the Grand Canal. She and Lizzie were alone and a foreigner, not Italian, had taken Lizzie by the hand and was leading her away.

"Mummy was mad at Art." Lizzie bit into another potato chip. "She was just standing on the bridge looking at the water. The man said he'd buy me an ice cream."

Sarah pulled Lizzie to her. "We had the stranger danger talk after that. Europe's a dangerous place when you're alone and don't know the language people are speaking."

"Is that why you left?"

Sarah looked over Lizzie and fixed Connie with the kind of stare she used when they were teenagers arguing over George. "You wanted me back. To see our mother."

Connie turned away from the stare and put her arm around Lizzie. "*Our* mother and Lizzie's grandmother. You could have stayed in Europe and just come for a visit in Florida."

"Europe isn't home. The only people we talked to were store clerks and waiters and docents. My French wasn't good enough. Swiss German is impossible. Italians talk too fast. Even in London I got pegged as an American as soon as I opened my mouth. I got tired of sightseeing. I was just another rich American tourist."

"And so here you are. Back in Freedom. Queen of the home front."

"Better a queen here than a peasant in Paris." Sarah stood up. "Time for Cotton to Cocktails. I'm hungry."

"Aunt Connie didn't tell us about Granny yet," said Lizzie.

"We'll listen at dinner," said Sarah.

"I'll tell you all about Granny. We'll work on Mummy to come to Florida." If Sarah delayed a Florida visit, she'd threaten to send George's suicide note to her insurance company. She took Lizzie's hand and they got off the sofa together.

When they entered the foyer of Cotton to Cocktails, Connie glanced at the coat check counter. It was made from a piece of mill machinery whose use she had forgotten. In the restaurant, a hostess led them toward a long bar softened with rounded corners. On a dais adjacent to the bar, a pianist was playing tunes from *The Great American Songbook*. Nice, but nothing like the jazz improvisations David used to play. Connie and Lizzie followed the hostess while Sarah stopped at the bar to say hello to an assortment of people Connie didn't recognize. The hostess left them with menus at a table along a brick wall. It was broken up with half a dozen twelve-foot rectangular windows that had once let air into the stifling room where workers ran machines for carding cotton. The rest of the tables were scattered within a circular wall of windows and a ceiling whose wood created the illusion of a canopy. Connie felt none of the construction's openness, only the claustrophobia that encased mill workers and would engulf her if she returned to Freedom.

Eventually Sarah joined them. "Sorry. You should have stopped to say hello. You remember Dottie Barnes and Matt Wilson. They're married now. The others were also in high school with us."

Connie handed Sarah the children's menu she had been looking at with Lizzie. "Do you know everyone here?"

Sarah set the menu on the table without looking at it. "Most everyone who comes to the bar."

A waiter came to the table with a loaf of bread and some olive oil. "Nice to see you, Sarah. And you, too, Lizzie."

"Connie, this is Roy. Roy, my sister Connie."

"Sarah told me you're a writer. Should I buy your book?"

"Come to Zach's tomorrow at seven o'clock and you can decide."

Sarah handed him the menus. "A bottle of the BV sauvignon

blanc. That okay, Connie? It's not as good as the French we had, but it's okay."

"That's fine." Connie had more to drink in Sarah's apartment than she needed, but it would help her get through the meal.

While they waited for the wine, Sarah talked about the architectural plans for the house she was having built.

Lizzie interrupted her coloring to tell Connie about the swing set she'd have. "It has two swings and a slide and a playhouse. That's where me and Gretchen will have tea parties."

Connie pictured Lizzie in a rope swing, not an expensive display of conspicuous consumption. "Is Gretchen your best friend?"

Sarah spoke before Lizzie could answer. "Gretchen is Martha Greenleaf's daughter. You remember her. She married someone from Concord descended from a family connected to all those Transcendentalists we were forced to study in high school. She convinced him to settle in Freedom."

Connie was saved from saying she didn't remember any Martha Greenleaf by the arrival of their wine. Roy poured Sarah a taste. When she nodded okay, he poured for them both. "Ready to order?"

Lizzie whispered to Connie. "The shrimp and grits like you said."

Sarah heard and ignored her. "Lizzie will have her usual. Hamburger and fries. I'll have veal marsala. Connie, you ready?"

Connie hadn't done more than glance at the menu, so she ordered the one item she remembered. "Baked haddock."

Apparently Roy knew Sarah's choice of soup or salad because he only asked Connie which she wanted.

As they drank their wine and ate their way through the salads and their dinners, Connie listened to Sarah talk about her house plans, the people from high school she had reconnected with, and more about her time in Europe.

Sarah was describing the jazz club she and Arthur frequented in Paris, when Lizzie interrupted. "One night the babysitter didn't come so they took me. I liked the piano player. He said I look like you."

"I don't know any musicians in Paris." With her rounded features, strangers would have thought Connie, not Sarah, was her mother. The way she leaned close to her coloring book said Lizzie also had her eyes, brown and myopic, not blue with the perfect vision of Sarah's. Lizzie would be wearing glasses before she got out of elementary school.

Lizzie set her crayon on the table so hard it broke. "Mummy said he knew you."

Sarah rummaged through the basket of crayons and found Lizzie an unbroken one. "She's right. One night when we were talking with him, he said he used to know someone from Freedom. The piano player was David. You never told us about him."

Connie swallowed a last piece of haddock and washed it down with a gulp of water. After they stopped seeing each other, he had gone to Chicago to try the jazz clubs there. She wished he had told her he was going to Paris. He had written her after her father died. Told her she was a fool to go to Florida with her mother. She should come to Chicago. They could try again. "He was a good friend."

"More than that," said Sarah. "What happened?"

"The usual. Too much time apart while he slept days so he could play at night and I slept nights so I could work during the day." Connie found the lie. "I never think of him now."

"I liked him," said Lizzie.

The pianist in the corner was playing "Come Rain or Come Shine" with little expression. David would have been offended enough that he'd have left the restaurant. Connie missed his talent. When he played he channeled some god she couldn't reach.

"Anyone in your life now?" Sarah had finally stopped her own stories to probe Connie's. She'd been in Europe. Maybe she'd understand about Will.

Connie didn't want to get involved in a conversation about sexual identity in front of Lizzie. "Like I can sandwich in a relationship between watching Mum and hiding in the Bayview College library so I can get some writing done."

"You chose it," said Sarah.

"Not much of a choice, as I recall."

Roy appeared at their table. "Ready for dessert? Chocolate ice cream for you, Lizzie?"

"Not tonight," said Sarah. "My sister's tired. She had a busy day in Boston."

Connie joined Lizzie's protest. "It would taste good with coffee." She craved a cup of coffee. "A little sweet to settle the dinner as Mum used to say."

"Not tonight," Sarah repeated. "Lizzie has school tomorrow." She signed for the meal. When they passed the bar, she stopped, gave Connie the keys to her condo. "I'll be up in a minute. You can read Lizzie a story. She'd love that."

Connie welcomed the break from Sarah's self-absorption. She got Lizzie into her pajamas, admired her Mickey Mouse toothbrush, and squeezed next to her on her bed. She read *Make Way for Ducklings* and told her about the Public Garden and the swan boats. When she finished the story, Lizzie checked underneath the bed.

"Nothing there?" Connie remembered the monsters she checked for at Lizzie's age.

"I look to be sure."

Connie tucked her under a bedspread designed with images of Paris. "Next time I visit, I'll take you to the swan boats. But first you need to come to Florida. Granny and I can take you to Disney World."

"I love you, Aunt Connie."

"And I love you." Connie kissed her on the forehead and went into the living room. She lay on the sofa planning how to tell Sarah about George's suicide note. It was another hour before her sister appeared.

"Thanks for taking Lizzie." Sarah plopped onto a chair that matched the sofa.

Connie had stopped planning and was reading. *Angle of Repose.* If she had Sarah's freedom, she'd have explored Wallace Stegner's West instead of Europe. "I enjoyed reading to her. You're lucky to have a daughter."

"You sound like our mother. Don't think my life is easy. Except when Lizzie's in school, I never have time alone. I could have stayed at the bar until midnight."

"Don't you hire a babysitter?"

"Lizzie complains about them. She misses Arthur. The creep."

"You'll find someone nicer than Arthur. Maybe even get married again." Connie imagined her sister married to someone who knew her when she was prom queen.

"Don't get me wrong. I love Lizzie to pieces. It's just that everyone we know is married with kids."

"Be patient. You've only just gotten back. Get that house built. Lizzie needs a yard to play in. Hire yourself a sexy gardener. Like Lady Chatterley's lover."

"Who's that?"

"Just a character in a novel. It doesn't matter."

Sarah straightened a copy of *People* magazine that lay on the coffee table. Apparently she liked the gossipy magazine that launched a year ago. "You're the one who should get married. Move into a house near Mum so you don't need to be with her every day."

"You need to come see her. While she still remembers you."

"Is she that bad?"

"Not yet. She forgets things. Can't follow the plot of a TV show. She focuses on the past a lot. Especially Charlie."

"Who's he?"

"Mum's brother. You should remember. He disappeared when Mum was thirteen."

"Who cares? He's dead and gone."

"Mum cares. There's some kind of secret. She has a box that she keeps looking at and then hiding. I'm sure there's something in it about Charlie." Connie waited for an opening to tell her she knew what Sarah was hiding about George.

"Ask her."

"I have. She says she promised her mother never to tell."

"So look in the box when she's not around."

Connie saw herself opening George's suicide note. When Sarah wasn't around. "I'm tempted. One of these days she's going to forget where she hid it."

"I really can't be bothered about some long ago secret. I'm going to bed. Anything you want to do tomorrow before it's time for your reading at Zach's?"

"Visit Dad's grave. And George's."

"You can go in the afternoon. Lizzie has a half-day at school. You can pick her up and take her with you."

"Don't you want to come?"

"I have an appointment with Andy Therrien." Sarah paused before she added. "My contractor."

Connie heard a note of defiance in her sister's voice. She

remembered Sarah talking with his wife the day they were at Zach's before she left for Europe. "Get here early enough so we can call Mum."

"It will have to be a short call. I won't get back until six with the babysitter. Lizzie won't like it, but she can't come with us."

Connie braced herself to tell Sarah about George's suicide note. "There's something else."

Sarah walked away. "Not tonight. I'm too tired. Save it for the morning."

In the morning, Connie drove to her parents' old house, knocked on the door, and explained who she was. The young woman who answered holding a baby invited her inside to see what she and her husband had done with the house. A toddler sat coloring at a table Connie recognized as one her father built. Inside she saw evidence of him everywhere. The bookcases surrounding the fireplace, the mantle of thick pine, the cabinet over the bathroom sink, the kitchen counter. She left, happy to know that Hannah sold the house to someone who loved it.

The afternoon with Lizzie passed too quickly. Lizzie planted rust colored chrysanthemums on George's grave, talking to him about how she remembered the rope swing and how he'd set her on the counter to watch him shave. Already she was losing most of her memories of her father. Listening to her, Connie knew that she'd never share George's suicide note with anyone except Sarah. Her sister needed something to force a visit to Florida, but she didn't need her life ruined.

Lizzie planted yellow chrysanthemums on Sam's grave. She said she wished she still had the dollhouse he built for her.

She remembered more about her grandfather than her father. Connie knew these memories, too, would fade. She took Lizzie's hand and walked her around the family plot, telling her about her great-grandmother Molly, her triple great-grandparents whose three little girls died of scarlet fever. Maple trees that had just begun to turn to fall colors shaded the graves. Lizzie made bouquets from the leaves and laid one on each of the graves of their ancestors. Connie felt the umbilical cord of her ancestry tighten around her. She and Lizzie each found a stone at the edge of the cemetery to place in an indentation on top of Sam's gravestone. Connie kissed hers before she set it down.

After the cemetery, they drove to Kimball's Ice Cream stand. It was an institution. Since Connie's childhood, it had grown into a place that sold hotdogs and hamburgers and huge baskets of seafood or chicken and chips. An adjacent gift shop sold T-shirts, mugs, stuffed cows and an assortment of ice cream related paraphernalia. Connie relived her childhood by eating a hotdog with Lizzie. They finished with single scoop chocolate cones that were double the size of the scoops at most ice cream stands. The reading at Zach's would be stressful and the long book tour to Florida tedious. She'd start on her diet when she left Freedom.

Connie enjoyed her reading at Zach's more than she expected. People were there from her class as well as from Sarah's. They asked questions, told her they knew in high school that she'd do something big with her life. Sarah stood quietly next to Andy and Brenda Therrien. For the first time since childhood, Connie felt the attention on her, not her sister.

When they returned from Zach's, Lizzie was asleep, cuddled with the stuffed cow Connie had bought her. Sarah paid the babysitter then opened the door to a cabinet Connie recognized as one her father had built when Sarah first married George. It was filled with wine and liquor bottles. She pulled out a bottle that reminded Connie of a bell jar.

"It's an Aberfeldy scotch," said Sarah. "I learned to drink single malts the month we spent in Edinburgh. This isn't the best. Aged just sixteen years, but it's good."

Connie never drank anything stronger than a gin and tonic. A scotch would fortify her for the conversation she needed to have about George. "Just a small one with ice."

Sarah handed her a squat glass with an inch of scotch. "You drink it straight up. Never with ice. It will help you sleep."

Connie sipped. It burned all the way to her chest. "This will knock me out. These readings are exhausting."

"You were a success. It was nice to see all those people from your class."

"It was nice of you to invite Andy." Connie paused before she added, "And Brenda."

Sarah raised her glass, sipped and sat on the chair. "He's my contractor."

Connie moved onto the sofa and put her glass on the coffee table. "Are you friends with Brenda again?"

"Not really. Never mind about her and Andy. Did you sell any books?"

"Eleven."

"Is that good?"

"Not bad. I should do better on my tour because Random House does the marketing."

"Someday I'll have a famous sister. You always were the smart one. All your high school friends seemed to think so."

"No smarter than you."

Sarah pulled her legs onto the chair and sat Buddha style,

holding her glass in the cross of her ankles. "I'm glad I'm not driving alone and reading in all those strange cities. Europe cured me of wanting to travel. I think I'll never go further than New Hampshire now."

Connie was tempted to ask about Andy's place on Winnipesaukee. She swirled her scotch and took another burning sip. "You need to come to Florida. Mum needs to see you. And Lizzie."

"She sounded okay when we called. You're taking good care of her."

Sarah hadn't heard the part of the call when Hannah was asking if she'd seen George. "Phone calls aren't the same. She forgets things. Confuses a lot of names. Except for her brother Charlie. The secret she's keeping is bothering her but she won't let me help."

"We all have secrets. Like the one you kept about David. He's good looking. He could have tempted me to stay in Paris."

"You don't need to seduce another man I cared for."

"What's that supposed to mean?"

Connie swallowed the last of her scotch. "Like you said, we all have secrets. I know about George."

"Know what? That he preferred me to you?"

"How he died."

"We all do. A train hit his truck."

"He let it hit him."

Sarah unwrapped her Buddha pose and went to the liquor cabinet and refilled her glass. "What's that supposed to mean?"

"I have the note."

"What note?"

"The one that says 'I'm going to the train.'"

Connie read Sarah's body language. She assumed the posture she took when they were teenagers and she was lying to their parents. A slight stiffening of her shoulders. An elongation of her neck. "He'd never do that."

Connie stood up to face her sister. "You left the note in your car. The Mercedes dealership mailed it to Florida."

"I never saw a note."

"Don't lie. You read it and taped it back into the envelope."

Sarah's eyes flashed the defiance she had never been able to hide if someone challenged her. "You had no right to open it."

"You were in Europe. I thought it was junk."

"You threw it away, right?"

"Wrong."

"Please, Connie. He's dead. Insurance wouldn't pay for suicide."

"I'm glad you admit it."

"Give me the note."

"It's in Florida."

"Destroy it. Please."

"No. Lizzie doesn't need to know about her father. But she needs to come to Florida. Bring her to see her grandmother and maybe I'll give it to you."

Connie swallowed the last of her scotch and put down her glass. She left Sarah standing alone in the middle of the living room. In the bedroom she looked at Lizzie sleeping with the cow clutched in her arms. She bent to kiss her cheek, warm in the peaceful sleep of childhood she couldn't destroy by exposing her mother.

Chapter 12

Late October 1975

Philadelphia, Washington, Charleston, Atlanta, Jacksonville, each bookstore displaying *Secrets* alongside year-old titles like *Carrie* and *Jaws*, each reading a little more crowded than the last. *The 158-Pound Marriage* and *The Hair of Harold Roux* were Random House titles. Neither John Irving not Thomas Williams was famous, but they were on their way. Reviews of *Secrets* were coming in, including ones in the *New York Times Book Review* and *The New York Review of Books*. More than once Connie was compared to Joyce Carol Oates, suggesting that she might eventually win a National Book Award. Her hosts wined and dined her to an added five pounds. In Philly, it was cheese steak, in Charleston She-crab soup. She visited Eva's son in Atlanta. He served her a slice of peach pie large enough for two and topped with a double scoop of vanilla ice cream. Despite her success, on each leg of her journey, she felt more lost. The further she got from New England, the less she felt at home.

Jacksonville started out better. She had grown used to Florida. After her reading, she went to the bar in her hotel with her host, Bobby Randall. She thought only a grown man in the South would call himself Bobby instead of Bob. They ate fish and chips, drank beer, and talked about the future of Patty Hearst who'd been arrested a year and a half after she'd been kidnapped by the Symbionese Liberation Army. Connie identified her as a victim, Bobby called her a terrorist.

Bobby brought up Squeaky Fromme's attempt to assassinate Gerald Ford. "You know that the guy who pushed the gun so Squeaky missed is gay."

"Oliver Sipple. So what?"

"It's disgusting. The media was all over it."

"He didn't deserve to have his privacy invaded." She stood up to leave. Bobby walked her to the elevator and got inside. He kissed her, his mouth tasting of beer and cigarettes. He pushed so hard against her that all she felt was pain from the hand railing that lined the elevator walls. He followed her to her room, expecting to come inside. She turned him away. He might have a southern name, but he wasn't a southern gentleman.

In the morning, she drove in silence along the straight road across Florida's midland, the radio's steady diet of religious stations turned off. Her life spooled in front of her with the monotony of the road. She wasn't like Sarah. She couldn't go home again. Her future had no map.

She left the rental car at a dealership in St. Petersburg and took a cab to her mother's condo. After two years, she still couldn't think of it as hers. She opened the door to silence. The room was stifling. The back door and the windows were all closed. Her mother must be with Jane. She carried her bags into her bedroom and opened the window. The room was as claustrophobic as Lizzie's. She opened the door to her mother's bedroom.

Her heart fell when she saw Hannah asleep on her recliner, her chin touching her chest, a photograph album on her lap. She stopped breathing and rushed toward her, stumbling over the blue box on the floor. She let out her breath when Hannah jerked her head upright. Her eyes were vacant. "Mummy?"

"You were dreaming. It's me. Connie."

Hannah pulled the recliner upright. When she stood, the photo album fell from her lap. She was more wraith-like than when Connie left. Recognition seeped onto her face.

When they hugged, Connie could feel her mother's bones. She picked up the photo album and put it on the chair. When she reached for the box, Hannah grabbed it from her. Her strength surprised Connie.

"I'll put this away," said Hannah. "Take the album into the kitchen. We'll have a glass of lemonade and we can look at it together. Reminisce."

The idea of reminiscing stifled Connie as much as the air in the bedroom. She opened the window. "You must have been dying of the heat. No wonder you fell asleep."

"I don't notice it much. Go now. I want to hear about your trip. About Sarah and Lizzie. Did you see George?"

Connie stepped away from the window. Less than a month away and her mother had sunk further into Alzheimer's. Connie's future closed in on her. "Lizzie and I put flowers on his grave. And on Dad's." She left Hannah wiping her eyes with a tissue. She needed air to escape a suffocating room and a crying mother.

She went into the kitchen where she could feel the hint of a breeze when she opened a window. The refrigerator was nearly empty. One block of cheese was half wrapped and hard around the edges, the carrots in the vegetable bin were limp and the lettuce brown. The oranges were good and the jam and condiments all had their lids on. She smelled the milk, dumped it in the drain, and threw the carton and a doggie bag from The Lobster Landing with a half-eaten fish sandwich into the trash. There was no lemonade. She rummaged through the cupboard and found some instant iced tea and some nuts. She was sitting at the kitchen table, her head resting on her arms when Hannah came in. She lifted her head, jerking back when she saw an envelope on top of the oldest of her mother's photo albums. She thought it was George's suicide note until she remembered that the note was in a smaller envelope and safely hidden in her closet.

Hannah sat down, opened the envelope, and took out a photograph. "This is my brother Charlie." It was the same black and white photo Connie had seen dozens of times. Charlie in his World War I uniform, standing against the backdrop of an army barrack. Jacket with a high collar, four pockets, and a belt at the waist. Jodhpur pants and puttees. He was holding a ranger hat stiffly at his side. His hair was dark and cut short, his face rounded like Connie's. As a child, she thought his image handsome. Today, she thought his eyes looked slightly mad.

Hannah took the photo back. "Did you see him in Massachusetts?"

Connie did a quick calculation. "He'd be eighty-six years old. He's probably dead. Do you know where he disappeared to? Where was he in the photo?"

"Don't get all snippy. He was in Alabama. That's near Florida. We could go look for him."

Connie recoiled at the prospect of hunting down a man who didn't want to be found and who was likely dead. "I just got back. Let me settle in first." One good thing about Alzheimer's was that Hannah would forget her idea.

Hannah put the photo into the envelope and set it on the table. Her hands trembled. Connie reached across the table and cradled them. "Tell me what you've been eating. There's no food in this house."

"There is. I've been eating pasta and chicken soup. I finished the last of the bologna yesterday. I went out with Jane a lot and brought home leftovers. Do I look like I've been starving?" Hannah pulled her hands away and put them in her lap. She straightened her torso and shoulders.

"You look thinner than when I left."

"You don't. Sarah must have fed you well."

Connie pushed the bowl of nuts toward her mother. "My hosts in every city fed me too well. Diet starts tomorrow. For me. I want you to gain a pound for every pound I lose. Or, better, two pounds."

"Don't harass me about food. Tell me about Sarah and Lizzie. When are they coming to Florida?"

Connie spent the next two hours telling Hannah about Sarah's plans for a new house, about all the friends she had reconnected with. She described her and Lizzie's trip to the cemeteries and to Kimball's, and made up a story about when they would come to Florida.

At four-thirty Jane opened the screen door. Her tiny figure bounced into the kitchen. "Connie. You're back. How was the trip? Sell lots of books?"

"I did."

"I'm not surprised," said Jane. "I saw a review of *Secrets* in *Time* magazine. I have my copy, ready for you to sign."

"You didn't need to buy a copy. I would have given you one."

"I'm more than happy to add to your royalties. Come to dinner with us. Tell us about the trip."

Connie was too tired for Jane's perkiness and an Early Bird special. "Thanks, but I'm exhausted. I'm going to go to the grocery store and restock this empty refrigerator. Then I'm going to take a bath and collapse into bed with a good book. I'll catch you up tomorrow."

Hannah picked up the photo album and the envelope with

the picture of Charlie. "I'll just get a sweater. Connie thinks I need to eat more." She went into the bedroom.

Connie put the iced tea glasses into the sink and faced Jane. "Was she difficult for you while I was gone? She looks terribly thin and there's no food in the house."

"She's been fine. We went out a lot and I took her to the grocery store every few days. Sometimes she forgets to eat. She's obsessed with her photo album. The pictures remind her of stories about the past."

"It's not the past I'm worried about. It's the present."

"Don't worry. She's got a long way to go before she needs anything except an occasional reminder to eat."

Hannah came out of the bedroom. "Did you say 'eat?' I'm ready."

Connie watched them drive away. She found the car keys in her room and started for the Piggly Wiggly. Already she felt the threatening fog of depression. The moment she relaxed, she'd fall asleep. She'd want to pull the covers over her head and never get up.

"Thank you for checking on my mother. Jane said she's mostly okay, but she looks terrible." Connie and Eva were sitting at the edge of the pool dangling their legs in water that had started to cool down with the late October air.

"I did. Every day when I came home from school. Even had her over for dinner a couple of times."

"Did she eat anything? She's skinnier than you are."

Eva splashed water onto Connie. "I'm short, not skinny. Your mother's got six inches on me and no extra pounds."

Connie sucked in the belly that was holding all the extra weight from her trip. "I'm worried about her. She looks frail and

Jane told me she's obsessed with her photo album. When I got home yesterday, she showed me a picture of her brother Charlie then hid it away in that box she keeps."

"The one with the secrets? Old people dwell on the past even if they don't have Alzheimer's."

"She's barely sixty. Not much older than you."

Eva splashed her again. "Fifteen years can be a lifetime."

"I hope in fifteen years, I'll be like you."

"What's that mean?"

"With your energy. Your contentment. Don't you ever want another relationship?"

"Men only complicate your life. I've got my son. Got all my students. I went on a few dates while you were away."

"A few meaning a few guys or one guy and several dates?"

"One guy. Turns out he's married. Seriously, I'm quite happy being a middle-aged single woman."

"Not yet middle-aged."

Eva swung her legs out of the pool. "At least not menopausal. I'll be glad when I can stop buying stock in the Tampax company. I need to go make repairs and hit the stack of papers I have to grade."

Connie lowered herself into the water and floated so she could see Eva's face. "Did you sleep with him?"

"What?"

"Did you sleep with him? The married man?"

"You need a boyfriend, Connie." Eva picked up her towel. As she walked away, she said, "And, yes, your mother ate."

Connie dove under the water. She remembered kissing Bobby in the elevator. She half-wished she had invited him into her room. She needed to feel something besides water and chaste hugs on her skin.

She found Will at their usual spot on The Groaning Board's patio. He was drinking coffee and reading *Secrets*. He didn't look up until she sat down "It's wonderful. And thanks for the Acknowledgment. 'Will, my first and best reader.'"

"Notice I didn't say my only reader. The next one will be dedicated to you."

"How's it coming?"

"I was too wrapped up in *Secrets* on my tour to make any progress. It's got Aunt Charlotte, scenes in Massachusetts, a swindler, a Florida orange grove, and a hurricane. The Massachusetts woods and the Florida orange groves are becoming characters. I could use a good Florida botanist."

"How was the tour?"

"Exhausting."

Their regular waitress, Lily, appeared at the table and asked for their order. She saw Will's copy of *Secrets*. "You did it. I knew you would. If I buy a copy, will you sign it?"

"I'll bring you a copy next week, all signed." Connie knew she shouldn't give too many copies away, but she liked Lily, who assumed she and Will were having an affair.

"You're in for a treat." Will handed her their menus. "Chowder for me."

"Me, too. I was in New England and I assure you that The Groaning Board's chowder is every bit as good."

Lily wrote the orders on a slip of paper. "I'll tell the cook. And I'll tell him to buy a copy of *Secrets*."

Connie watched her walk away. "I wonder if she'll read it."

"She will. She's listened to us talking about it for a whole year."

"Why are you reading it? You must be sick to death of hearing about a smart botanist and a boy who talks to trees."

"It's different reading it all printed up. I love the cover. The lake more gray than blue, the line of trees darkening, the title

Secrets rising out of the empty rowboat. Your name is in the perfect spot, in the right hand corner just below the boat. The reviews are wonderful."

"Where did you see reviews?"

"In all the papers and magazines the library gets. 'A stunning debut novel.' 'Far more than a page-turning mystery.' 'Brilliant.' 'Glorious.'"

"Except for the *New Yorker*." Naomi Rhinebeck was wrong. The magazine did review *Secrets*.

"They don't like anything not set in a city, preferably New York."

"Maybe, but the 'stuck in a rural mentality' hurt."

"Forget it. Bask in the good reviews."

"I am. Makes me nervous about the next one, though. You know. Successful first book. Promise not fulfilled."

"Don't be nervous. I'm your advisor."

"That helps more than I can tell you."

"How was the rest of your trip? Your sister? Your niece?"

Before she could answer, Lily came onto the deck. She rested a tray at the edge of the table as she moved Will's copy of *Secrets* out of the way. She put the chowder in front of them and patted the book. "I love the cover."

"And I love your chowder," said Connie as Lily left to wait on another table. She lifted the spoon to her mouth and felt the chowder's warmth. It was milky, unthickened by flour, with bits of bacon adding a taste of salt, and a hint of tarragon spicing it. She inhaled the steam like a memory.

She began to tell Will about Sarah's reintegration into Freedom, about Lizzie's need to get out of a condo into a house with a yard, about how they met David in Paris. She told him about Boston and how she already felt disconnected from the friends she had there. When she mentioned the Moonies, Will said, "Everyone needs to feel part of a group. That's why people join churches or clubs or cliques at work."

"What's your group?" Connie had never seen Will with anyone except his colleagues and Sid.

"Not a bunch of gay guys trolling the bars, if that's what you're asking. My colleagues are my friends. I'm having a turkey leftovers party Thanksgiving weekend. I want you to come. The botanist you're looking for will be there. He's new. I think you'll like him."

"Are you playing matchmaker?"

"You'd suit each other."

"It's a date, then." Maybe Eva was right. She needed a man in her life. Something more tender than an aggressive kiss in an elevator.

Chapter 13

Thanksgiving 1975

Thanksgiving Day arrived, splendid in the Florida sun. Connie got up at six o'clock to stuff the turkey and put it in a slow oven to be ready for two o'clock dinner. She worried through the next hour about introducing her mother to Will. With Eva, Jane, and Sid away, she invited him, so she could avoid the church dinner organized for the lonely that her mother suggested. Hannah beamed at the idea.

When Hannah got up, they called Sarah. Lizzie answered the phone. "Aunt Connie. I miss you."

"I'd love to eat turkey with you." Connie held the phone to her ear while she stuffed celery with cream cheese.

"We're eating at someone's house with a bunch of people Mummy knows. The only one I know is Andy. First we're going to the football game. It'll be my first one."

"I remember those games. Your Mummy was a cheerleader." In her maroon skirt and heavy white sweater with the FHS for Freedom High School, Sarah was the best looking of all the good-looking cheerleaders.

"Are you eating with a lot of people?"

"Just Granny and one of my friends."

"Did you cook? Mummy made apple pie. That's what I'm supposed to say. Actually, she bought it at the farm stand."

Figures, Connie thought. Sarah was always too interested in the football game to help with the cooking. "Let me talk with Mummy. Then you can both talk with Granny."

Sarah came onto the phone. "How's Thanksgiving in Florida? Warmer than here, I bet. We'll be wearing winter jackets to the game."

Connie remembered George's final Thanksgiving game. It was so cold people in the stands wrapped themselves in blankets. The cheerleaders blew icy smoke along with their cheers. George was the quarterback and scored the winning touchdown. Connie watched from the bleachers when he and Sarah hugged at the end of the game. "I'm surprised you still go to the games."

"Everybody does. What are you and Mum doing?"

"Cooking dinner. I have a friend coming."

"Male or female."

"Male. A friend, not a boyfriend, though I'm afraid Mum will think differently."

"That should be amusing."

"Will Brenda be with Andy?" Connie suspected her sister was having an affair.

"And three other couples. I'm the only single one. Let me talk with Mum. We're leaving in ten minutes."

Connie was glad to give the phone to Hannah. It was hard enough having Thanksgiving in the warmth of Florida. She didn't need to hear about football traditions that were lost to her.

When Hannah finished her Thanksgiving wishes, she seemed confused. "Why are we here? Sam and I never came to Florida for Thanksgiving."

"We live here now. We'll have a nice day. Help me set the table before Will arrives."

"Will? Oh, yes, that friend of yours. I hope he's as nice as George."

Connie stopped herself from saying George is dead. "You'll like him."

They finished preparations and had just taken the turkey out of the oven when Will arrived carrying cranberry sauce and a pumpkin pie. They sat down for a glass of the beaujolais he brought. Hannah kept talking about how interesting it was to meet a man who knew how to make cranberry sauce and pumpkin pie. She said he was taking Sam's place carving the turkey. Will winked at Connie. Hannah had them married.

Throughout the dinner, Hannah picked at her food. Consumed by her interest in Will, she kept forgetting to eat. She wanted to know where Will and Connie first met. When they explained, Hannah said, "Probably it was fate. What's the word? 'Serpety'?"

"Serendipity. Whatever it was, Will's been a great reader for me. And an even better friend." Connie emphasized the word "friend." Will might be amused at Hannah's matchmaking, but she wasn't. She put a fork into her mother's hand, reminding her to eat.

After the table was cleared, Connie suggested a walk along Edgewater before dessert.

"The place where you met? You should go alone," said Hannah.

Connie was tired of matchmaking. "No. You need to come with us. Digest all that turkey."

She and Will led Hannah out the door and down the road to Edgewater. The boardwalk was filled with people walking after dinner or before. The air felt good, warm but not hot, with enough of a breeze to stave off humidity. The walk refreshed her, made her appreciate a climate where she didn't have to worry about a snowstorm or a gathering where the women worked in the kitchen while the men watched football. She thought about what she'd make with the leftover turkey for Will's party. She'd been imagining the botanist ever since Will told her about him.

Back home, they brewed coffee to drink with the pumpkin pie. Hannah didn't notice when she spilled pumpkin on her shirt. "This pie is better than mine. Almost as good as Jane's."

Will bit into the pie. "I'll have to meet Jane. Have her help me get rid of the 'almost.'"

Hannah took too big a bite and spoke with her mouth full. "I'm glad you serve it the right way."

"The right way?" said Will.

"With cheese instead of whipped cream. Jane's my best friend in Florida."

Will blew on his coffee before he sipped it. "It must have been hard to move here. Leave all those years in Massachusetts."

Hannah stood up and started to clear the dessert dishes until she saw that Will and Connie were both still eating. "Don't hurry. I'm going to get one of my photo albums. Show you some pictures of our family. You'll want to get to know them."

Connie finished her last bite. In every photo, she'd look chubby and nerdy with glasses while Sarah grew from adorable to cute to beautiful. "Spare him. No one but us is interested in old family photos. It's almost as bad as watching two hours of home movies. Remember that night at the Donaldson's?"

Hannah picked up the plates and stacked them. "I sure do. They had spent a week on Newfound Lake teaching their daughter to water ski. Two hours of movies before she finally made it around the lake."

"I've had to sit through a few nights like that," said Will. "At least it wasn't fishing. That's what I got the last time I visited my brother."

"You have a brother?" Hannah called from the opening into the kitchen.

"I do. He lives in Portsmouth with his wife and two kids. Actually the movies were pretty cute. The oldest, a girl, was learning to put a worm on a hook. She thought it was pretty gross."

"I hope you want kids," Hannah said as she came out of the kitchen and walked toward her bedroom.

Connie rolled her eyes at Will. He grinned.

When Hannah came back to the table, she was carrying the newest of her photo albums. "Just a few pictures. I promise."

Half an hour later, Hannah had stopped at every picture of Connie. Connie holding the newborn Lizzie, sitting on a swing next to her, kneeling in the garden with Hannah, posing with Sarah and George in front of the Cotton to Cocktails sign. Only one picture showed her with her father. They were holding the sign Lewis Hardware Store. Hannah had taken it and it was slightly blurry. He had just sold the store and claimed he was ready to retire. It was the last photo in the album. When he died, the photos died with him.

Eventually Hannah brought out the photo of her brother Charlie in his army uniform. "Do you think Connie looks like him?"

Will held the photo and studied it. "A bit. The shape of her face. Not the eyes."

"They're the eyes of a madman," said Hannah.

Her comment startled Connie. The taste of pumpkin pie regurgitated in her throat. She swallowed it back with a sip of water. "I've never heard you say that. Is that the secret you've been keeping? Was your brother insane?"

Hannah took back the photo. "Never mind. I loved my brother. When he left, I was heartbroken."

"Where did he go?" asked Will.

"Don't know." Hannah picked up the photo book. "Why don't

you two go for another walk. I'm going to close my eyes for a bit. What's that stuff in turkey that makes you tired?"

"Tryptophan. It's a myth," said Will.

"Doesn't matter. I need a nap. You young people go out and enjoy yourselves." Hannah spoke as if she were eighty, not sixty-one.

Will stood up and looked at Connie. "How about we drive to Pinellas Park and walk around there."

Connie grabbed a jacket from the coat rack. "Don't sleep too long, Mum, or you won't sleep tonight."

"I'll set an alarm. Don't hurry back."

Outside Will took hold of Connie's hand as they walked to his car. He looked over his shoulder. "She's watching at the door. I love how she's playing matchmaker."

"I'm sorry. She feels guilty that she'd dragged me to Florida where I haven't found a boyfriend."

"It's kind of cute, actually. I hope she's not disappointed when she finds out why we won't get married."

"She'll never figure that out. If she does, she won't remember."

"She remembers everything about the past."

"If she could only remember what happened yesterday, she'd be in great shape."

Will opened the car door for Connie. He got into the driver's side and started the engine. "I loved today. If you hadn't invited me, I'd have spent the day alone."

"None of your friends on the faculty invited you to dinner?"

"Actually I had several invitations. I preferred yours. You're coming Saturday aren't you?"

"To be your cover? Pretend my mother's matchmaking is working?"

"Don't talk like that. You've met everyone before. Except the new guy from botany. Everett Eaton. I think you'll like him."

Connie watched a couple on the sidewalk stop to kiss under a live oak tree. She hoped Will was a better matchmaker than her mother.

After Will dropped her off, Connie went inside, expecting to find her mother asleep on the recliner in her bedroom. She wasn't there. The bathroom door was closed. She called in. No answer. She knocked, knocked louder. Still nothing. She tried the door. It opened easily. Her mother was in the bathtub asleep. Her head rested against the back of the tub, her hair gray and wet against the white porcelain. Her mouth was open enough to show the gold fillings of her back teeth. Her frail body was sunken beneath the water. Connie had never seen her mother naked. She recoiled, her gasp involuntary when she saw the scar that ran from her left breast down to her stomach.

Hannah's head jumped erect, her eyes startled open. She sat up in the tub, trying to cover herself with a facecloth. "Get out of here."

"I'm sorry. You didn't answer when I called."

"Just get out. I'm awake now."

Connie retreated, remembering Dr. Wilberforce's question about the scar. Her body quieted even as her mind raced. Where could her mother have gotten it? How could she have kept it a secret?

When Hannah came out of the bathroom, dressed and awake, Connie was blunt. "How did you get that scar? When?"

"Fell out of a tree onto a splintered log. When I was a kid." Connie knew she was lying. The scar was too savage.

"From now on, no baths unless I'm here. You could have drowned."

"Don't be stupid. If my head went into the water, I'd wake

right up." Hannah went into the bedroom and closed the door.

In the morning, Hannah was confused. She didn't remember falling asleep in the bathtub. About the scar, she only said, "Ask Sam."

Connie stood alone on the deck where Will first told her he was gay and where Annette, the woman who seemed too glamorous to be an English professor assumed they were having an affair. The moon floated above her, waning just above the clouds.

A voice sounded from behind her. Everett. "Tired of shop talk?" His voice was deep, mid-western. She wanted to look at him closely, remember the color of his eyes. Blue maybe. Or hazel. His hair was red, more rust than carrot. Maybe 5'10". For sure not six feet. Freckles, she thought. The light inside when Will introduced them was too dim for her to see. Outside, despite the half-full moon, it was dark. If she passed him on the street tomorrow, she was afraid she wouldn't recognize him.

"How do you know Will? You're the only one here not in his department."

He moved a step closer to Connie. She could smell his aftershave. Subtle, just a hint of menthol. "Will and I play racquetball together."

"I feel like a gate crasher."

"They all admire you."

"Some of them want me to teach. I couldn't do it. Read all those personal essays they're promoting in the curriculum. There'd be too many papers about dead grandmothers or triumphant touchdowns. Writing process or not, I wouldn't have the patience."

"If you become a teacher you'll waste your talent. *Secrets* is a wonderful novel."

"You read it?"

"A book with a protagonist who's a botanist? I sure did. You got all the botany right, by the way."

"Thanks. I researched it some, but most of it was familiar. I grew up in Massachusetts. Spent many vacations on the New Hampshire lakes and in the woods."

"Scene of the next novel? Another one with Maura Appleton?"

"Starts in Massachusetts. Different characters. Ends in Florida. Right now I'm researching orange groves."

"I can help with that. Not the writing. That's Will's department. He likes you."

"We're not in a relationship," Connie said. Maybe too quickly.

"I know. More than you think."

Connie took her hands off the railing. She risked a question. "Have you met Sid?

"Indian Sid? I have. They're pretty closeted. It's hard for them. Will appreciates being able to talk with you."

"I'm not his cover, if that's what you mean."

Annette appeared on the deck. She wore a flowing dress like the green one she wore at Will's party nearly a year ago. Thanksgiving colors this time, yellows and reds and oranges. She still wore the emerald ring, but tonight her nails were painted red. She displayed clothes as if she taught in the Art Department. "Come inside. We're playing charades. Connie's good at that," she said to Everett.

When they started to play, Connie was distracted. She did a poor job of acting out *Brideshead Revisited*. She missed guessing "Leda and the Swan" and *Who's Afraid of Virginia Woolf.* But she guessed Everett's charade, "Puttin' on my top hat." His movements were as fluid as Fred Astaire's.

As the party wound down, Everett walked her to the door. "Goodnight. I'll get your phone number from Will and call.

Give you a lesson in Florida botany."

Connie drove away. The car radio played familiar lyrics, "The First Time Ever I Saw Your Face." The song Eva named when they were talking about her attraction to Will. The song David played in jazz clubs. She took one hand off the steering wheel, touched her face, let her hand move onto her neck, over her breasts and stomach. She held it on the top of her leg until she needed to turn. Maybe the song was an omen.

Chapter 14
December 1975

Connie spent Sunday wandering between the condo and the pool, listening for the phone and reminding Hannah to find her if a call came. By the evening when she picked Eva up at the Tampa airport, Everett still hadn't called and she had given up hope.

Eva greeted her with the announcement that her son was engaged and that he intended to stay in Atlanta. She was filled with stories about his fiancée and his job working for the Coca Cola company in the city of its birth.

While Eva talked, Connie thought about a friend in Boston who had gone to a dozen weddings and liked to observe the first dance of the bride and groom. The friend would use her fingers to guess the number of years the marriage would last. So far, she'd been right about a two year, a four year, and a seven year marriage. Marriage was a study in hope. It too often came with the pressure to have children. Connie would settle for a love affair. Better heartache than the complications of divorce and child custody battles.

They were entering Dunhill before Eva asked about Connie's weekend. "How'd the dinner go? Your mother have you and

Will married with children?"

"It was pretty funny, actually. Will was great. He and my mother bonded right up. We're sorry to disappoint her."

"Anything interesting happen while I was away?"

"I went to a party last night at Will's. Met a bunch of his colleagues. And their spouses."

"None divorced or eligible?"

"A bachelor from the science department."

"A possibility?"

Connie stopped at Eva's condo. "He said he'd call."

"I'd label that a possibility." Eva got out of the car and retrieved her suitcase from the back seat. "Thanks for the ride. I'll catch up with you in a few days. Hope you've gotten that phone call."

The call never came. Instead, on Monday Everett found Connie in the library and invited her to drive to a swamp on the St. John's River. He wanted to arrange a field trip for his Intro to Botany students. "It'll be a long day, but it might be useful for your new novel. I'd love company."

"Will we go on one of those boat tours? I took one with my mother when we first arrived in Florida."

"Hell no. Ever paddle a canoe?"

"I have. Never in an alligator and snake infested swamp."

"Not to worry. A canoe paddle is a great weapon."

"Against alligators?"

Everett winked. "Or any other swamp predator."

If Everett was a predator, Connie wanted no weapon. "Okay, then. I'll see you on Saturday."

"These are air plants. Epiphytes, plants that live off another plant," said Everett. "This type lives off the moss hanging from the cypresses."

"They look like a swarm of hummingbirds." Connie had been listening for an hour to Everett's identifications of monstrous aureum ferns and trumpet vines so strong they could climb them. The thick canopy filtered the sun into sparkles of light onto the narrow canal where they had been paddling. Everywhere silvery moss hung from trees like bridal veils. They paddled through an alcove formed by the green roof of trees and trailing silver veils. The air was thick, the scents so powerful she could taste them. Insects and birds orchestrated the trees in a cacophony of competing sounds. Everett led them through the labyrinth into unmapped channels where they watched cottonmouths swim past them and alligators sun themselves on cypress knees or lumber onto the land. The swamp was dangerous and seductive. She wanted to lie down in the canoe next to Everett and give herself to the miasma.

"Why would you take students here? It's so seductive, they'd never find the energy to leave."

Everett leaned forward and touched her arm to stop her paddling. "I'll bring them in March and get them to search for the ghost orchid. They'll be so busy cataloging they won't get seduced."

"What's the ghost orchid?"

"An endangered epiphyte. They live mostly on tree trunks, growing in clusters on short stems. If you think air plants look like hummingbirds, you'd say the ghost orchid looks like a frog. The flower ends in two bowed legs. They smell wonderful, kind of like an apple."

"I'd like to come back in March to see one."

"We will. I'll invite you to join my students."

"It's like a fairy tale in here." Connie turned so she could see Everett. His shirt was soaked with sweat and the humid air. His hair and face glistened. She faced front again then looked to the side at a rustling coming from the thick foliage along the shoreline. A deer came to the water and drank. It lifted its head, studied them, and bounded out of sight. What looked like a log moved. The deer had roused an alligator that swam toward them.

"Enough fantasizing," said Everett. "It's not just swamp sleep and alligators we need to worry about. The wind is shifting. There'll be a storm."

They began paddling as the first clap of thunder sounded in the distance. At a junction, Everett said "Left." Before they had paddled a dozen strokes, he said, "Not this one. Turn the canoe around."

Connie looked at what she could see of the sky above the tree canopy, its blue gone, replaced with the gray of ominous clouds. She glanced behind her at Everett. He looked worried, his face red from the effort of paddling. "Do a sweep," he said. "We don't want to lose the path."

They found their way back to the junction and paddled hard into the pathway on the right. Connie breathed heavily from the effort. She saw a lightning streak and counted the seconds before the clap of thunder. Ten. The storm was still a couple of miles away. She felt more exhilarated than afraid, as if electricity were pulsing through her. She paddled harder. "We should have Ariadne's thread," she called into the wind.

"What?" Everett yelled from behind her.

She twisted to speak along the path of the wind. "Ariadne's thread."

"No minotaur in this swamp. Sweep right. We'll just beat that storm."

They aimed the canoe into the last of the narrow passages. No alligators sunned on the cypress knees. No turtles slid from the banks. The frogs had stopped their loud croaking. Even the birds had gone silent. The only sounds were the wind and the thunder and the paddles stroking the water. Connie matched her breath to each stroke and to Everett's rhythm. They passed under a drapery of hanging moss she remembered from when they first entered the marshes. They were almost home. Another dozen strokes and they shot into the open water. Paddling became harder, the wind trying to blow them onto the shore. They were in sight of the dock when the rain hit. Neither of them spoke. When they reached the dock, they tied the canoe and ran into the rental shop. The man who rented them the canoe and warned them about a possible storm stood up when they came in. He took off a pair of oversized glasses and stared at them from underneath dark, bushy eyebrows. "Warned you, didn't I? Rules say you need to clean off the canoe. Empty the rain water out of it."

Outside, thunder sounded overhead, closer now. "As soon as the storm passes." Everett took a map from a shelf.

"Costs a dollar," said the man.

Everett looked at Connie. "Don't need one, but it'll pass the time." He reached into his pocket for the wallet he had zipped into it. He smashed a wet dollar bill on the counter, then motioned Connie to a bench along the wall. They sat, soggy, next to each other. Everett pointed to various inlets on the map, explaining where different stands of vegetation provided habitat for animals and birds and bugs.

Connie cared more about how his wet sleeve touched hers than about his explanations. The weather had turned cold, but she could feel the heat of his body. "You've only been here a few months. How do you know so much about the swamps?"

"I spent a semester here in grad school working on my dissertation. Got as far away from Buffalo as I could."

"You grew up there and stayed to go to college?" She was surprised. She pegged him as a wanderer, someone who would have left his hometown to go to college.

"No. I went to undergrad at Tulane. University of Buffalo made me a grad offer I couldn't refuse. It was worth another five years of Buffalo winters."

"You still have family in Buffalo?"

"Folks from Buffalo are an odd lot. They pride themselves on surviving the winters. It's tough to get anyone to leave. My parents are there and my brother and sister. My sister's married with a baby. Brother's a senior at Niagara University."

"Folks in Buffalo sound like my sister." Connie told Everett about Sarah's experiment with Europe, about Lizzie, about Hannah. She said nothing about George and his suicide note. His swamp had been Vietnam, something to survive, not study.

The man at the counter watched them. They could have been the enemy. When the rain stopped, he pointed at the clock. He wanted to go home.

They went outside into the teeming air. They took the life jackets and their cooler out of the canoe, then tipped it over, drenching themselves again. They got dry clothes from Everett's car. Inside, the man still scowled at them but said they could use the restroom to change. "One at a time," he said, as if they were going to huddle naked in what proved to be a tiny room with only a toilet and a sink. Connie stepped out of her clothes. She scanned her body. Heavy, but not flabby. She forgot George and Vietnam. She wanted to embrace the botany of Florida, embrace its swamps and live the life it promised.

The night before Everett went to Buffalo for Christmas, they went to dinner at L'Orange, named after one of Florida's earliest citrus plantations. Everett promised to tour her through an orange grove when he returned. She wanted every pulp of information for her novel. They ate oysters, drank champagne, and ordered a bottle of wine to go with their dinner steaks. They drank coffee with their crème brûlée. After dinner, they walked through the back streets of Clearwater until they reached the house Everett was renting. Connie saw it dimly, a craftsman style bungalow. Pale yellow or maybe beige. She couldn't tell in the light. She didn't care. It was lovely.

Everett invited her inside. He unlocked the door and pointed Connie to a sofa arranged so it faced a window that looked out on a garden flooded with light from a full moon. "Wait here," he said.

She sat down and looked around the room. The walls displayed a dozen botanical prints. She recognized ferns and orchids, but would have to be closer to read the identification of some of the other plants. The only furniture was a bookcase overflowing with books, a sofa covered in dark green, and a coffee table. No TV. No music cabinet. If she was lucky, she wouldn't be like she had been with David, playing second fiddle to a passion for music. If passion ever happened.

She looked through the books and magazines on the table. *Secrets* sat on top of copies of *Plant Physiology* and *The American Journal of Botany*. Everett came out of the door that must lead to a bedroom. He had changed into jeans and a T-shirt. He reached down and pulled her off the sofa. "This is it. Let me show you around. It's small, but it's home."

He took her first into a dining room where the table was strewn with papers. She looked at the cover of a manuscript, "Endangered Epiphytes in the St. John's River." She pointed to it. "This must be what you've been researching in the swamp."

"Research is done. I'm revising now."

"I envy you a private space to write."

"Don't envy me until I get something published. This is a spin-off from my dissertation on the ecology of Florida's swamps. We need to pay attention before we destroy them."

"That's more important than anything I'll ever write."

"The mind needs science, but the heart needs art. Without art, no one will care about science."

"Is that why you have all these wonderful botanical prints?"

"Partly." He led her to one on a windowless side wall. "This swamp illustration is a reprint from *Appletons' Journal*. Done by a man named Thomas Bangs Thorpe. More imagined than real, but I like it."

"Me, too. It reminds me of our day on the St. John's." Connie felt desire more intense than that day in the swamp.

Everett walked her into the kitchen. "Want anything? Another glass of wine?"

"Not unless you want to carry me home."

He took both her hands. "How about I carry you to the bedroom? We've waited long enough. This won't be a one-night stand."

They kissed, held together as they moved to the bedroom, Connie stepping backwards, Everett laughing, steering her so she wouldn't bump the tables. She saw nothing in the bedroom, just closed her eyes and let herself feel as he removed her dress, her bra, her panties. Holding her with one arm, he took off his clothes. He lowered her to the bed. He was a gentle lover, releasing their passion slowly.

Afterwards she lay still and whispered, "Thank you."

"Has it been a long time?"

"Three years. Ever since David left."

"The jazz musician. Will I be chasing a ghost?"

"No. This felt more real."

"For me, too. Will you stay the night?"

She sat up and put her feet on the floor. "I can't. My mother will get confused if I'm not there in the morning."

"At least have some coffee. I have Christmas cookies my

neighbor baked. And I have something for you."

Everett turned on the light as Connie got out of the bed and picked up the clothes that lay scattered on the floor. She felt awkward about her body until Everett said, "You're beautiful."

She smiled. The two words were almost as satisfying as the sex.

"Bathroom's straight ahead."

When Connie came into the kitchen, she was surprised at her hunger. Everett brewed coffee and set out a plate of sugar cookies shaped like Christmas bells. She dipped a cookie in the coffee and wrapped her free hand around the warmth of the cup.

"You're a cookie dipper, too?" said Everett.

"I am. These are wonderful. Be sure to tell your neighbor."

"I will. I'll be right back." Everett went into the bedroom. He returned with a package wrapped in Christmas paper. Not expertly. He put the package on the table in front of her.

She was embarrassed. She had nothing for him. "I didn't buy—"

Everett stopped her. "Don't. You've given me yourself."

She opened the package. It was a copy of a novel called *East Angels*. She remembered the name of the author from her stop at Fatio House in St. Augustine. Constance Fenimore Woolson. It was old, its cover brown with darker brown etchings of vines. She opened the cover. It wasn't a first edition, but it was close. 1886.

"This is old. It looks valuable."

"Old, but not valuable. Almost no one these days has heard of Constance Woolson."

"How do you know about her?"

"She exchanged letters with my great-great grandfather. Daniel Eaton. He was a botanist at Yale and she was an avid fern collector. The novel's a little tedious for me, but it has a wonderful chapter on the Florida swamps."

"Was this your great grandfather's copy?"

"Great-great. It was. I want you to have it. My first novelist lover."

Connie flinched at his phrasing. "Sounds like you've had a lot of lovers."

He hesitated before answering. "None worked out. I hope we'll do better."

"So do I." Connie opened the next page of the book and read the inscription. "To Connie, my fellow explorer of the swamp. Fondly, Everett Eaton 12/1975.

Connie wondered if someday "Fondly" would turn to "Love."

Driving home, still glowing from their lovemaking, she realized they hadn't used a condom. In the morning, she'd find a doctor who prescribed birth control pills without asking questions about her marital status.

Chapter 15
Christmas 1975

Two days before Christmas Connie sat with her mother and Sarah and Lizzie around the condo's swimming pool. It was seventy-five degrees. Lizzie took off her glasses with the rose-colored frames shaped like an octagon. "Andy told me I look like a writer. I want to be one like you, Aunt Connie." The glasses were large for her face, but she looked cute in them.

"Whatever you do when you grow up, I'll be proud of you."

Lizzie stepped into the water at the shallow end. She wasn't shy of it as she moved deeper and bobbed under, then practiced what was more a doggie paddle than a crawl.

Hannah sat on a pool chair knitting a new blanket for Connie's bedroom. The mottled red yarn would make the green fern pattern of her bedspread look like a Christmas tree. She looked up from her knitting. "Who's Andy? Another tutor? I thought Lizzie was in school where she should be."

Sarah rubbed on tanning oil. She was pale from the Massachusetts winter but faint lines from a summer tan still showed around the edges of her bikini. "She's in school. Andy is my contractor. Andy Therrien. I went to high school with him." She closed her eyes as she circled her hand slowly around her belly, rubbing in the oil.

Connie was sure now that her sister was sleeping with Andy. "He married Brenda Jacobs. You remember her, Mum. She was a cheerleader with Sarah."

"The pretty one with the curly hair? I never liked her. She always flirted with George." Hannah put away her knitting. "Too much sun for me out here. Whoever thought we'd be sitting around a pool at Christmas."

Lizzie stopped her bobbing. "Bye, Granny. When I finish swimming, you can teach me that game you showed me."

Hannah looked down at Lizzie as she stood up to leave. "Clue. Best game ever. Grampy and I played it every Saturday night when your mum and Aunt Connie were your age."

Connie hadn't played Clue since she was in junior high school. She'd been good at it, able to remember who asked about which weapon, which room, which murderer. She could piece together what three cards were in the answer envelope. At seven and a half, Lizzie should be almost ready for the game.

"I hate Clue," said Sarah when Hannah left.

"Really? It was my favorite."

"That's because you always won." Sarah lay back on the lounge and closed her eyes.

"Indulge her. She'll ask every turn if Miss Scarlet did it."

Sarah opened her eyes and pulled the back of the lounge chair up so she could sit. "Clue has that envelope with the solution. What about the envelope you opened? It belongs to me."

Connie watched Lizzie exploring the pool. "It's tucked away somewhere. I won't use it. It would hurt Lizzie."

"What about me? Haven't I been hurt enough?"

Connie twisted on her lounge to face Sarah. "You've got Lizzie, a new house, I'm guessing a boyfriend. I don't think you're hurt."

"You don't know anything. It wasn't easy living with George

when he came back from Vietnam. The war killed him and all we got out of it is a bunch of refugees pouring into Lowell. They're coming in droves since the airlift out of Saigon."

"Most didn't make it on planes. The ones in Lowell were probably boat people. You're seeing the lucky ones, the others drowned." Connie cringed at the horror George must have seen while she and Sarah went on with their easy lives. "Forget the note. No one will see it."

Lizzie splashed in the pool. "Mummy. Watch this."

"I'm watching, Lizzie."

Lizzie did a front somersault under water. Connie and Sarah applauded.

"She never gives me a break," said Sarah.

"She's awfully sweet. Easier to watch her grow than to watch Mum decline."

"She seems fine to me. Are you sure she has Alzheimer's?"

"Didn't you notice how many times she called George 'Charlie'?"

"That's normal. Old people mix up names all the time."

"She's only turning sixty-two in January. It's not normal. She gets lost, forgets what she needs to buy at the grocery store. Look at the ten jars of peanut butter in our cupboard."

"I should say thank you for being here. You know I couldn't do it with Lizzie to take care of."

Connie knew she could have. "It's not been all that bad. I actually feel closer to Mum than I have since I was a kid."

"Watch me, Mummy." Lizzie tried a backwards somersault. Crooked, but complete.

"Good job," said Sarah. "Five more minutes and you should get out of the water for a bit."

"There's something else about Mum," said Connie. "She has a scar. From her nipple down to her stomach."

"Has she been cutting herself? I heard some people do that."

"No, it's old. Did you ever see it?"

"No."

"I think it has something to do with Charlie."

"That's your obsession. I didn't even remember that she had a brother until you said something about him when you were in Freedom. Forget it."

Connie got off the lounge and jumped into the pool beside Lizzie, wishing she could wash away memories as easily as Sarah did.

As soon as they finished dinner, they put up the scrawny Christmas tree. Lizzie hung most of the decorations. When it was time for the star or the angel, Sarah rummaged through the box of decorations that were too many for the pitiful tree. "Where's the angel?"

Connie handed her the star. "Put this on instead. We couldn't find it last year."

"Figures," said Sarah. "We should go shopping tomorrow and find another angel. Another tree, too. This one is awful."

"I like it," said Lizzie. "Especially all the tinsel."

"Forget the tree," said Hannah. "It's time to play Clue. I almost didn't bring it to Florida. Then I remembered how much fun we had playing. I know Lizzie will love it."

"Granny says I get to play detective. Like Nancy Hardy. I don't know who that is."

"Nancy Drew. She's a teenage detective in a story you'll be able to read by next Christmas."

"Lizzie reads quite well," said Sarah.

Lizzie picked up a book she had put face down on the table. "I read all the time."

Connie read the cover. *Ramona the Brave.* She'd never heard of it, but it looked suitable. Tomorrow, she'd make a trip to the bookstore and find a copy of Nancy Drew to add to Lizzie's Christmas gifts. She picked up the Miss Scarlet figure and handed it to Lizzie. "Time to play the game. We'll be detectives together."

While she sorted the cards into three piles for the murderer, the weapon, the scene of the crime, Lizzie sounded out the names of the rooms. "Library." "Hall." "Dining Room." "Palór." What's a Palór?"

"A parlor is a fancy living room." Connie anticipated the next question. "And a conservatory is a place for lots of plants. I guess these are rich people."

"Like Mummy and me."

"One of these rich people has committed a crime." Connie watched Sarah, who showed no recognition of her own crime.

Sarah reached for the piece that represented Mrs. Peacock. "I'll be this rich lady. She's probably the victim, not the murderer."

Hannah took the yellow piece. "I'll be Colonel Mustard. He was your grandpa's favorite."

Connie put three cards into the envelope and handed clue record-keeping papers to Hannah and Sarah. She showed Lizzie what the papers looked like. "Next year you'll be able to be your own detective. Right now, I'm glad to have you on my team."

Lizzie caught on quickly. If they checked off one of the rooms as the scene of the murder, they moved Miss Scarlett toward another. Lizzie loved checking off the clues and didn't ask about something they already knew. Hannah sat next to them, fumbling when she had to show a card. Only after the sixth round did she start to show confusion. Every turn, she'd ask if Professor Plum was the murderer and every turn Sarah would show her a card that Connie and Lizzie had figured out was the Professor Plum card.

Sarah lost patience and snapped at her. "Use your wits, Mum. I showed you this card six times already."

Hannah snapped at her. "I have no wits. I have hard arches."

Sarah threw down her cards in frustration. "Arteries, not arches."

Hannah pushed back her chair and stood behind her, putting her hands on her shoulders. "Whatever they are, they're hard. Last time I saw Dr. What's His Name, I peeked at his records. I can still function most of the time."

Connie got off her chair and stood behind her mother. "It's okay, Mum. We're here for you."

Hannah's voice cracked. "You are. Eventually I'll forget you all. Sarah and Lizzie first, but then even you. You'll be changing my diapers and spoon feeding me until I don't even know how to swallow. I'd rather die. Swallow a whole bottle of pills."

Lizzie started to cry. She put her arms around Hannah. "Don't die, Granny. I love you too much."

"Family hug," said Connie, motioning to Sarah.

They stood together, arms entwined, mother, daughters, granddaughter. Four women faced with lives that showed too few clues for their future. Hannah was the first to speak. "I'm sorry. I shouldn't talk like that in front of Lizzie. Let's finish the game."

They sat at their places again. After a few more rounds, Lizzie and Connie declared they were ready to guess. Lizzie made the accusation. "Miss Scarlet in the dining room with the rope."

Sarah opened the envelope. She placed the cards on the Clue board. "You got it. Why I hate Clue. Your Aunt Connie always wins."

Hannah stood up and looked around vacantly. "I told you it wasn't Charlie." She went into her room. Connie and Sarah said nothing until Lizzie asked, "Who's Charlie?"

Sarah began to pull out the sofa bed where she and Lizzie slept. "Charlie was Granny's brother. I'll tell you about him in the morning."

In the morning, Lizzie was full of plans for Christmas Eve and Christmas day. She had forgotten about Charlie.

Two days after Christmas, Lizzie and Hannah went outside to the pool while Sarah packed to leave. Connie was in Hannah's bedroom putting away Christmas decorations. Sarah found her and said, "The note, Connie. Please can I have it?"

Connie wasn't ready to give it away. It was a last message from George, one that showed his tender side. *You'll be better without me.*

"It will take too long to find it. You need to get Lizzie, say goodbye to Mum. It's time to go to the airport."

Sarah took a step toward Connie. "Promise me you'll destroy it."

Lizzie appeared at the doorway. "Promise what?"

Connie remembered George's line. *Love Lizzie for me.* She took her niece's hand and walked her out of the bedroom. "That you'll visit Florida again. It's a promise."

PART IV

Release

Chapter 16

November 1977 – January 1978

Connie took the exit into Dunhill and found her way to Edgewater. She parked the rental car near the spot she first met Will, got out and walked along the water's edge, needing to collect herself before she faced her mother. She'd been gone all of October promoting *The Orange Grove*. Woolson's *East Angels* and Everett had both influenced it and she knew it was a better book because of them. Her protagonist felt the passion she had shared with Everett for almost two years. She wanted to see him before she checked in on her mother, tell him how people had praised her descriptions of Florida's botany. Their outings always found their way into *The Orange Grove*. Canoe trips in the swamps and on the rivers, walks among the sea grasses on the Atlantic and Gulf coasts, hikes on the myriad trails in The Everglades. She recreated the scent of orange blossoms, but didn't include the time they made love under the trees, the blossoms falling softly around them smelling like a bridal bouquet. It had been a month since they made love.

The month had been worth the separation. The tour was successful and even her visit with Sarah was pleasant, perhaps because Andy had left his wife. Connie still found him self-absorbed but he was good to Lizzie, who was filled with stories about Andy's house on Winnipesaukee and how she had learned to water ski. At nine, Lizzie had Connie's muscular build and had joined a swim team at the Freedom Y. Walking along the Gulf Coast, feeling air as moist as the enclosed air around the Y pool, Connie thought of Lizzie. Sarah complained about how boring the swim meets were, but Connie loved watching the kids who worked so hard and splashed too much with each of their strokes.

She walked back to her car, hoping that Hannah's Alzheimer's hadn't progressed even further than when she left. She drove to the condo and parked in the space reserved for guests. Laughter sounded through the screen door. When she opened it, she saw Hannah, Jane, and Eva in the kitchen rolling dough to make pizzas.

Hannah's appearance shocked her. From painfully thin, she had progressed to withered. Wearing a sundress that sagged against breasts that seemed to have disappeared and that drooped around her, she looked like a child playing dress-up.

"Come in, come in," Hannah said in a high-pitched voice.

Jane set down the pizza dough and led Hannah to Connie, who managed to say "Mum."

Hannah looked at her blankly. "Sarah? We've been waiting for you. Where's Charlie?"

Connie held her mother's hands, feeling the bones. She looked directly into her confused eyes. "Charlie's your brother, Mum. He left a long time ago. Sarah's back in Freedom. I'm Connie. I live here."

Hannah snapped her hands back. "I know who you are. You shouldn't have left me." She stalked out of the kitchen and went into the bedroom.

Connie faced Eva and Jane. "Why didn't you call me? She's much worse. I would have come right away."

Jane rolled the pizza dough. "You know that she gets these moments when something startles her. Then she rallies."

"I've checked in every day after school," said Eva. "Most of the time your mother and I talk about New England history. I love her stories, especially the one about losing you in the secret staircase at The House of the Seven Gables."

"I never got lost there. It was her brother Charlie. She's told me that story a million times."

Connie looked over the kitchen counter and surveyed what she could see of the living room. Nothing was different. The coffee table still held Hannah's knitting and her latest blanket project was still folded on the back of the sofa. The TV and stereo cabinet still displayed the photo of her and Sarah. She still hated it. In the corner where they put up their sad Christmas tree, the ficus had survived, though it looked like it could use water. "I shouldn't have left," she said, thinking "I shouldn't have come back." She wanted space, air, some place more expansive than the claustrophobic condo.

"She's been the same as when you left," said Jane. "I check on her every night and every morning. The housecleaner came once a week, our minister and women from the church visited. She's been looked after. You needed to go. Hannah's proud of her daughter the writer."

Hannah heard Jane as she came out of the bedroom. She walked slowly into the kitchen, put her hands on Connie's face, and looked into her eyes. "My daughter the writer. When I get so bad that I don't know you, I'll still love you."

Connie hugged the body that was all boney angles. "I'll stay with you, I promise."

"You're a good daughter."

Connie pulled away, found a tissue, and wiped her eyes, half wishing she weren't the good daughter.

They were in the swamp on the anniversary of their first canoe trip. Although the day was a little cooler than the December of two years ago and no rain threatened, the air was still sultry. Instead of wanting to lie down and give herself to the miasma, Connie wanted to escape. They paddled into an alcove of trailing moss that she once likened to a bridal veil. Everett stopped paddling and said, "Turn around. I want to look at you."

She pulled her paddle into the canoe, steadied herself with her hands, and swung her body around. The face she had grown to love was tightened the way it got when he was concentrating. Behind him, she watched a blue heron swoop under the moss and fly toward its nest in a dead tree.

When he spoke, his voice was soft against the sharp buzz of the insects. "I need to tell you something."

"'Tell,' not 'ask'?" She breathed in air that felt like a weight in her chest.

He stopped his drumming and started to pull on the hair that curled along his neck. "I'm going to Washington in January."

She breathed out, the weight in her chest lifting. "A conference? Some work with the government before your semester begins?"

"Not D.C. Washington state. I'm doing a faculty exchange. There's a botanist there studying the ecosystem of the San Juan islands. It's an opportunity I couldn't turn down."

She calculated. A faculty exchange. January to June. Six months. "I wish you had told me earlier. I can find a caregiver for my mother. I can come with you."

"I thought of that. It won't work. I'll be living in a one room efficiency apartment. Between teaching and researching, I'll have no time. You need to stay here. Keep writing. Keep using Will for feedback. You need to get the next novel out. We managed for the month you were away. We'll manage for one semester. I'll write, I'll call, I'll be back."

"I'm not sure I'll manage." For the first time since Everett came into her life, Connie felt the dark cloud of depression that descended on her after she published *Secrets*. Since *The Orange Grove*, she'd felt energized, not debilitated. She had a good idea for novel number three. The title, *Homeward Bound*, expressed perfectly the theme of her character's search for a home freed of the bondage of provincialism and family obligations.

"You're strong. You'll be okay. When I get back, you'll have that third novel all written."

Connie swung around again to face the front of the canoe. Too fast. The canoe listed to the right, nearly tipping them into the murky water. Everett counterbalanced it. "Jesus, that was close. If we went in, that alligator on the cypress root would have had us for dinner. Let's go back. We can talk about this later."

Connie slapped her paddle into the water. She no longer synchronized her strokes to Everett's. The force of her paddling matched her churning thoughts. Six months seemed like forever. She'd find a way to get to Washington. Maybe ask Random House to set up a West Coast book tour so she could visit. Jane and Eva could manage her mother for a couple of weeks. Her paddle snagged in a weed. She tugged it free and thought of her freedom when Hannah died. She slowed her paddling to match Everett's, trying to stroke away the guilt of wishing her mother dead.

The first postcard came from New Orleans, a picture of The French Quarter and a one line message. "Happy New Year from The Big Easy. Everett. January 1, 1978." A new one came every day for the next two weeks. Connie traced his route, through Texas, north into New Mexico and Colorado, west to Utah, Idaho, and Oregon. She wanted to follow him into Carlsbad Caverns, climb in the orange cliffs of Bryce Canyon, hike along the great length of the Columbia River. When he reached Seattle, he called.

"I miss you," Connie said at the first sound of his voice.

"You would have loved all the places I stopped."

"I should have driven with you. Flown back."

"I wish we had thought of that." He told her more than she wanted to hear about the university's botany program and his first trip to the major islands he'd be studying. She wanted him to ask about her, about her mother, about her writing, about whether she walked through the orange groves.

Too soon he said, "I have to hang up. These telephone minutes cost a fortune. He gave her his address and phone number and promised to call on Sundays and to write every week.

That night, she slept badly. She hadn't shared Everett's drive, but she could share a few weeks by his side on the San Juan Islands. In the morning, she called Naomi Rhinebeck to ask if Random House would support a series of readings in the Northwest. Naomi talked her out of the idea. Her settings were Eastern and her name still not big enough to draw crowds in the West. She should be working on the third novel. They'd set up tours through all of the United States when it came out.

Naomi was right, but Connie didn't care. She'd go on her own. She called a travel agent to check on plane flights. Expensive, but her royalties were good. When she met Will at The Groaning Board, she told him her idea.

"Forget the surprise part," he said. "You need to talk with him, co-ordinate a time when he's not giving exams or camping out on those islands doing research. You need to find the names of bookstores. See if Everett can set you up at the college."

"I'll tell him on Sunday."

"Tell or ask?"

Connie pulled her sweatshirt tighter against the occasional

dampness of Florida's January. "Ask."

"Will Jane and Eva take care of your mother? How's she doing?"

"She gets angry more often, but mostly okay."

Will handed her the opening chapters of her next novel. "You don't need to rush to Washington. You can get the whole novel drafted while Everett's away. Give yourself space. Everett will keep. Your mother won't."

When Connie returned to the condo, Hannah accused her of stealing what she called her memory box.

"If you had a memory, you wouldn't keep losing the box."

Hannah slammed into her room. Connie went into the bathroom to cool her anger and her guilt with a wet cloth. The mirror reflected a face that resembled Hannah's, a terrifying reminder that she might be looking at a future of her own Alzheimer's. She went outside to calm herself. When she came back, Hannah was in her room, the blue box on her lap, the fight forgotten.

Sunlight poured onto the desk Connie used in the Bayview library. It felt good against one of the few cold days in Florida. It was more cheerful than the chapters of *Homeward Bound* she was revising. The novel opened with the death of a teenage boy and she had started to develop her two main characters, girls who were friends of the boy. She liked how the title captured the theme, one girl bound to home, the other searching for home. She didn't know yet where it was going, but she knew she was modeling the town on Freedom and the characters on herself and Sarah. The girls were becoming women, were disguised enough and moving in directions different enough that they were taking on identities of their own.

She returned home to find her mother outside, huddled on a lounge by the swimming pool. Hannah struggled to stand up. "I was worried about you. The lake's choppy. You and Charlie shouldn't have been out in the canoe. Is he in the house?"

Connie put her arm around her mother. "It's too cold to be out here. Come inside. We need to make dinner."

They walked across the grass and into the condo. "I got confused," said Hannah.

"We're in Florida."

"Is Sam here?"

"Not today," said Connie.

On Sunday when Everett called, Connie didn't ask to visit.

Chapter 17
Easter Weekend 1978

A volleyball landed on the sand a foot in front of them. "Sorry Mrs. Swenson," said the gangly teenager who picked it up and ran back to his game on Clearwater Beach.

"One of your students?" Connie asked Eva. They had taken off their shoes and were walking to the hard sand along the water's edge where the waves were merely ripples.

"They all are. That boy is new. Gave me trouble the first week until the others told him the deal."

"The deal?"

"Shape up or ship out." Eva pointed to a ship barely visible on the horizon.

Connie used her foot to splash water onto Eva's leg. "How do you control a guy like that? He's easily a foot taller than you."

"Grades. They're my weapon."

"Is that ethical?"

Eva splashed Connie back. "I just hold them accountable. Paper comes in on time or the grade gets lowered. If the dog ate it, they have to bring me the tattered pieces. Ted, you met him, makes them bring in an obituary if they say their grandmother died."

"That seems harsh."

"You'd be amazed at the excuses they think up. They respect you if you hold them accountable. If they respect you, you can respect them, know when to accept an excuse, to show some sympathy."

They moved aside to let a couple holding hands pass them. Children were building sand castles in puddles left from the high tide. Others were chasing the shallow waves while their parents watched from the shore. Older people sat on towels or beach chairs, their faces turned to books or the sea.

"I could never teach. I told Everett that the night I met him at Will's. Will's colleagues were trying to get me to teach creative writing." The wave at Connie's feet carried a pang of loneliness that swept up her body.

"His appointment's half over. Will your draft be finished?"

Connie picked up a shell. Everett had missed last Sunday's call and a couple of weekly letters. Since he left, she'd been writing furiously, surprised at how quickly the words came. *Homeward Bound* opened with the teenage friends, Stephanie and Eileen, riding their bikes along a road that bordered a corn field. It was a perfect September morning, the sun fully shining, the coolness of the night still lingering in the air, the corn already picked and brought to the farm stand. A perfect day, until at the edge of the field they saw a pair of sneakers and, curious, stopped to look at them. They belonged to their friend Joseph, who was found hours later in the farmer's barn, his body naked, his neck broken. The girls prowled through the fields for weeks trying to find something the police overlooked. Joseph's death went into the cold case files.

"It's going okay. I'm trying something new, alternating points of view. Eileen leaves Massachusetts and travels all over the United States looking for something she can't name. Stephanie refuses to leave the borders of New England."

"So you're like Eileen? Stephanie's like Sarah?"

"They're taking on lives of their own. I'm beginning to understand Stephanie. She lives in the moment, treasures what she has, lets go of what she can't change."

"Do I hear a note of reconciliation with Sarah?"

"She's happy. I envy that."

"Doesn't writing make you happy?"

Connie ran her fingers along the shell, searching for the right word. "More like satisfied. Or fulfilled. At least I will be when I get this draft finished."

"How will it end?"

"I'm not sure. Eileen will come home. One of them will find the truth behind Joseph's death."

"Which is?"

"I don't know. Maybe he fell from the hay loft after having sex, maybe with a girl, maybe a boy. Or maybe he was the victim of a pedophile and was thrown from the loft. Maybe a suicide. I'll know the answer when I get to the end. I'm writing by the seat of my pants, trusting that the writing will lead me where I need to go."

They reached an area where the beach bordered the ubiquitous construction along Florida's Gulf shore. They turned back, away from the noise that continued even on Good Friday. Eva picked up a stone and threw it into the water. "Snowbirds from the North are ruining Florida. Pretty soon Clearwater Beach will be bordered with nothing except high rises."

"I plead guilty. At least my mother and I stay all year now."

"I didn't mean you. You never came down dragging a bunch of kids wearing Mickey Mouse hats."

"I'm almost thirty-five. Too old for kids."

""How's Everett feel about that?"

"He'd like kids, but Lizzie's enough for me." When Everett returned, Connie would explain again why thirty-five was too old to start a family. How she was mothering her mother. Hannah wasn't good, but she was compliant. Connie had enrolled her in a program three days a week where she spent her time knitting or playing Bingo with the help of an aide. Jane and some women from church helped out on the days Hannah stayed home. She wasn't incapable and she wasn't a danger to herself, though Connie knew she would eventually need to find more help.

She dropped the shell she was carrying into a wave. "My novels are my children, birthed in pain and raised to fruition."

"Spoken like the writer you are," said Eva as they continued toward where they had started on the beach.

On Easter Sunday, Connie went with her mother and Jane to church. She half listened to the minister talk about how Christ sacrificed for all of God's people. When she looked around the congregation, she wondered if he considered only whites as God's people. With the influx of Vietnamese, even Freedom had become more diverse than Dunhill. Florida was still erecting monuments to Civil War generals.

After church, they stopped at Clearwater Beach to walk. It was quieter than when she was there on Good Friday with Eva. They saw only a few parents with young children kicking balls or trying out bikes on the boardwalk. A little girl pushing a doll carriage reminded Connie of Lizzie five years ago. She wondered if Everett was celebrating Easter with anyone in Washington.

Hannah had been quiet in church, had recognized the hymns and tried to sing them, her voice halting and off key. Without the familiarity of the church ritual, she lost her bearings. She watched the child with the doll carriage move beyond them and called after her, "Sarah, wait for me and Grandma."

"She's fine," said Jane. "Just a little confused in a strange place."

They took off their shoes and stepped onto the sand. Hannah stumbled. Connie caught her before she fell. Hannah looked at her blankly. "Do I know you?"

"It's me, Mum. Connie. Your daughter."

"I have a daughter? Does Charlie know? He's my brother. Gone away."

Connie took her mother's hand. "We'll just walk for a bit. We're having Easter dinner at Jane's."

Jane took Hannah's other hand. She and Connie kept her from falling as they walked along the hard sand at the water's edge. Hannah sang to herself, softly and out of tune, words to "Easter Parade." Despite all her confusion, she remembered what day it was.

When they finished their walk, they brushed sand from their feet, got into the car, and drove back to their home. Connie opened the door to the condo just as the telephone rang. She reached it before Hannah and said hello. Her heart somersaulted when she heard Everett's voice. "Oh good. You're home." He cleared his throat. "I need to tell you something."

Tell, not ask. Her legs went rubbery, the way they did at her first book reading that seemed eons ago. "You're scaring me. Something's wrong."

"I accepted a full-time position at the University of Washington. I'm not coming back."

Behind her, Hannah started yelling at Jane. "Why are you in my house? You took my box." She pushed Jane onto the couch then slammed the door to her bedroom. Jane signaled Connie that she'd take care of Hannah.

Connie clutched the wall to keep her legs from buckling as she spoke into the phone. "I can't come right away. My mother's Alzheimer's is worse."

She strained to hear Everett's next words. "I didn't ask you to come. You need to stay in Florida. Get that book written. Tend to your career."

"My career can take me anywhere." Her shock was turning to anger. "So can yours if you wanted it to."

"That's not fair. Washington is a huge step up from Bayview College."

"A step you prefer to take alone."

"Yes." Everett spoke louder.

"Your choice." Connie wouldn't plead with him. "Read my next novel," she said, and slammed the phone down.

"What's the matter?" Jane asked as she led Hannah out of the bedroom.

Connie spoke through clenched teeth. "I'm tired of being the good daughter." When Jane touched her arm and said "I'm here to help," she pulled away. Hannah stopped in front of her. Connie studied her mother. She had shrunk to under a hundred pounds, she needed new clothes that she wouldn't disappear beneath, she needed a haircut to disguise the thinning of her hair that had become a dull gray. Except for the garnet she refused to take off, she looked like a stranger, not the mother Connie had driven with to Florida five years ago.

Hannah looked vacantly around the room. "Is it time for ––" She paused, searching for the word. "Time to eat."

Connie watched Jane walk Hannah out the door. She went into the bathroom, took off her glasses, and splashed cold water on her face, willing herself not to break down. She grabbed two of the towels on the rack behind her. The wall was so close to the sink she didn't need to take a single step. The bathroom was as claustrophobic as her life. She studied the frames of her glasses. Brown plastic shaped in an oval too big for her face. So different from the John Lennon glasses she wore when she left Massachusetts. She put them on and looked at her face in the mirror. The same brown eyes peering from the glasses that sat on the same narrow bridge of her nose, the same round face, the same dark hair that she had grown a bit longer because it waved in Florida's humidity. She could change the style of her glasses, the style of her clothes, the length of her hair, but she couldn't change her life or the possibility that she carried the Alzheimer's gene. She opened the bathroom door, walked past copies of *Secrets* and *The Orange Grove* that Hannah insisted on keeping on the coffee table, and out the door of one tiny condo into the door of another.

Connie woke on Monday to the heavy cloak of depression that had wrapped itself around her all through her restless sleep. She heard Hannah in the kitchen and forced herself out of bed. Before she went into the bathroom, she checked on her. One of the stove burners was glowing red and Hannah was trying to crack a hard boiled egg into a frying pan.

She held it toward Connie. "These eggs are all different colors. Do the chickens lay them this way?"

"Yesterday was Easter. We colored them."

Hannah tried to crack the egg again.

"Let me help you, Mum. They're all cooked. Go sit down and I'll bring you breakfast."

Hannah started to go out the front door. "Not that way." Connie pointed her toward the table in the dining area.

She fixed a plate for her mother and watched her while she called Will. The college was closed for a long Easter weekend so he should be home. He answered on the first ring.

"Will. It's Connie. Can I come over?"

"He told you."

"You knew?'

"Come over. We can talk."

She hung up. Hannah sat blankly at the table, her food untouched as if she had forgotten how to eat.

She dressed rapidly, leaving her door open so she could hear her mother. Hannah's periods of confusion were getting worse. She'd have to find a facility for her soon. She wanted to call Everett. Say she could find one in Washington.

When she finished dressing, she coaxed Hannah to eat her eggs and toast, got her into a shirt more appropriate for Florida than the heavy turtleneck she had put on. She combed the tangles out of her thinning hair, promising herself that she'd help her mother wash it later.

They drove in silence to the adult day care center, aptly named Sunset Manor. "You have a nice tan," Hannah said to the Black woman who greeted them. She looked at her own hands. "I used to tan. Got as dark as a Negro."

Connie gave Hannah her knitting bag and pointed toward a cushioned chair. She faced the aide. "I'm so sorry. She's really confused today."

"Don't worry about it. Happens all the time with older white people." Connie heard a note of contempt when the aide added, "Especially if they're from the North."

Connie waited to see that Hannah was settled then drove to Will's. When he answered the door she felt a surge of attraction she hadn't felt since before she'd learned he was gay. How different her life would have been with him instead of with Everett.

"Want coffee?" he said. "I'll bring it onto the deck."

"Please."

Sid came out of the kitchen. "There's Easter bread left if you want some." He touched Connie's arm and went back to the kitchen. It wasn't only Will who knew about Everett. She went to the back deck, feeling betrayed by everyone. When Will came outside with a tray, she blurted, "You knew. Why didn't you tell me?"

"At least let me sit down before you attack me." Will put the tray on the wicker table and sat on a chair opposite Connie. "He wanted to tell you himself."

"How long have you known?"

"Just a few weeks. He had to formally resign. He asked me to tell some of our friends before the news became public."

"Public except for me. I should have gone with him in January."

"In January he thought he'd be coming back."

"So why didn't he ask me to move to Washington? I can write from anywhere. I could take my mother. Half the time she barely knows where she is. Florida or Washington wouldn't matter."

"He didn't tell you everything?"

"What's more to tell? He got a new job. He's not coming back."

Will reached across the table. "He's seeing someone else. He wants to start a family and he knows you don't want children."

The depression that had been stalking Connie all morning lifted into the energy of rage. She spit out her words. "Three months. He couldn't wait that long. He couldn't ask if I would change my mind, have a child."

Will handed her a napkin and she wiped the spit off her chin. He took her hands, holding so tight she couldn't move them. He leaned forward, his blue eyes starring into hers. "He should have told you."

"He left it to you."

"Guess so. Fucking coward."

"Fucking asshole. What's with you men? Chasing whatever skirt's most convenient."

"Skirts don't interest me, remember."

"Sorry."

"He asked me to look after you."

Connie erupted, angry sobs wracking through her. "Who does he think he is? I've been taking care of myself ever since I went away to college. I'm not my mother. I don't need someone to take care of me."

"I've seen that since the first day I met you. You were so confident when you gave me those directions."

She spoke in a low pitch to control her voice. "I'll get over it. Get on with the sad state of my life."

"Forget Everett. He's not worth your love."

"I thought he was your friend."

"He was. Sid never liked him. Thought he was an opportunist. Thought he was using me because I'm on the tenure committee."

"He won't get tenure now."

"He'll find a way."

Connie bit into some Easter bread. She had trouble swallowing. She choked down coffee. She gave up trying to eat and stood to leave.

Will jumped up next to her. "Where are you going?"

She didn't know. Inland where the heat and humidity would smother her or to the ocean where the salt air would sting. "Anywhere. Nowhere."

"I'm coming with you."

"No. I need to walk alone."

"Connie, please. I know how you feel."

"No you don't. Sid never betrayed you."

"We're both here for you. You have friends. You have your writing. Your novel will be wonderful."

"*Homeward Bound*. Home is a chimera. It's elusive or it's a trap." She ignored Will's protests, pushed past Sid who was clanging on something in the kitchen, and got into her car. When she started it, the radio blared out Roberta Flack. "The First Time Ever I Saw Your Face." She hated that song. She was done with men. Forever.

Chapter 18

June 1979 – May 16, 1980

Like the humid air, lethargy enveloped Connie until Eva convinced her to hire a caregiver for the days Hannah didn't go to Sunset Manor. Jenny was a nursing major at Bayview College. Hannah often mistook her for a boy because of her cropped hair and sometimes called her Charlie. What Jenny lacked in experience, she made up for in her good humor and her patience when Hannah asked over and over if she wanted to look through the family photos. If Hannah ever showed her what was in the blue box, Jenny never told Connie.

One afternoon in June, she returned home to find Jenny looking through one of Hannah's photograph books. Beside her Hannah dozed. Slumped and emaciated in a patterned shirt, she seemed to disappear into the floral pattern of the sofa. The only thing familiar about her was the garnet she still wore around her neck.

Jenny set the book on the coffee table. "She remembers everything about every picture in this book. Told me how she met Sam when he came into a restaurant where she was working. Even remembered the name. Bickford's. By the look of his photos, he was a handsome man."

Hannah jerked awake and slammed the photo book onto the coffee table. "I'm not deaf. I'm going for a nap." She stomped away, opened the bathroom door, slammed it, and found her way to the bedroom, slamming that door shut.

"Three slams," said Connie. "Has it been a bad day?"

Jenny gathered her things to leave. "Up and down. It must be hard on you."

A knot cramped Connie's stomach as it did whenever Hannah turned angry. A month ago she had locked away all the scissors and knives so her mother wouldn't turn her anger against herself. Or Connie. Hannah could no longer be left alone. "Having you here helps."

Connie paid Jenny and went into Hannah's bedroom. Hannah was sitting in her recliner looking at the photo of Charlie she kept unframed on her dresser, her anger forgotten. She looked at Connie as if she were a stranger. "Have I told you about my brother Charlie?"

Connie gently took the photo from her. Its edges were disintegrating. "He was a handsome man. Why did he leave?"

Hannah murmured "I forget."

Connie knew the chance of learning the answer was as likely as the chance that Everett would return. If she didn't move beyond her own grief, she'd end up disappearing under a blanket. With an hour before dinner looming unfilled, she went to her room where a handwritten chapter lay untouched beside the typewriter. She rolled in a piece of paper and forced herself to type.

She regained her will to write even as her mother continued to decline. Hannah still tried to knit blankets and didn't notice that they unraveled from all the dropped stitches. She had to be coaxed to eat and had to be reminded to go to the bathroom so she wouldn't soil herself. When Connie helped her bathe, she tried not to look at her mother's scar. If she asked about it, Hannah would thrash in the water and swear at her. Her bouts of anger increased, but she was too weak to do more than slam the cover of her photo book or throw a dish on the floor. Connie began to serve her on plastic plates. Only holding the photo of Charlie calmed her.

In April Jenny gave her notice. She'd be graduating, class of 1980 she proudly announced. Connie advised her to get out of Florida, see something of the world, seize her youth while she was still untethered by what life might toss her. With Jenny leaving, Connie accepted that it was time to place her mother in a facility dedicated to the care of Alzheimer's patients. She called Sarah. She wanted her involved.

Lizzie answered the phone with "Hello," none of the "This is the Lewis house" that Connie and Sarah had to say when they were twelve.

"Lizzie. This is Aunt Connie." In the background she heard the laughter of young girls. "You're not in school?"

"Teacher workshop day. I'm having my birthday party."

Connie had called on her birthday. The Sunday after Easter this year. One day it would fall on Easter. Every year she and Lizzie calculated the date. 2031. Connie would be eighty-seven and Lizzie sixty-three. Every year, they vowed to be together. "Did my gift finally arrive?"

"I love it. My very own writer's book. I haven't started *Silver on the Tree* yet, but I know I'll like it. Susan Cooper is my favorite writer." Lizzie paused. "Except you, of course?"

"You read my books?"

"This year. Mummy said I was old enough."

"Is Mummy there? I need to talk with her."

"Bye," said Lizzie, adding, "Tell Granny hi."

Connie heard her in the background calling for Sarah, who picked up the phone and said, "What's up. We just talked last week."

"It's Mum."

"Is she worse?" Sarah had no idea how much Hannah had deteriorated since her and Lizzie's last visit.

"Jenny is graduating. I can't handle all the care. We need to talk about an Alzheimer's facility for her."

"Can't you hire more help?"

"She's not safe. I can't leave her alone because I'm afraid she'll hurt herself. I have to lock her bedroom so she won't wander in the middle of the night. She eats so little she weighs only seventy-six pounds. She has fewer and fewer days when she knows me. I want you to come down, be part of choosing a place."

"Can't you do it without me?"

"I can. But I need you here. She's our mother, not just mine."

"I'll need a few weeks. I'll need to arrange for Lizzie to stay with someone so she doesn't miss school."

"Can't Andy take her?"

"I'll ask."

"Jenny leaves the end of May, so come as soon as you can." Connie put down the phone. Hannah came up behind her. "Were you talking to Sam? Is he coming home soon?"

Connie was covered in flour, making a pie while Hannah looked on. She had to explain about the dough, the rolling pin, the strawberries and rhubarb she was cutting up for the filling. She brushed off the flour when she heard a taxi arrive with Sarah. She and Hannah went outside to greet her.

Sarah emerged from the car, tall, slender, groomed as if she had just come from the beauty salon instead of an airplane. Connie wished she had changed her flour-covered T-shirt. Hannah leaned into Connie. "Who's that woman? She's beautiful."

"That's Sarah, Mum. Your daughter."

"I remember. I have a daughter."

"You have two daughters." Connie accepted Sarah's hug.

Sarah and Hannah faced each other as if they were strangers until Sarah said "Mum" and bent to kiss her. Hannah rested her head on Sarah's shoulder. Sarah pulled away, took her mother's hands, and studied her. "She looks so frail. Is she eating?"

Hannah let go of Sarah's hands and touched Connie's stomach. "She's a good eater. Always has been." She went into the condo, leaving Connie and Sarah standing next to a suitcase too large for a three day visit.

"She seems really confused," said Sarah. "And she looks terrible."

"Why I called you down. I don't want to decide on a place by myself."

Sarah picked up her suitcase. "You've done more than your share."

Connie heard the catch in her sister's voice as she went inside. Sarah was Hannah's daughter, too.

A laughing gull shrieked in the distance. It didn't sound joyful.

On Thursday, they took Hannah to Sunset Manor and visited the half-dozen nursing homes within an hour's drive of Dunhill. The Alzheimer's units were awful. Warehouses for men who needed a shave and wore shirts holding remnants of their last meal and pants stained with pee. Most of the patients were women, their hair pulled back and tied with pink yarn, their frail bodies lost in dresses or shirts and pants that had once been fashionable. The clothes smelled of moth balls. The facilities smelled of stale food and urine and half-washed bodies, the rancid odor of death. Some of the patients moaned, others laughed, most sat quietly, heads drooped and torsos collapsed in a half-curved fetal position. The staff, most nurses' aides, helped them move from wheelchairs to sofas, gave them drinks of juice, assured them that no one had stolen anything from their rooms.

When they left the last facility, all Connie could say to Sarah was, "These are houses of the dead."

They went together into Sunset Manor. Hannah was sitting quietly in front of a window watching goldfinches at a feeder. "Sam makes bird houses," she said when they approached. "Do you know him?"

"We do," said Connie. "Let's get you up. Time to take you home."

"To my big house on Dunstable Street. You'll like it."

Sarah shook her head and shrugged. She whispered to Connie as they exited Sunset Manor. "You need to get her into one of these facilities. Fast."

That night with Hannah safely in bed, dosed with a Valium, Connie and Sarah sat at the kitchen table drinking gin and tonics, going over their options. Sarah had a piece of paper in front of her with the name of each facility in one column, the cost in another, pro and con columns ready to be filled in. "Dunhill Haven is closest."

Connie turned her glass around and around on the table. "Cross it off. Jenny worked there before I hired her. Said they let their patients lie in wet beds for hours."

"Then why did we look at it?"

"I don't know. I suppose because it's close. I wasn't thinking."

Sarah crossed it off the list. "What about Fair Point Manor? It's the farthest away."

"Also the most expensive."

"Don't worry about it."

Connie stopped twirling her glass and wiped her cold fingers on her pants. "If she runs out of money, Medicaid will take over. I don't want to put her in one facility and then have to move her to a place like Dunhill Haven."

"Don't you have Power of Attorney? How much money does she have?"

"She used Dad's insurance money to pay off the mortgage here and manages to live on his Social Security, eight hundred dollars a month. The money she got from the house in Freedom is in a couple of different bank accounts."

"Her Social Security will cover most of the cost and she can use those investments." Sarah sipped her gin and tonic. She sounded as cold as the drink when she said, "She won't outlive her money."

"Don't wish her dead." Connie pushed aside the feeling that rose into her heart when she anticipated the freedom she'd have when Hannah died.

"I'm just being realistic. Fair Point Manor's possible. Three left. Harborside, Oak Knoll, and William Loring."

"Not William Loring. They had his portrait hanging in the dining room. Bayview College has a statue of him outside the library. The woman who showed us around was bragging about how he was a hero in the Civil War."

"She wouldn't notice."

"I would. Too many people around here are reacting to desegregation by defending the proud history of the South in the Civil War."

Sarah crossed off William Loring. "You got more sensitized than me and Mum when you did that march on Washington."

"If you spent time in the South, you'd know what I mean, though Florida's better than many of the other states. Too many northerners flocking here in the winter to risk offending them. What other facilities are left?"

"Harborside and Oak Knoll were both adequate."

"I'm favoring Harborside. I can take her for walks along the Gulf. Is it more expensive?"

Sarah drew a circle around the name. "Fifty dollars a month more. She'll manage. You'll manage."

"I guess I'll have to. She drives me crazy half the time, but it already feels lonely without her."

Sarah pushed the paper to Connie. She finished her gin and tonic, rinsed the glass in the sink, paused behind Connie, and squeezed her shoulder. "Accept your freedom and don't feel guilty. I'll watch Mum tomorrow and you can go to Harborside to get her on the list. Sometimes it takes a while. Andy's grandmother had to wait three months. She died less than a year later."

Connie got out of her Volkswagen. In the carport that once housed her father's black station wagon, its yellow seemed a mockery. The air was still hot in the late afternoon sun. Florida's spring was already turning into its summer heat. She smelled the star jasmine that crept along the back of the carport. Her head ached with the flowers' perfume and the stress of signing her mother into Harborside. She hoped for a month to help her choose what to take with her, what to sell, but there was an immediate opening. Sarah had one more day in Florida. They'd spend it listening to Hannah's confused litany about the photographs in her book. They'd go through her closets and her drawers. Somewhere the blue box would appear.

The front door was locked. Sarah must have closed it to turn on the air conditioner and forgotten to turn the latch to keep it unlocked. Connie fumbled for her keys. She dropped them into the bed of impatiens she had planted on Valentine's Day while the weather was cool enough for them. Red and white, the colors of love and peace she told her mother. When she stooped to pick up her keys a gecko scurried over her hand.

She stepped inside. The windows were open and no air conditioner was running. The sliding back door was closed. She called, "Sarah? Mum?" No answer. She noticed a towel designed with blue fish draped over a dining room chair. They must have gone to the pool and forgotten it. She dropped her purse and keys on the table and went to the door. When she tried to slide it open, she was surprised that it, too, was locked. She opened it and went outside, pausing next to the azalea she had replanted after the tropical storm six years ago. Sarah was lying in a lounge chair next to the pool. Hannah must be with Jane.

Connie wanted company and thought of Will. She could drive to Will's, have a drink with him, and return before Hannah came home. She stood over Sarah, who had fallen asleep. Next to her a half-full glass with a lime floating in it reminded Connie that she could have a drink with her sister instead of Will. Sarah had been more helpful than she had imagined. Massachusetts and a relationship with Andy that was public after his divorce had mellowed her. She tapped her on the shoulder.

Sarah opened her eyes, closed them again, and said, "How'd it go?"

"It was awful. Go back to sleep. I'll get into my bathing suit and join you for one of those gin and tonics. When will Mum and Jane be back?"

Sarah jumped up. "She's not with Jane. I gave her one of her pills and left her taking a nap. Locked the doors in case she woke up and wandered."

"She's not supposed to take Valium in the afternoon. She'll never sleep tonight."

"What time is it?"

"Four-thirty."

"Shit. I was going to check on her at two-thirty. I fell asleep. It's stressful being around her, seeing how bad she is."

"No kidding. I'll go wake her. Wait a bit before you come inside. She'll be groggy as hell." Connie left, cursing Sarah for letting Hannah sleep. Sarah got her nap while she signed their mother into the hell of a nursing home. Sarah could stay up while Hannah was awake all night. Feel a little more of the stress she had been sheltered from in her Massachusetts comfort.

The photograph album lay on Hannah's recliner. She wasn't there. She wasn't in her bed. She must have woken while Connie was at the pool and gone into the bathroom. Connie knocked on the bathroom door. "Mum, are you in there?"

No answer.

She knocked again. "Mum?"

Still no answer.

She turned the knob. The door was locked. Connie had tried to break her mother of the habit she developed after the day she found her asleep in the tub, her scar shining beneath the water. When she coaxed her into the bathroom, she'd tell her to leave the door open. Too often Hannah would close it, lock it, and forget how to unlock it. The key now hung on a hook next to the door. Connie knocked one more time before she turned the key in the lock.

The bathroom light glared onto the counter and Hannah's plastic pill case. Connie registered the compartments. Today was Thursday. Friday and Saturday's pills were gone. The closed shower curtain loomed in front of the bathtub, its forest design turned into a landscape of fear.

"Mum?" Her voice came out a whisper.

She pulled aside the curtain. Hannah lay under the water, her face contorted, fine strands of hair rising from her scalp as if from an electrical shock, the scar along her torso shining through the stillness. The garnet still hung around her neck.

She felt screams coming from some deep uncontrollable source. "Mum, Mum, wake up." She felt Sarah's arms pull her away. She heard the tap of Sarah's fingers on the phone and her sister's voice, controlled and efficient. "Yes, there's been a death. Twenty-seven Magnolia Place." By the time she heard the sirens, she was sitting on the sofa, staring at the picture of her and Sarah on the stereo, dimly aware that her strongest tie was broken and too filled with grief to wonder what that would mean.

Chapter 19

May 1980 – June 1980

Connie and Sarah faced each other across the kitchen table. A pot of tea Jane insisted on making before she left lay steeping under a tea cozy designed as a rooster. Sarah raised her cup, sipped, put the cup back on the saucer, and pushed it away. "I hate tea. Want something stronger?"

Connie tasted her tea. "It's not bad. Chamomile. It's supposed to make us sleepy."

Sarah went to the cupboard and opened the bottle of gin she used in the afternoon for her gin and tonic. She filled a tumbler with ice and poured a glass. "Want some? This is what will help you sleep."

"No. I need to stay clear-headed. *We* need to. We need to figure out funeral arrangements."

"We can't do anything until morning. We'll go to that funeral parlor Jane suggested, pick out a casket, and arrange for it to be flown to Freedom."

"Her, not it."

Sarah pushed away her tea cup and set her glass of gin in its place. "I'm sorry. I don't know how she got those pills. I put the case back in your desk drawer after I gave her the Valium."

"You're sure?"

"Absolutely. She was watching me and going on about Charlie again. Something about his desk and his pill box."

"She watched you? I never let her see where I keep those pills."

"Oh God. It's my fault." Sarah rested her head on the table, nearly knocking over her glass. Her body convulsed in sobs.

Connie let her cry. It was an accident, not a suicide. There'd be no question of that. They had given the empty pill box to Eva before the medics arrived. She pushed Sarah's glass of gin to the side of the table and studied her hair. It was soft with no hint of the coarseness that had invaded Hannah's. "Mum's hair was like an electric halo in the bathtub."

Sarah lifted her head, all the beauty drained from her face. She took a wad of tissues from the box on the table and blew her nose. "I couldn't look. It's my fault. I shouldn't have fallen asleep."

Connie exploded. "One time, Sarah. One time I ask for your help. You couldn't sit with her for a few hours."

Sarah found her glass and drained it of gin. "At least you won't have to watch her deteriorate in a nursing home. I released you."

"Just like you got released from George."

Sarah jumped up so fast her chair fell over. "That was cruel."

Connie followed her into the living room where Sarah was pulling out the hide-a-bed. "I'm sorry. We're both tired. I'll see you in the morning." She knew Sarah was right. She was released. But tonight their mother's death felt like a vise of pain cranked close against her entire body.

The earth gaped open in front of the gravestone marked Samuel Mattson Lewis, March 4, 1912 - January 24, 1973 and Hannah Anderson Lewis, January 20, 1914 - . The blank would be filled in after the funeral. May 16, 1980. More people than Connie expected had come to the funeral. People Hannah hadn't seen in the seven years she had lived in Florida spoke of her as if she still lived on their street or they sat next to her in church. Andy was with Sarah, acting as if he were part of the family. Their friends were there gushing condolences. Connie accepted sympathy from people she vaguely remembered. Even Lizzie had friends who came to support her in a grief for a grandmother she barely knew.

Connie stared at the coffin that would soon be lowered into the earth. A minister she hadn't met until she and Sarah talked with him about the funeral service stood at the grave's edge. His words at the service had been canned. A verbal portrait of Hannah given to him mostly by Sarah. Comforting phrases about the loss of a mother and grandmother. Now he was saying something about commending Hannah's spirit into God's hands. When he finished, he extended Sarah's invitation to join them at Cotton to Cocktails for an informal luncheon.

Sarah and Andy approached a wreath of roses, plucked one out and together dropped it onto the still raised coffin. Connie and Lizzie waited until everyone was walking to their cars. They each took a flower from the wreath and placed them on the coffin.

"I remember when we came to Grampy's grave before Mummy and I went to Europe with James. He was awful. James, I mean, not Grampy."

"You said Grampy and your dad could hold hands in the dark."

"I hardly remember either of them." Lizzie picked more roses from the wreath. "Let's put these on the other graves. Especially that one with the three dead children. I remember you telling me they died of some disease. It made me afraid I was going to get sick and die."

"You should have told me."

Lizzie handed two roses to Connie. "You were gone. I thought of it for months. That I'd die and get buried in one of the cemeteries behind the ancient churches we kept visiting."

They found the graves of the three children, silently put a flower on each one, and returned to the gaping hole. Connie took two more flowers from the wreath. "We'll put these on your father's grave tomorrow."

"I'd like that," said Lizzie.

Connie gave Lizzie the two roses and took one more from the wreath. Its thorn pricked the palm of her hand. She placed it on the coffin and licked off the spot of blood. It tasted like iron. They walked past the backhoe that would bury her mother. A man stood beside it, waiting for them to leave. Connie wanted to jump into the grave and let the grave digging machine bury her.

She unlocked the door and stepped into a condo as hollow as a tomb. Until she saw the dish garden on the dining room table. She opened the card that was propped against it. An image of a gull flying toward sunrise and the sea, the inside free of a Hallmark sentiment. It was signed simply, "We're here for you. Love, Eva, Jane, Will," each name in the handwriting of her friends. She moved the dish garden to the coffee table and still holding the card, reclined on the sofa. She felt as empty as the house. Eva. Jane. Will. These were her only anchors to Florida. She had no other anchors in no other place. She was free to leave, but she had nowhere to wander.

She dozed, then woke to a voice calling through the screen. Jane came inside, sat next to her, and choked out, "I miss her."

Connie took her hand. "You were a good friend."

"She died for me a year ago when the Alzheimer's invaded so much she didn't know us. But that doesn't lessen the grief. We should feel relief."

Connie put the card she was still holding onto the table. It had crinkled in her hands. "The plant helps. And the card. You remembered how much I hate Hallmark platitudes."

"Eva and Will remembered. Eva will come over as soon as school's out. I fixed dinner for us. Will says to call."

The idea of dinner exhausted Connie. She'd rather crawl into bed and sleep but if she did that, she feared she'd never find the strength to get up. She needed to claw her way through the cobweb of depression that infiltrated the condo. "I'll call Will now, take a shower, then come over." She watched Jane leave, carrying her own weight of sorrow.

"Closet's empty," said Jane. "Sure you don't want to keep any of these clothes?"

Connie stood up from kneeling in front of Hannah's dressing table. She had only the bottom drawer to empty. She moved beside Jane. Coat hangers dangled from their rod, metal, plastic, wooden, all emptied of every reminder of Hannah. The shoe rack curved its holders above a floor covered only in dust. Jane had pulled out the two suitcases Hannah hadn't used since leaving Massachusetts and filled them with clothes they'd take to Goodwill. Connie imagined them packed for a trip in some vehicle other than a coffin to some place other than a grave.

"Do you want to go through this box?" Jane used her foot to push a cardboard box away from the closet door.

"I know what's in it. I helped my mother pack it when we moved. Things that belonged to my father. His toolbox, his trophy for catching the biggest trout in some fishing derby, his high school yearbooks, his watch and his cufflinks. Even a couple of his ties. I can't face it right now. Let me finish this last drawer. You can help me load my car and I'll drive it all to Goodwill."

Jane sat on the bed and waited while Connie pulled sweaters too heavy for Florida from the drawer. She smiled as she reached for the last one. She and Sarah had given it to their mother one Christmas while they were in elementary school. Their father let them pick it out and helped them pay for it. Hannah didn't ski, but they said she was always cold in the ski lodge where she'd sit in front of a window waiting for them to appear over the lip of the slope. Connie fingered its wool as she picked it up. It must have been horribly scratchy and its snowflake design was hideous. As she pulled it from the drawer, its blue sleeve brushed against the blue of the box that lay beneath it. The snowcapped mountain on the box appeared as if Hannah had coordinated a winter theme.

Connie quickly closed the drawer. Her mother's secret would have to wait until she was alone.

She sat against the headboard on Hannah's bed, the box resting in her lap. The bedding smelled of laundry soap. She lifted the box to her nose to try to find the scent of her mother's hand cream. Paint. Wood. The hint of something herbal. The breeze coming through the open window filled the room with the strong scent of star jasmine.

She studied the room. Two reproduction paintings of a country road in New England, one in summer, one in winter. They hung in cheap frames on the wall in front of her. She remembered one of her mother's last lucid moments when they talked about how Sam would drive them along country roads for an adventure. She and Sarah would take turns telling their father to go left or right until they believed they were lost in the deep woods. When Connie suggested they buy better frames for the photos, Hannah accused her of wanting to steal them. Connie was haunted by her cruel answer. "Damn it, Mum. Cheap reproductions aren't worth stealing." She left the room and her mother crying. She needed to move her memories through her moments of anger at a deteriorating mother to the times when Hannah was whole.

On the dressing table beneath the photos, a silver-backed hairbrush and mirror lay next to a jewelry box Sam had made for Hannah when they first married. Inside the box was the garnet necklace and the diamond wedding ring the mortician had removed from Hannah's body. Connie shook away the image of her mother's hands crossed in her coffin, left over right so her wedding band showed. On the floor beside the dressing table lay the cardboard box with Sam's things, on top of that Hannah's photo books. Connie wasn't ready to sort through them, decide what to keep, what to sell, what to donate.

She ran her hand over the smooth surface of the painted box. She could leave it unopened, throw it in the dumpster, drop it into the Gulf or into the swamp where she and Everett had canoed. She could, but she wouldn't. Whatever secret Hannah had been keeping wouldn't go with her to the grave.

The box had no lock, not even a clasp to keep it closed. Slowly she lifted the lid. The inside was empty except for a large envelope addressed to Molly Anderson, Freedom, Massachusetts. It was postmarked from Ashland, Oregon, December 2, 1939. Connie knew that her grandmother Molly died early in 1939 and that her husband disappeared eleven years earlier. Whatever was inside, only Hannah had seen. She opened the envelope and pulled out the single page of a yellowed newspaper. The masthead read *Ashland Daily Tidings*, the date November 22, 1939. She unfolded it to read whatever front page article Hannah had been keeping so secret.

The headline read, LOCAL MAN JUMPS FROM GREEN SPRING ROAD:

> Charles Anderson, 42, died Thanksgiving afternoon in an apparent fall on Oregon's Route 66. An unnamed source reported that Laura Anderson found her husband in the morning holding their infant daughter and a rifle. He appeared to be having a conversation with someone named Ing. No Chinaman was in the room.
>
> Benjamin Wallace, a neighbor, told *The Tidings* that Mrs. Anderson ran to his house for help. Wallace left her at his home with the baby. He then transported Anderson to Ashland Hospital where Dr. Stephen Davis administered a sedative and released him.
>
> Wallace stated that he slowed at one of the steep curves on the treacherous road back to Green Springs. Anderson opened the door. Wallace said he screamed something about flying before leaping over the edge.
>
> It took Fire and Rescue four hours to recover Anderson's body from where it landed against a boulder. He likely died as soon as he went over the edge.
>
> Anderson had worked at Siskiyou Lumber Company since 1927. His wife and child are unharmed.

The article didn't identify the child as a girl or a boy. It gave no follow-up to who Ing might be.

She looked inside the envelope to see if there was some clue about Charlie's wife and child, about why Hannah had the news clipping. She found a folded piece of notepaper, marked with the name Kam Wah Chung. She unfolded it and read, "Charles was a good man and a good father. He often spoke of you. I am returning the garnet that belonged to your mother. Our baby Molly is all I need of him. We are safe and he is at peace."

The note was dated Dec. 1, 1939. There was no return address.

Molly. Charlie and Hannah's mother's name. He left home stalked by more than hereditary depression. Within three years he found his way to a job in Oregon. When and where he married remained a mystery. It wasn't until sixteen years after he left Massachusetts that there was evidence of a child. Whatever propelled him to leave, however it connected to the scar Connie still could see on her mother's dead body, he hadn't forgotten his family.

Chapter 20

June 1980

Connie carried the box into her bedroom and rested it on her desk. Her mother's awful scar must have come from the brother she loved. The family legacy of depression had exploded with the war. Shell shock. Or schizophrenia. Or both. Was the voice of someone he called Ing real or imagined? Why Chinese?

She started toward Hannah's bedroom then caught herself. Her mother was dead. Ever since she got back from the funeral, she'd been going to the room to call her to dinner or to say she was going out. Hannah's clothes were gone to Goodwill and her jars of peanut butter to the Food Pantry, but her spirit permeated the house.

She went outside and walked the few blocks to Edgewater, her mind racing. What did he do to you, Mum? Did you never hear from him again? Why didn't you tell us? With every thought, she waited for an answer until she reached Edgewater and realized she was acting like Charlie talking to whoever Ing was.

She found a bench and sat looking at the Gulf. A half-dozen sailboats moved quietly in the wind as if they had no destination. She watched gulls diving into the water. With each one, she thought of what held her to Florida. She whispered names. "Hannah," the reason she came. Dead. "Everett," gone to the Northwest where Charlie had gone. She was free. She could follow him. Fight to get him back. A seagull rose from the water, a fish in its mouth. It dropped the fish then dove again. "You're gone, Everett, like that fish. I don't want you back." Another seagull dove and she whispered, "Jane." Jane was Hannah's friend. She wasn't enough to keep her in Florida. Only Will and Eva mattered. Everyone else she knew was more an acquaintance than a friend.

She walked again, giving in to the rhythm of her pace and the warmth of the breeze. She remembered the day Will asked her if she was capable of joy. Like the tide, her emotions had been ebbing and flowing between sorrow and a sense of freedom. Her step became more buoyant.

Eva was unlocking her door when she walked past. A canvas bag loaded with student papers rested by her feet. Connie managed a wave and continued walking.

Five minutes later, Eva was at her door. She opened the screen without knocking and sat next to Connie, who was on the sofa staring at the photograph of herself and Sarah.

"Bad day?" said Eva.

Connie rested her head on her knees in a fetal position. The buoyancy she felt outside was drowned by the narrow walls of her mother's condo.

Eva sat until Connie lifted her head. "Want to talk about it?"

Connie blew her nose. She sucked in air between her words. "I don't know where to go."

"You don't need to go anywhere."

"I have no life here. Mum's gone. Everett's gone. I hate living in a condo. I need a yard, trees, cold air."

"You have a life here. Me, Will, your writing. I'll help you find a house to buy. Maybe something on the water."

Connie thought of Charlie's baby, her cousin, close to her own age. Somewhere in the West. "You're my best friends, but right now I'm too restless to buy a house. I might travel."

"As long as that's not running away. Travel and come home again."

"Like Sarah."

"Freedom is not your home. You've told me that a million times. Wait until summer's over. You can't travel now. There's too much gas rationing. With the lines, it'll take you a week just to get out of Florida."

"Makes me hate Jimmy Carter."

"Better than the alternative. Go get ready. We're going to dinner and a movie."

"What about that bag of papers I saw on your doorstep?"

"It's Friday. They can wait. I want to see *Urban Cowboy*."

"Isn't that the movie with the song 'Lookin' for Love'?"

"Don't worry about it. You wouldn't be looking for love in Texas."

"Maybe Oregon."

"Why there?"

"Forget it." Connie wasn't ready to tell Eva about the newspaper article and Laura's note.

Every day, she sat in front of blank papers at the library before putting them aside and walking along the beach. When she met Will at The Groaning Board, she was empty-handed.

Will found a pen and a clean paper napkin to write on. He handed them to her. "You can't just mope. You need a plan. Make a list. Set a goal."

Connie pushed aside the salad she had been picking at. "You're ridiculous."

"I'm not. When I get overwhelmed, I make a list. It puts things in perspective. Helps me gain control."

Connie wrote down the number 1 and showed it to Will. "Now what?"

"Number 1. Wait a year before traveling. Gas is too expensive. Number 2. Make no decision about your condo."

"Why?"

"It keeps your options open. Keeps you from making a mistake. Number 3. Spend a year finishing *Homeward Bound*. You've got a contract. You owe it to your publisher."

Connie wrote, 3. Finish novel. "That's not much to keep me grounded."

"Okay. Number 4. Do a longer book tour."

Connie wrote it down and listed a number 5. She pushed the napkin to Will.

He read, "Go to Oregon. Why? The book tour doesn't need to take you three thousand miles away."

"I have a cousin there."

"How can you have a cousin? Your mother's brother disappeared or died or something."

She looked at Will, the familiar curl in his hair, the blue of his eyes as bright as the sky. He trusted her with his secret. She was ready to trust him with her mother's. "I found a newspaper clipping my mother was hiding."

"In that box you told me about?"

"Yes. It described Charlie's death." She told Will about the child in his lap, the gun, Ing. "He heard voices. Maybe because of the war. I don't know, but I'm afraid that will happen to me. When I get involved in writing a scene, it sometimes feels like I'm in a different place, like my characters are really talking."

"That's called creativity."

"There was a note. From his wife. Laura. She sent it to my

grandmother, but my grandmother was dead, so my mother got it. She also sent that garnet my mother wore all the time."

"So Charlie told her about your family?"

"He must have. The baby's name was Molly. She'd be just a little older than me. Around forty. I want to find her. Find out if she knows what my uncle did to my mother."

Will pushed the napkin back to Connie. "Why do you think he did something to your mother?"

"I never told you. She had a scar. From her breast to her navel. I saw it one day when I found her asleep in the bathtub. It was terrible. Violent. She said that when she was young she fell out of a tree onto a splintered log, but I'm sure that was a lie."

"What difference does it make? It's over. Your mother is dead. Her brother is dead."

"And I have the family genes. What if I start to hear voices? What if I become violent, hurt Lizzie or someone else? Like you or Eva."

"You won't. You didn't go to war. You aren't like the Vietnam vets with PTSD living on the streets in Tampa. You've got an outlet in your writing."

Will was right. Disturbed veterans were now officially labeled with post traumatic stress disorder. She had no trauma. "Maybe that's why I write murder mysteries. They help me cope with anxiety, deflect it into my writing."

"And they're an outlet for your readers. You have a huge audience. Finish the book you're writing."

"I'll try. You were right. A list helped. I'll get the book done and talk my publisher into sending me to Oregon."

"And you won't sell your condo."

"Not yet." Connie put the napkin into her briefcase. She could pretend that a goal gave her joy.

The writing didn't come easily. *Homeward Bound* was a novel written out of despair. With Will's help, she managed to send it off to her editor in February. Naomi said it was the best she had written. It had the same strong setting and plot of *Secrets* and *The Orange Grove*, but *Homeward Bound* had a new depth of feeling.

"Can depth come only out of despair?" She was walking with Eva along a path in Pinellas Park. It had rained the night before, another of Florida's torrential downpours that she had grown used to. Heavy rain hit often, but nothing as severe as the storm in 1974 when she huddled with her mother and Eva and Jane in the middle of the living room floor. With each heavy rainfall, she thought of her mother.

Eva kicked a stick out of the path. "Despair paralyzes. What you had was grief. You managed it by writing. Otherwise you would have stayed in bed all day and I'd have been spoon feeding you chicken soup."

"Without you and Will, I might have done an Edna Pontellier and walked to my death in the Gulf."

"Who was she?"

"A character in a novel. *The Awakening.* She leaves her husband and her children, has an affair, and when she awakens to the futility of her life as a woman in the nineteenth century, she chooses death."

"Well, don't choose it for yourself. It's a selfish act. You've got more life to live, more books to write."

Connie wondered if George committed suicide out of pain or to free Sarah and Lizzie from the pain he was inflicting. "It's more complicated than that. Think about my mother and her brother Charlie."

"Your mother had Alzheimer's. She was too confused to commit suicide. Her death was an accident."

Connie saw the Valium on the bathroom counter. Her mother had enough memory to find it in the bedroom where Sarah gave her a pill. "She had moments of clarity."

"Not at the end. Put that idea out of your mind. All you know about Charlie is that he fell off a cliff."

"Jumped, I think. He wanted to free his wife and daughter from the pain he was giving them."

"You don't know that. Forget him until you finish *Homeward Bound*. Follow through with the idea you told me last spring. Get your publisher to set up a book tour to the West Coast. What's the publication date?"

"June 1981."

"School will be out. I'll go with you."

Connie and Eva moved to the side of the path to let a mother and an infant pass. The baby was facing outward in the mother's backpack. She smiled at them from beneath a pink bonnet. Connie waved at her. "We could find Molly."

"Solve a mystery. It will make a great plot for your next novel."

"Book tour or not, let's do it." They came out of the path to where The Yellow Sub glistened in the dampness left by the rain. Wherever it took her, it would be an adventure, a respite from Florida. It was time for her to move on.

PART V

The Journey Forward

Chapter 21

July 1981

"I see why you want to stay in Freedom," Eva said to Sarah. Porch lights and a full moon lit Sarah's yard and the swing set Lizzie, at thirteen, had outgrown. Fireflies blinked through the flower bed. "People have an independent spirit. Whoever named the town, named it well. You've got a beautiful house and yard and you have friends everywhere."

Sarah slapped a mosquito. "Only problem are the mosquitoes. Can't even sit on this deck at dawn or dusk."

Connie couldn't imagine herself returning. "Mosquitoes are just as bad in Florida. While Eva and I drive across the country, I'm going to find the place with the fewest bugs and move there."

Lizzie was playing with a Rubik's Cube. "You should come back home, Aunt Connie. Isn't that what your novel is all about? Those sisters are like you and Mum. One stays home and one leaves."

Connie studied Lizzie's face. Her teeth sparkled with metallic braces. She wore oversized glasses and had her hair permed into an Afro in a look that didn't suit her. All week she had an edge to her. Maybe being thirteen. Maybe she felt the tension between Connie and Sarah. Connie missed the little girl she used to read to. "They're not based on me and your mother."

Eva pulled a sweater over her shoulders. "Freedom seems like a perfect place for someone like Connie's wandering character to return to. Clear and sunny in the daytime, cool at night. Like Florida in March before the heat and humidity invade."

"Come in a few weeks and you'll feel right at home," said Sarah. "You should come back, Connie. This is your home."

Connie didn't know where she was going, but she knew she'd never come back to Freedom. Maybe Boston or some other New England city. Or the mountains of New Hampshire. Some place far away from the sprawl of suburbia. "I've been gone too long. It doesn't feel like home any more."

"What was it like giving a reading at your old high school? It's so much nicer than the one I teach in," said Eva.

Connie sipped from the expensive wine Sarah had opened. "It was new the year Sarah and I started high school. I recognized only a few people. Sarah's friends. My senior English teacher and the biology teacher we all had a crush on."

"I didn't," said Sarah. "He used to hang out at cheerleading practice."

Connie looked at Eva. "She's exaggerating."

Sarah defended herself. "No I'm not. Brenda reported him. After that, he stopped."

Connie had watched the biology teacher as she spoke about her novel. He was still good-looking. She wondered if he was married. It didn't matter. She wouldn't come back to Freedom. Mostly at the reading she thought about George. When she signed a book to the teacher who had been advisor to the newspaper, she wrote *To Christine Booth, who taught all of us on The Lion's Pride to write.*

Miss Booth had said, "I remember you and George. I thought you'd both become writers. Such a shame, his accident."

A clock chimed inside the house. Eleven. Connie finished her wine. "I need to go to bed. Eva and I want to start early tomorrow. Figure out how to negotiate the streets of New York City."

Sarah poured herself another glass of wine. "Tell me again where you're reading. It's some place famous."

"The Eighth Street Bookshop in Greenwich Village. First reading I ever did was there. I'm not as nervous as I used to be."

"Why didn't you read there before Boston? Wouldn't it have been closer when you were coming up the coast?"

"Just a scheduling issue. Eva and I aren't in a hurry." Connie carried her glass into the house.

Lizzie followed her. She hugged her the way she used to when she was five years old. "In case I'm still sleeping when you leave. You should come back here. I miss you."

Connie kissed her Afro, smelling the chemical scent of the permanent that held it in place. "Maybe I'll find a place closer to you."

Connie had just gotten into bed when Eva came into the room. "You didn't need to worry so much about this visit. Sarah's been gracious and Lizzie is wonderful."

"I miss little girl Lizzie. She seems so distant."

"She's thirteen. Trust me, I work with teenagers. She's more open with adults than most of them."

"She said she might be asleep in the morning when we leave. Why wouldn't she get up for five minutes to say goodbye?"

"What difference would it make?"

"None, I guess. At least Sarah will get up." Connie rested her head on her pillow.

Eva got into the other twin-sized bed. "Make peace with Sarah. This is the right life for her. She thrives on her connections the way you thrive on your writing."

Connie turned on her side, hiding her tears from Eva.

In the morning, Lizzie staggered out of her bedroom and gave Connie one last hug before she went back to bed. Eva went to the car, leaving the two sisters to say goodbye in private.

Sarah stood, wrapping a silk bathrobe around her slender body. "You destroyed the note, right?"

"George has been dead for ten years. Stop worrying about it." When she hugged Sarah, she felt the silk like the luxury of Sarah's life. "I'll call when we get to Oregon."

"You'll never find that daughter of Charlie's. Who cares if he was crazy anyway. We're not. Well, maybe you are to think you can find her."

"Doesn't matter if I find her or not. Eva and I will see our country and I'll sell a few books."

"I guess we're different. Traveling to Europe left me content to stay home. Maybe this trip will convince you to find a home of your own."

"Maybe." Finding Molly or not, Connie had committed herself to staying in Oregon for a year. She was embracing the idea of travel, trying out new homes. She picked up her suitcase and walked to the car. Eva opened the door for her. With a new sense of exhilaration, she pointed The Yellow Submarine heading toward the unknown.

At the Eighth Street Bookshop, Connie read to an overflow audience. Later, Naomi Rhinebeck brought her and Eva to the coffee shop where she had taken Connie after her first reading. The same man was playing his guitar, a little more gray, but with the same youthful intensity. Connie wanted to tell him to leave Greenwich Village, find success in a larger venue. While she and Naomi talked about her next novel, Eva listened to decade old folk songs. Connie confessed that she had no ideas for a new one.

Naomi handed her a piece of paper. "Here's your itinerary. You'll have plenty of time to think of a new idea. You'll need to start soon on a novel if you win the Pen New England Award. I nominated you."

Connie swallowed the sip of coffee, feeling her stomach somersault at the news. "I'm not that good."

Eva stopped listening to the music. "She'll win. She keeps getting better and better. We'll talk about ideas every night."

"I hope so," said Naomi, standing to leave.

Connie found her wallet and a five dollar bill. She dropped it into the tip jar for the guitar player and mouthed "Thank you."

Outside, Naomi hailed a cab for Connie and Eva. As they got into it, she said, "Check in after each of your readings. Let me know how the sales go. You'll have plenty of free time. I hope you brought your typewriter."

The acid taste of the coffee rose in Connie's throat. "I did. And plenty of paper."

When they got out of the cab, Connie and Eva walked to a liquor store near their hotel and bought a bottle of champagne. Eva insisted on celebrating the nomination. Connie was more interested in the adventure of searching for Molly than in starting a new novel. If she won the Pen Award, the pressure to write only about New England would be paralyzing.

She maneuvered The Yellow Sub onto the exit for Niagara Falls. The sign flashed her back to driving with her mother out of Massachusetts and into New York. "My mother honeymooned here."

Eva turned down the radio that was filled with news about the upcoming wedding of Prince Charles and Lady Diana Spencer. "It will probably be crawling with honeymooners today."

"My mother talked for days about her honeymoon. She wanted to know if I ever slept with George."

Eva glanced at her. "Did you?"

"No. I've not been thinking about him."

"Thinking about Everett? He's from Buffalo, right?"

Connie's pain rose as sharp as it had been a year ago. "I thought I was over him. If we married, the wedding might have been here."

"Grief rises and falls. You learn to live with it."

"Do you ever think of your ex-husband?"

"At times like this I do. We had a wonderful honeymoon in Key West. We thought we'd stay married forever."

"You never told me what happened."

"Nothing dramatic to tell. I didn't turn into the woman he thought he married. When Jimmy, Jr. was born, I stayed home for a year. I needed more, so I found a nanny and went back to work. Jim found the nanny, too. I was relieved, actually. We shared custody of Jimmy and I became a better mother when I didn't feel trapped in a life of domesticity."

"I'm learning to embrace my freedom. Like now. Whoever thought we'd be two women traveling across the United States with no one except ourselves." Eva pointed to a sign announcing Niagara Falls State Park. "We're here."

Connie circled the parking lot twice before she found an empty space. She watched a group of senior citizens getting off a bus. "It's going to be overrun with tourists."

"It's July. All those honeymooners."

"And senior citizens on group trips. Better than school kids."

"Lay off them. I like my school kids."

They got out of the car and walked into the Visitor Center. The place was packed. Lines had formed for tickets to The Cave of the Winds and The Maid of the Mist. They exchanged looks that said "skip those." Connie took two maps of the park out of a rack near the entrance. She handed one to Eva and they went outside. They found their way to a path that led to a viewpoint for Horseshoe Falls.

Connie gasped at a power that assaulted her senses. A horseshoe of raging falls plunged a hundred and eighty feet into a roiling pool. The sound drowned out the din of gawking tourists. She smelled the water, felt a mist on her arms and face that she never felt in Florida from the Gulf of Mexico. There could have been thousands more tourists and still the power of nature would dwarf them. She imagined what it must have been like when the tribes of the Iroquois Nation farmed and fished along the Niagara River.

Two men in wheelchairs came up beside her. They wore Vietnam veterans caps. They reminded her that the tribes warred with one another, chose sides, warred with encroaching French or English. She thought of her mother and father and their honeymoon. Had Hannah wondered if Charlie, damaged from World War I, had seen the Falls? She looked down at the two veterans, both missing their legs. What would George have been like if he returned from Vietnam physically damaged? She turned her attention back to the Falls. Nature this powerful dominated. It didn't heal. She touched Eva's arm. "Let's go."

They left the throng of tourists, young couples holding hands, a tour group of mostly gray-haired women, a Japanese man crouching to take a photo of a blond-headed toddler wearing rubber boots and looking for puddles left by the mist from the Falls.

"It's overwhelming." Connie turned her eyes away from The Falls whose sound echoed around her with a force as loud as an Atlantic hurricane.

Eva looked down at her map. "Let's follow this path along the river. It will be quieter."

It was quieter, but not quiet. The water churned as it was sucked toward the waterfall. Connie remembered being in the Florida swamp with Everett. Its seduction had been sensuous. Here the seduction was toward violence, toward what led to George's suicide, toward whatever had propelled Charlie to hold a gun along with his child. She put her arm around Eva. "It makes me sad."

"Me, too. The landscape's been ruined with commercialism."

"It's not that. It's the violence. Nothing could overwhelm such power. Let's keep walking. I need to clear my head for tonight's reading."

They wandered for another hour through the landscaping of Frederick Law Olmsted, stood at the viewpoint at Bridal Falls, decided not to go to the Canadian side. When they came back into the parking lot, Connie gave the keys to Eva. "Your turn to drive. Let's find us a quiet place for lunch. Maybe get some beef on weck."

"What's that?"

"Everett told me about it. Roast beef on a kimmelweck roll."

"I'm good with the roast beef. Never heard of a kimmelweck roll."

"Just a soft roll covered with salt and caraway seeds. The beef is sliced thin, dipped au jus, and spread with horseradish."

"Sounds as good as those Buffalo wings we had last night."

"Without the blue cheese dip." Connie remembered her dream. The wings had morphed into alligators and Niagara Falls became a Florida swamp. She pointed The Yellow Sub toward Buffalo and the ghost of Everett.

Everett had been right. The Albright-Knox Art Gallery was beautiful. Its columned front entry overlooked Olmsted's Delaware Park and its holdings boasted paintings by artists ranging from Albert Bierstadt to Pablo Picasso and Georgia O'Keeffe. When the host arranged by Random House led them into the auditorium, Connie's legs wobbled. "It's enormous," she whispered to Eva.

"The front rows are already full. You'll be fine." Eva pointed her to the table that was set up with copies of *Secrets*, *The Orange Grove*, and, the largest pile, *Homeward Bound*.

More people came in. A few of the bolder ones shook Connie's hand and mumbled platitudes about how they loved her work. Several mistook Eva for Connie despite the poster displaying her photograph.

At seven o'clock, Connie spoke from the auditorium floor instead of the stage. She invited everyone to move to the front so they could hear. Only a woman with a young child stayed at the back. Connie assumed the woman was poised to leave if the child made noise.

As she began to speak, the venue felt more intimate. Eva kept nodding and giving her a thumbs up with the hands she held in her lap. Connie recycled the same remarks she had been using along the seacoast from Florida to Boston and New York. How in high school she wanted to be a journalist, how she had been encouraged in a creative writing class at the University of Massachusetts, how she forgot her desire to write until the death of her father and the care of her mother freed her to pursue what she discovered was her life's passion. She introduced Stephanie and Eileen, the sisters in *Homeward Bound,* and described how they responded to the death of their friend Joseph, Stephanie remaining bound to the borders of New England while Eileen wandered, haunted by the death of Joseph. She read from the opening of the novel, the scene where the girls ride their bikes on a perfect September morning, the sun fully shining, the coolness of the night still lingering in the air, the corn already picked and brought to the farm stand. She read through how they found Joseph's sneakers, how they went to his house, how his mother called the police.

She ended her reading with the opening of the barn door. *The door creaked on its hinges, sunlight seeping through onto the space that had been empty of farm animals for years. The smell of new mown hay permeated the air. A barn swallow flew from the loft and perched on the rusted edge of a wheelbarrow. Next to it Joseph lay, face down, unmoving on the wooden planks of a floor strewn with pieces of hay.*

Connie closed her copy of *Homeward Bound*. She heard the intake of breath from the audience, then the applause. She moved a little closer. "Thank you so much. We have time for a few questions."

An older man sitting in the front row asked the question that someone had been asking at every one of her readings. "Do we learn how Joseph died? Does one of the sisters find the truth?"

Connie pointed to the books spread out for sale. "I'm afraid you'll have to read the book to find out."

More questions followed, about which sister she was most like, about Eileen's travels and whether Connie had been to these places, about themes that connected her three novels, about her writing process and what authors influenced her, about her plans for the next novel. Only the question about whether there was an unsolved mystery in her life surprised her.

"We all have mysteries in our lives," she answered. She ended the questioning. "Thank you all for coming and thank you to the Albright-Knox Art Gallery for hosting. It's a wonderful gallery overlooking a beautiful park."

Some of the audience left the auditorium, but many stayed to form a line to buy books. The woman and child still sat quietly at the back. When Connie finished signing and began to pack up the remaining books for the gallery to return to Random House, the woman approached her, holding the child's hand. Connie could see now that the child was a boy, red-haired, she guessed about four years old.

The woman let go of the child's hand. He wandered into the rows of seats and began pushing each one up. The mother glanced at him and left him to his task. She had the same rust-red hair as the child. "I'd like two copies."

Connie picked up her pen. "Shall I sign them?"

"The first to me. Eileen Kobel."

"Like my character." Connie signed. "To Eileen Kobel. Enjoy. Constance Lewis, July 10, 1981." She picked up a second copy and waited for Eileen to speak.

"It's for my brother. He told me he knows you. Wanted me to get a signed copy." She looked over her shoulder at the boy. "My husband's at work so I had to bring my son. I was afraid he'd make a racket."

"He was fine. He's having fun now." The boy stopped putting up chair seats and as he started to walk toward them, Connie knew what the woman was going to say.

"Sign it to Everett Eaton. He said you'd remember him."

Connie's hand trembled as she opened the book to sign. Her voice faltered. "I do remember him. Where is he?"

"In Washington State. He's married. Has a new baby girl. He named her Connie."

The child reached his mother's side. He looked like a miniature Everett. "Can we go now?" he said.

"In a minute."

Connie steadied her hand, remembering Everett's gift of *East Angels* and how he had signed it "Fondly." She signed. "To Everett Eaton. With fond memories. Constance Lewis."

She wrote no date. She closed the book and handed it to Everett's sister. That chapter of her life had to be over.

Chapter 22
July 1981

Cleveland. Chicago. Des Moines. Lincoln. Cheyenne. Salt Lake City. The miles unrolled beneath The Yellow Sub. Connie spoke to audiences in bookstores, libraries, churches and on July 28th, to a full auditorium on the campus of Boise State University. She and Eva were hosted by Phil Maynard, a faculty member in the English Department and sat now with him and his wife, Maggie, in their living room, trying to wake themselves up with cups of coffee. It was 4 AM and they were watching the wedding of Prince Charles and Lady Diana Spencer. The room was small, furnished with two small sofas that faced the television, in a house not much different from Connie's Florida condo. Phil and Maggie were an older couple, well-matched except that Phil was double Maggie's size, the indentation where Connie was sitting telling her she was in his place. Bookcases lined a side wall, overflowing with books and photos of the Maynard family. It was a home of the long married. Settled. Comfortable. A little bit dull.

The camera panned onto Lady Diana as she got out of the glass coach that delivered her to St. Paul's Cathedral. She took a long time to emerge. Her dress billowed around her and, according to the announcer, the tiara she wore was a Spencer family heirloom. Her cascading bouquet contained a mélange of white flowers. Everything, even the attendants' dresses, was too bouffant, too white. The camera followed Lady Diana as she entered the cathedral and walked down the red-carpeted aisle accompanied by her father. Prince Charles, in his full dress navy commander uniform, greeted her at the altar.

Connie thought of Sarah and George's wedding. In a simpler dress with a shorter train, Sarah had looked every bit as lovely walking beside their father down the tiny aisle of the Congregational Church of Freedom. Not so her five attendants. Connie as the maid of honor wasn't flattered by the dress that washed out her complexion. Sarah still hadn't forgiven her for calling it puke green. Connie sometimes thought the color foreshadowed the disaster that ended their marriage.

The room was silent as Charles and Diana exchanged vows. When Diana mixed up Charles's name and called him Philip Charles instead of Charles Philip, Eva said, "This isn't a good omen. They barely look at each other. He doesn't look like he loves her."

"He doesn't," said Phil. "Marriage of convenience for the Royals. She'll be a good baby factory for him. Wouldn't surprise me if they tested her fertility before the official engagement."

"Don't be so cynical," said Maggie. "It's romantic."

Connie remembered how Lizzie loved the fairy tales about Sleeping Beauty and Snow White and Cinderella, all women rescued by a handsome prince, none of them ending with a story of women trapped in a marriage where their roles were no more meaningful than their sleep had been. "My niece is probably watching, imagining herself growing up to be a princess."

"Lizzie's too smart for that," said Eva.

Connie hoped so.

Phil stood up. "I've seen enough. You women can keep watching while I make us some breakfast."

When he left, Maggie said, "He's a wonderful husband, but he hasn't a sense of romance."

Connie leaned forward on the sofa toward Maggie. "But congratulations for marrying a man willing to cook for three women."

They watched through the rest of the ceremony and to the aftermath when Prince Charles and Lady Diana came onto a balcony. He took her hand, his white gloves stark against the navy of his sleeve. Already Prince and Princess seemed separate, more tuned to the crowd than each other. When they kissed, Connie ticked off a four on her fingers. Enough years to produce an heir to the throne. There wouldn't be a divorce. Queen Elizabeth would see to that. But the marriage would be one in name only.

The smell of bacon cooking drew the women into the kitchen. It was five o'clock in the morning and still dark. Phil put a plate of bacon and eggs in front of each of them. "You're crazy to get up to watch a silly wedding. Clips will be repeated all day."

Connie agreed. She was ready to get back to the freedom of the open road and their four-hour drive through Oregon's eastern high desert. They'd check in early to one of the few hotels they found in a town called John Day. They weren't in a hurry. They had plenty of time to let their journey lead them where it would.

When they finished breakfast, the sun had risen and the day promised to be picture perfect. They said goodbye to Maggie in the kitchen. Phil walked them to their car, carrying the cooler they had cleaned and that Maggie had loaded with fruit and homemade cookies. "Be sure you have a full tank of gas. Some of these areas you're driving through are pretty remote."

"Filled up yesterday when we arrived. Thank you for

everything. Boise State seems like a wonderful place to teach." Connie unlocked the stuffed trunk and found the only spot for their suitcases.

Phil opened the driver's side door for Connie while Eva got into the passenger seat. "It is a good place. If you ever want a job teaching creative writing, we can find you a spot."

"I'm afraid I'm not suited for teaching. But thanks for the offer." Connie closed the door and glanced at the back seat. It was filled with evidence of their weeks on the road. A box of her novels, now half empty, jackets for cool weather, hats to shade them from the sun, hiking boots and sandals, a blanket for picnic stops. The pile of T-shirts they'd been accumulating at different stops was spilling onto Connie's typewriter that took up the middle of the seat. Whether she found Molly or not, the trip was giving her something to write about.

As they backed out of the driveway, Eva said, "Nice couple, though a tad on the traditional side. Maggie thought that wedding was real."

"Wedding was real enough. The marriage won't be." Connie thought of the bridal-like epiphytes in the Florida swamp. "There are no fairy tale endings."

Phil was right about services on the roads through southeastern Oregon. Route 26 was straight, flat, and hot, running through prairies inhabited by nothing except jackrabbits and towns that were unincorporated. When they hit a town called Unity, the road started to curve through a green mountainous landscape before it descended into John Day. It felt like another world, vast and empty. As they entered John Day, they saw a white building with a small sign that read Paleontology Center. Connie pulled her car into the driveway. A man was sitting at a picnic table eating his lunch. They got out of the car and approached him.

"Is this a museum?" Connie asked.

"Not yet," said the man. With a straggly sandy colored beard, he looked like a prospector. "We're the headquarters for the John Day Fossil Beds. Planning a museum. You can see the beds, though. Blue Basin is just up the road. An hour west and you can see the Painted Hills. Then head north to the Clarno Unit. All different. Too late for Clarno today, but you can see the other two. Florida license plate. You're a long way from home."

Connie shaded her eyes from the noontime sun. "Just exploring the West. We'll stay here tonight. Any place you can suggest?"

The man continued to speak in the clipped sentences of someone not used to conversation. "Miner's Lodge. Only place. Check out the Blue Basin first. Just up the road along the river. You've never seen anything like it." He drank from his water bottle. "Better take water."

Connie realized how thirsty she had become in air so dry that Eva had lost the curl in her hair. "Thanks. Maybe I'll come back when you get that museum built."

When they got back to the car, she reached into the cooler and took out the two water bottles they had filled at the Maynards'. She handed one to Eva. "Not very cold, but I'm glad we remembered to fill them. Want an apple or a cookie?"

Eva swallowed half the water before she took a cookie. "At least he said to follow the river. A blue basin sounds like a pool. I could stand to see water after that high desert."

They drove a half mile until Eva saw a tiny sign announcing "Blue Basin Trail." In the distance a blue-green formation rose to a peak of dark rock on its top. It looked like a wedding cake. They got out of the car and followed a path into a basin of blue-green rock formations, their sneakers getting covered in the stony dust of the trail. They could have been on a planet suitable for the rumored second sequel to *Star Wars*. Cake-like structures rose all around them. Connie bent to look more closely at the texture of the rock. It was porous, more like cracked clay than rock.

"This is surreal," said Eva. "Look at those caves on the rock faces."

"I don't think they're deep enough for caves. Probably filled with birds."

"And fossils. I can't imagine anyone living here."

"Doesn't look like anyone does." Connie reached to feel the rock face. "It's harder than it looks. What a contrast to its soft colors."

They walked in silence, feeling the foreignness of the landscape. After a lifetime in Massachusetts and Florida, Connie felt a new world opening before her. "Maybe I could live here after all."

"No you couldn't. It's too isolated."

Eva was right. It wasn't the isolation but the starkness of the landscape that would wear Connie down. Intense to look at, but the blue-green rocks were barren of water and trees. When they left the basin, parched and hot, even the green edges of the flat, slow John Day River seemed empty of life.

It was still too early to check into The Miner's Lodge, but they stopped anyway and rang a bell at the counter. A woman appeared wearing a T-shirt with the imprint of some type of invertebrate. Under it were the words "Blue Basin Fossil." The woman was old, her face lined with wrinkles. If she had been a fossil, she would have been a sturdy one. More dinosaur than fish.

"Can we get an early check-in?" said Connie. "We got up at four o'clock to watch The Royal Wedding."

"You must have been in Boise. I had to get up at three to watch it. You from Idaho?"

"Florida," said Eva.

Connie picked up a pamphlet labeled John Day that lay on the counter. She unfolded it. One column showed a photo and information on The Blue Basin. The other showed a photo of miners under the words John Day's Chinese. She held it closer and saw that the miners were all Chinese. "There are Chinese in John Day?" She rubbed her hand along the photo, waiting for the answer.

"Not any more. Used to be at least a thousand a hundred years ago. Locals called where they lived Tiger City. They stopped coming when our government excluded Chinese. Some went back to China. Only one I ever knew was Ing."

Connie grabbed Eva's arm. "Ing? I'm looking for someone named Ing."

"Ing Hay. Doc Hay. He was a healer. Gave me some of his Chinese medicines when I had postpartum. Saved my son's life. He's up in Portland now."

"Ing or your son?" Connie took her hand off Eva's arm. Whoever Ing was, he held clues to Charlie's death.

"My son. Ing's been dead nearly thirty years."

Connie calculated. "So he was here in 1940."

The woman took out her registration book and began copying information from Connie's driver's license. "That was the year his partner died. Lung On. Ing went away for awhile but he came back. Their graves are in Rest Lawn Cemetery." The woman handed them keys. "I'm Thelma if you need anything. Room seventeen's just down the hall. Go have yourselves a nap. That wedding was mighty early."

Connie took her key. Thelma called Ing and Lung partners. Had they been like Will and Sid, another couple keeping secrets? "Were Ing and Lung married?"

"They may have had wives in China. They never said. People didn't ask. We just called Ing when we needed one of his medicines.

Why so interested?"

"My uncle may have come through here. Used his medicines. Charlie Anderson. Did you ever meet him?"

Thelma closed the registration book. "When would that have been?"

Connie clutched the key so hard it cut into her hands. "1924. '25 maybe."

"When I had the post-partum, I was just eighteen. I don't remember those years much."

"It could have been later," said Connie.

"Lots of people used to come through. They'd ask for Ing, get some of his medicines, and leave. Go take your naps. Then go down to Kam Wah Chung. Back down 26, take a left on Canton. It's where Ing and Lung had their Chinese grocery and herbal shop. It's open for touring until four o'clock. You've got plenty of time." Before Connie could press her further, Thelma disappeared through the door she had come from.

"We have to go. Now." Connie walked ahead of Eva to the car.

"We could at least take in our suitcases."

"You can if you want. I'm going. Ing must have been with Charlie. He went missing the same year Charlie died."

Eva got into the car. "Okay. I'll go with you. But then can't we please take naps?"

Connie found the way to Canton Street. She parked in front of a small blue building with red trim and a prominent sign that read Kam Wah Chung & Co. A notice on the door told them they needed to go across the street to sign up for a tour. Connie checked her watch. One-twenty. They found the building. No one was waiting for a tour. A woman whose name tag read Heather said they were lucky. It was usually busy in July, but too many people had gotten up early to watch the Royal Wedding. They could take the two o'clock tour.

They walked around the small room reading pamphlets about the town of John Day, about the three locations of fossil beds spread out over a hundred and seventy-five miles, about the Chinese gold miners and railroad workers who stopped coming to John Day after the Chinese Exclusion Act of 1882. Connie poured through the brochure about Kam Wah Chung and its owners whose skills had allowed them to integrate so fully into the town that they never left. Doc Hay was a legend through half of Oregon.

"I guess this Ing Hay was better than any doctor out of medical school." Connie didn't expect information from Heather, who looked like she hadn't yet hit twenty.

"He died before I was born. But my grandpa used to tell me stories about how people came to see him from all over Oregon. He even carried on a mail order business."

"Can I talk to your grandfather?" said Connie just as an old man came through the door.

"This is him now. He'll be leading your tour."

The man looked close to eighty, slightly stooped with a head of still thick gray hair. From the cowboy hat he held, Connie pegged him as a rancher.

He reached out a veined and calloused hand. "Seth. You two interested in our famous Chinese?"

Eva took her turn shaking his hand. "It's fascinating. I teach history so I know that the Chinese helped to build the railroads and that they were ostracized. How did Ing Hay and Lung On manage not just to stay but to thrive?"

Seth pointed them to the door, put on his hat, and talked as he walked them to Kam Wah Chung. "They were smart. Knew the Chinese workers wanted Chinese food and medicines. Stocked a grocery store. When all the others were gone back to China or the grave, the whites around here had gotten used to them.

Especially Doc Hay. I don't go in for all this hippie healing stuff, but he was the real thing."

"Were you here in the late twenties, the thirties?" Connie's heart pounded as if she were race walking instead of strolling along the deserted road.

"Born in 1899. Never lived anywhere 'cept John Day."

Connie seized on the year. "1899. Same year as my Uncle Charlie. We think he may have come through here."

"I was working the ranch in the twenties and thirties. Didn't come to town much." Seth opened the door to Kam Wah Chung. They were assaulted by the smells of Chinese herbs that hung in the air as if it were still a working apothecary. It was a good smell, not the kind Connie associated with a modern medical office. Incense? Ginseng? Lavender? She couldn't unravel the smells any more than she could unravel the mystery of Charlie. As her eyes adjusted to the light, she saw dark wooden shelves lined with cans and jars. Some were covered in glass. Others stood open with boxes and tins labeled in English and Chinese. More boxes lay on the floor. One labeled LOBSTER displayed an image of a red cooked lobster that could have been shipped from New England.

A red chair rested in a corner with a small wooden table next to it. Seth pointed it out. "That's where Doc Hay read your pulse. He could tell what medicines to give you just from his reading."

"Placebo," said Eva.

"Don't matter. It worked." Seth led them into a back room. "This here's the bunk house."

Connie saw four wooden planks covered in some kind of animal skin as a mattress. "Did patients sleep here?"

"Maybe passers through. The room was mostly just for Ing and Lung."

Connie put her hand on one of the animal skins. No miracle told her she was touching a place where Charlie had lain.

Seth showed them one more room. "This was their kitchen." The room was big enough for a table, a sink, a cook stove that used wood, and more shelves with pots and pans and dishes in a Chinese design. Connie assumed that Ing and Lung used an outhouse because there seemed to be no bathroom.

Seth brought them back into the main room where ornate Chinese lights hung from the ceiling. He pointed at something prominently displayed on one of the shelves. "I always save this to last."

Connie stepped close to look at what was preserved in a clear bottle that held some kind of liquid.

Eva moved next to her so she could see. "It looks like a snake."

"It is. Preserved in rice wine. Ing used to give out small bottles of the liquid. Supposed to help with any kind of mental disorder."

"Placebo for sure," said Eva.

Seth opened the door and walked with them. "You girls staying in John Day?"

"At Miner's Lodge." Connie hoped that when she finally slept, the dreams she had been having wouldn't turn into nightmares about Charlie taking snake oil for his mental disorder.

"Thelma's place. Doc Hay helped her out when she had the postpartum."

"She told us," said Connie. "That's how we learned about Kam Wah Chung."

"John Day's got lots to offer. Eat at The Railroad Bar. Try the flat iron steak. Best in all of eastern Oregon."

Connie unlocked the door to The Yellow Sub. Seth pulled back his head and made a guttural noise. "This is John Day. No one locks doors. Where you heading tomorrow?"

"Through The Painted Hills and the Clarno site. We'll stay in The Dalles tomorrow then go to Portland."

"Connie's a writer," said Eva. "She'll be reading from her novel *Homeward Bound* in Portland. We have copies in the car if you want to buy one."

"Not much of a reader, I'm afraid. But good luck in Portland. Watch out when you go through Antelope. You might want to lock your doors there. Heard there's some kind of cult moving in, planning to buy ranch land. Won't work for them unless they grew up used to ranch life. Hard work in the dry climate. Hot summers. Cold winters. Bad soil. Cows that always need tending."

Eva reached out her hand to shake Seth's. "Thanks for telling us about Ing and Lung. I'm going to use all this information in the history classes I teach."

"Always a pleasure talking to outsiders. So long's you don't plan to stick around."

"Don't worry," said Connie as she got into the car. "A little too remote for me." She started the car and drove away, certain that Ing Hay was the man Charlie was talking to—or thought he was talking to—when he held baby Molly in his lap.

Chapter 23
July 1981

They drove the next morning through a landscape whose vastness measured how far Connie felt she had come. Massachusetts and Florida were behind her. She was no longer a woman depressed by the obligations of caregiving, but a successful writer on the road with her best friend. Route 26 out of John Day led them through greener countryside. In the distance, plateaus were layered against the sky like folded skin. Outside of Mitchell, they followed a sign to the Painted Hills. Nothing looked painted until softly rounded hills appeared, streaked in reds and yellows and oranges.

They parked the car and stepped out into the heat. Eva braced herself against a dry wind that threatened to blow over her hundred pounds. "It looks like Mars."

Connie took off her glasses. The hills blurred into impressionism. "I feel like I'm in an oil painting."

"Red, orange, saffron. They all represent fire burning away impurities."

"How do you know that?"

"I teach history, remember. Let's walk a bit. Feel purified."

They followed a path to a higher viewpoint. She and Eva had

spent nearly a month sharing stories about their childhoods, their love affairs, Connie's involvement with the Civil Rights Movement and the Vietnam War protests, Eva's way of introducing these to her mostly conservative high school students. They sang camp songs and outside Cleveland found a radio station playing Beatles' songs in a tribute to John Lennon. When "Yellow Submarine" came on, they opened the car windows and belted out the words. In Chicago, they'd completed their search for every state's license plate—Hawaii was the last— and started over again. They also knew when to be silent. Here in the purifying Painted Hills, neither spoke.

Despite the wind, Connie had never felt calmer. She stood next to Eva at the highest viewpoint, shading her eyes with the rim of a Boston Red Sox hat, then taking it off to soak in the colors. She removed her glasses and again enjoyed the feeling of being in an impressionist painting. When she put them back on, she saw a hawk circling around one of the hills, beneath the only cloud in the sky. There was no smell of bougainvillea or jasmine or the salt of the ocean. Only the dryness of the wind that blew its heat along her skin.

They were wrenched from their silence when a bus pulled into the parking lot below them. They turned together and walked to the lot where the busload of tourists were snapping cameras and sending loud voices into air that had been peaceful moments before. Inside the car, they stayed silent until they could no longer see the Painted Hills. Eva broke the silence. "What were you thinking about up there?"

"I wasn't thinking at all. I just felt peaceful."

"No thoughts of Charlie and Ing?"

"Not even of Everett or David or George. Maybe there's something to this meditation practice."

"Spiritual enlightenment?"

Connie's rational self reignited. "Just the strangeness of it all. I never imagined such a spot could exist on Earth, never mind in the United States. In a world like this, I'll never feel depressed again." The feeling surprised her. Even facing the need to start another novel, she felt hopeful.

They drove away from the Painted Hills on a road that wound through trees that blocked the view and felt more like the New England Connie had left. It opened into range land in a town called Fossil where they found one gas station. They needed a restroom more than they needed gas.

"Long way from Florida. Where you headed?" asked the lone attendant when they returned from the restroom. They were standing outside in what passed for a commercial district. Range land spread for miles to low hills that encompassed the valley.

"Clarno Fossil Beds." Connie reached for her wallet, hoping the man would take her credit card and not one of the few traveler's checks she had left.

"Nice spot. Careful on the road getting there." The man took Connie's credit card and went into the station.

Eva put her hands on the hood of the Volkswagen. "You can make it, Yellow Sub." She straightened when the man returned. "Will we find a place for lunch near Clarno?"

"There's a café in Antelope. If you're lucky there will still be some locals around. Some crazies from India or some place foreign are buying up more than sixty thousand acres of land. They come down here sometimes, wearing their red clothes and talking about the city they plan to build on The Big Muddy."

"The Big Muddy?" Connie hadn't seen enough water to make her think any of the land in the area could become muddy.

"Just a name for the sixty thousand acres. They want to farm. They want to build a dam. We just want to keep them out of Fossil. Like I said, there are probably some locals left in Antelope.

Café has good food."

They thanked the man and got into the car. "Careful on that road," he said as Connie closed her door.

He had been right. The road to the Clarno Fossil Beds was steep and twisting with no shoulder. Connie squinted through the windshield at a blinding sun. She avoided glancing over the edge. The wind blew so hard she struggled to keep the Volkswagen steady. One false turn of the wheel and they'd be rolling over a cliff. She wouldn't be like Charlie, imagining herself flying. Eva hung onto the front of her seat to keep her body from swaying with each curve. Her knuckles were white.

After forty-five minutes, they rounded a curve that opened into a view of pinnacles that rose into the sky like the turrets of a medieval castle. Connie looked quickly into her rear view mirror, then braked. "I didn't expect this."

Eva unclutched her hands. "How far have we driven since we left John Day? Two or three hundred miles? We could be on a different continent."

Connie took her foot off the brake and drove forward until they hit a turn-off marked Clarno Fossil Beds. They stepped out of the car into air cooler than in the Painted Hills. Between the pinnacles in front of them, a white cloud in a blue sky reached down as if it were lifting the land up. The orange-fringed rocks were steep, jagged, and flat at the top. They followed a rocky path into the heart of them, stopping where signs pointed out a fossil of a seed or a nut, a branch or a bone embedded into an edge of a pillar. Nothing large. Whatever mammals roamed the area forty million years ago, they weren't dinosaurs.

They walked up an incline to where they could see a natural bridge formed by the rocks. In the heat and air, Connie's nose was dry, her throat parched, her head dizzy. Eva had turned pale.

"You feeling it, too?" said Connie.

"Dehydration. We should have brought our water bottles."

"Not much water left in them."

"If The Yellow Sub breaks down, we could die out here."

"That's a bit dramatic." Connie started down the hill to the parking area. "Here's that busload of tourists. Maybe we can beg some water."

They reached the car as the tourists were getting off the bus. Everyone was talking and laughing and gazing up toward the pinnacles. They all carried water bottles. Through the bus door, Connie saw a plastic water jug. She found their water bottles and approached the driver, who was standing next to the bus. His face was weathered under the rim of his cowboy hat.

"Could we beg some water?" Connie asked.

The driver watched the tourists moving down the path. "Florida license plate. You Easterners never come prepared for the West." He took their water bottles and went into the bus to fill them. When he came out, he handed a full bottle to each of them. "Which way you headed?"

"Through Antelope, then north to The Dalles."

"I won't be able to help you again. We're going southeast, down to the Blue Basin. Stop in Antelope and buy a couple of jugs. Just stay away from the people wearing red. A few more arrive every day. Buying up The Big Muddy. They won't last through the first winter."

They drank half their water, thanked the driver, and drove away. The landscape changed again, opening into more ranch land. The wind howled and Connie struggled to keep the car steady on the road.

"Do we dare stop in Antelope?" said Eva.

"Aren't you hungry?"

"Starving, actually."

"We'll stop. What's the problem with wanting to buy up some

of this land? There's plenty to go around."

"Problem living in a small town. Everyone's suspicious of outsiders."

In the distance, they caught their first glimpse of a town rising out of the emptiness. They passed a Welcome to Antelope sign and turned right. The road skirted the town, revealing only open land and a few houses before it dumped them back onto Route 218. No children were outside playing. No one was walking a dog. They tried finding the center of town again, this time turning left off the perimeter road. They passed the school, cement Connie thought, and painted a soft green. Long windows spread across the front, making it look more inviting than institutional.

"That school is lovely," said Eva. "All that light coming in through the windows."

"Shall I leave you here and you can apply for a job?"

"Very funny. Town doesn't look big enough to support a school that size."

"Ranchers probably have lots of kids. How differently they must see the world growing up in a place like this." Connie turned onto another road that brought them to the tiny, rectangular restaurant. A sign running above a roof ledge announced Antelope Cafe and Store in gold letters against a hideous shade of turquoise. A lighted Open sign was set against one of two horizontal windows. On the opposite side of two doors, one white and one a darker turquoise, was a smaller square window.

Connie parked in front of the café. "Doesn't look like much, but we have to eat."

"And get more water." Eva grabbed both water bottles as she got out of the car.

Connie reached across the seat to open Eva's window. She rolled down the one on her side before she got out.

"Didn't that guy at Kam Wah Chung say to lock the car in Antelope?"

"It's too hot. We'll be able to watch from the window." Connie looked more closely at the building and saw that the blue was painted onto cinder block. She opened the white door and entered a small room where a half-dozen people had pushed tables together. Shirts, pants, one woman in a dress, everyone was wearing a shade of red. The only empty table was on the opposite side of the eating area in front of the section of the building that sold groceries. A woman in a tan dress, wearing rhinestone-studded glasses vintage 1950, stepped from behind a counter. She handed Connie and Eva menus and shrugged at the red-clad people. "I'm guessing you're not with them."

Connie opened her menu. "No. Are they the people we heard about who are buying some land?"

"More'n sixty thousand acres," said the woman. "Folks're already leaving. Used to have over fifty living right here in town. Now we're down to less than forty. Even some of the ranchers are gone."

"How can you support such a big school with so few people?" said Eva.

"Ranchers' kids. We do okay. Use it as a community center. Got a church, a library, a post office. Don't need nothin' else. It's peaceful here. 'Least it was." She took the water bottles that Eva had put on the table. "I'll fill these up for you. Get you some for the table."

Connie watched her move behind the counter, her slightly stooped body a sign of work and age. The woman's whole world would change if a new community was built on The Big Muddy.

"Guess there's some tension around here." Eva glanced at her menu.

"She should put up a sign. 'Outsiders not welcome.' What

are you ordering?"

"BLT. Menu says the bread's homemade."

Connie looked at her menu then closed it. "That should be safe. Not sure about the side of potato salad."

The woman returned with water for the table and their water bottles. "What'll you have?"

Connie handed her the menus. "BLTs for both of us."

"White or wheat?"

"Wheat," said Eva. "Toasted."

"Same for me." Connie picked up her water glass.

"Anything besides water to drink? Lemonade's good."

"Just water," said Eva. "I'm having trouble staying hydrated in this air."

"Same here," said Connie.

"Where you comin' from?"

"Florida," said Eva.

"Long way from home. Just passin' through, I hope." The woman left without writing down their orders.

Connie drained half her glass of water. "Guess I won't leave you here to find a teaching job."

Their sandwiches came quickly, piled high with bacon, lettuce, and tomato. The bread and the potato salad were both delicious. They ate in silence, trying to hear the conversation at the other table. They caught only scattered words. "Recruits." "Organic farm." "Irrigation." Something that sounded like "Rashee."

They were finishing their sandwiches when the group left. Except for one who approached their table. She was young, maybe thirty with a dark complexion and dark curly hair. She gestured to a chair. "May I sit?" Without waiting for an answer, she joined them. "I'm Sadhana."

"An Indian name?" said Connie. Unlike Sid's, this woman's manner was just short of aggressive.

"Yes. And you are?"

"Connie. This is Eva."

"License plate says Florida. You're a long way from home."

"We're just passing through." Eva stood up and went to the counter to pay for their meals, leaving Connie alone with this woman who was, like herself, a stranger in a stranger land.

Sadhana studied her as if she could see through to her restlessness. "We're building a community here. With our spiritual leader." The lilt in her accent rose as if in worship. "Baghwan Shree Rajneesh." Sadhana fingered a medallion with an image of an Indian man with long hair and a beard. "We all wear these malas. We live in community, everyone equal, male and female alike. We respect each other and the natural world."

The woman's ideas were compelling until she said, "No one will have to dye their hair like your friend."

Connie defended her friend. "Eva doesn't dye her hair. She's the most natural person I know."

"Then you and she should join our community. No raping of the land with industrial and chemical farming. Baghwan teaches us that when we get in touch with the land, we get in touch with ourselves. You should stay here. Help us turn The Big Muddy into the kind of community the world needs."

Sadhana stood up to leave when Eva started back toward the table. "Think about it." She opened the door and went out, her red dress flowing around her like a bridal dress for an alien culture.

Connie picked up the water bottles and started toward the door. "Thanks for paying. You wouldn't have liked her."

"What did she want?"

"To tell me about the utopia they plan to build. Everything peace and love and spiritual communion with nature. The goals are good ones. Everything natural. Everyone equal."

Eva stared at Connie across the hood of The Yellow Sub. "Are you tempted?"

"A bit." Connie looked at the horizon whose openness beckoned. A communal purpose might return her to the energy she felt in her twenties when she was joining protest marches.

"Is this woman the leader or is there still a man in charge?"

"Someone they call Baghwan Shree Rajneesh."

"It sounds like a cult."

"Maybe. She suggested we stay." Eva's comments tempered Connie's attraction.

"Forget it. You're not seeking enlightenment. You're seeking real answers about your Uncle Charlie and his daughter."

Chapter 24

August 1981

Connie closed her copy of *Homeward Bound* and smiled at the warm applause from the twenty people gathered in the space reserved for author readings. "Thank you. And thank you to Powell's for hosting me. Portland's lucky to have such an amazing bookstore. We have a few minutes for questions."

A man sitting in back raised his hand first. He wore a red jacket that seemed out of place among the bland colors on the rest of the audience. "Aren't both your characters––. What are their names, Stephanie and Ellen?"

"Eileen," Connie corrected.

"Whatever. Aren't they stuck in the past? Haven't all those nice rural farms been taken over by corporations lacing them with fertilizer and pesticides? They're bound to a myth."

"The novel is set in Massachusetts. I was there a few weeks ago and saw plenty of small farms still thriving." Connie knew they were sustaining themselves by selling farm-themed trinkets along with vegetables. She thought of the stuffed cow she bought Lizzie six years ago. Lizzie still had it, perched alongside the photo of Connie and Hannah next to her on the rope swing.

"If you say so. You should check out what we're building

in Antelope. Everything organic, everything outside of the corruption of corporate America and all the rules that take away people's freedom."

Connie heard in the man's comments the same disillusionment about industrialization she had heard from Sadhana. A new experiment in communal living sounded promising, but this was a book conversation, not a recruitment opportunity. "That conflict's outside the scope of *Homeward Bound*, but I'll keep it in mind for my next novel. Are there more questions?"

People raised the same kinds of questions Connie had been answering all across the country. When the event was over and they were leaving, the man stopped her. "We're looking for people who are interested in helping us build our city. You should think about it." He left and joined a group of others wearing red who were gathered on the sidewalk. Connie imagined they were all recruiters for their utopia.

"It looks like an invasion," said Eva.

"They make me think of the city upon a hill."

"Who said that?"

"John Winthrop in his speech to the Puritans on the *Arabella* when they were landing in America with a charter to build a new city."

"Look what happened," said Eva. "Wars with Indians. Killing of inconvenient women they accused of witchcraft. Get over it. There are no utopias."

"I'm the cynic, remember."

"A curious one."

"Why I'm a writer." Connie filed away her curiosity. Antelope would wait. First she needed to search for Charlie's daughter.

They spent the next five days driving along the changing

landscape of Oregon's coast. In Astoria, they saw where Lewis and Clark completed their journey west at the raging mouth of the Columbia River. They waded at low tide to Haystack Rock on Cannon Beach. The coast wound along cliffs that descended to the spectacular Pacific. It was wilder than the Atlantic in Maine until it calmed in an area of sand dunes that could have been part of the Sahara desert. In Coos Bay, they learned that the town's name rhymed with booze unlike New Hampshire's Coos County that was pronounced with two syllables and a long o on the accented first one. Connie felt like she was learning a language as foreign as the landscape.

On the last night, they stayed in a town called Brookings, close to the California border. When they crossed the border in the morning, they were surprised at a checkpoint for agricultural products. When Connie said they had nothing to declare, the man at the checkpoint waved them on.

"We must look like trusty middle-aged women," said Eva. "I wonder if he'd look through our cars if we were wearing red."

Connie reached across the seat and gave Eva a punch on the leg. "Lay off the red people. They want to work the land so vegetables don't need to be checked for contaminants."

"California's looking for bugs, not chemicals."

They stopped talking until they turned east on Route 199. When they reached a sign for the Jedediah Smith State Redwood Forest, they followed a narrow road into a parking area surrounded by massive trees. Eva opened her door and leaned onto the car to stretch her back.

"Place looks as busy as Niagara Falls."

Connie took a bag and water bottles out of the cooler in the back seat. "Everyone's congregated near the lot. We'll find a quiet spot."

They began walking through redwoods as unfamiliar as the

cypresses Connie had first seen in Florida. She stretched her neck to look up. The redwoods reached so high she couldn't see their crowns. Sunlight filtered onto ferns growing on a forest floor covered in the softness of decaying soil. A few fallen trunks were big enough for a stage. New trees sprouted from masses of burls on logs that looked like they should have been dead. More burls and ferns climbed up the trunks and into the highest branches.

They found a spot away from families and sat facing the river. Connie reached into the bag and handed Eva a peanut butter sandwich. "I knew redwoods were big, but not like this."

"I feel dwarfed," said Eva.

Connie nudged her petite friend. "You are."

"Very funny."

"We'd need a dozen people holding hands to make a circle around some of these trunks. But the ground feels open, not suffocating like the swamps in Florida."

"And no bugs." Eva bit into her sandwich and stopped talking.

They ate, watching a lone fisherman cast his fly line over and over in a smooth arc. The air was cool and moist and silent. Connie felt protected by the flow of the water, the high canopy of the trees, and the quiet of Eva beside her.

The respite faded when they got back into The Yellow Sub and drove along Highway 199. It wound through forest land until it came close to a city named Grants Pass. Connie wondered if the city was name for Ulysses S. Grant. The name surprised her because Eva had told her that Oregon was once so racist that Black people weren't allowed to live there.

They drove east through the city to I-5 and a sign that announced Ashland 40 Miles. The closer they got, the more Connie worried that her search for Charlie's daughter would yield no answers. She had only three more days before Eva left her alone in the enormous landscape of the West. All her life, depression stalked her. If it attacked, there'd be no one to force her out of bed. Her stomach knotted in hunger and anxiety.

When they drove under a railroad bridge at the entrance to Ashland, she rolled down her window and felt hot, dry air pour into the car. Eva reached across the seat and touched her leg. "You nervous?"

"Scared to death."

"Don't be. If you don't like it, you can fly home with me."

Connie stopped herself from saying that Florida was Eva's home, not hers. "I'm committed." She followed the main street past a school and a church and into the center of town. Her directions said to turn left off North Main Street onto Oak Street.

Midsummer Night Bed and Breakfast stood one block in on the left. A Victorian house that must once have been the private residence of one of the town's elite. Two circular bay windows framed the front door and an upstairs balcony. The yellow clapboards were accented with a soft green trim. Low shrubbery lined the foundation. Beside it, a tall oak tree shared its name with the street.

Connie parked in a designated spot behind the house. They stepped out of the car into air still hot at five o'clock. She willed her legs to stop shaking as she walked with Eva to the back entry. The door opened into a narrow hallway that led them into a sitting room. They set their bags on an oriental carpet whose blue, green, and red flower design showed off an oak floor laid out in a geometrical pattern of squares and rectangles. The workmanship on the floor was meticulous. The room was small and authentic in a late nineteenth-century style, fringed curtains on the bay windows, woodwork painted blue, furniture upholstered in blue velvet that looked better than the furniture was likely to feel. Antique pictures of people Connie couldn't identify hung in heavy frames on the walls.

The lighting was dim, the darkened room cool.

A woman Connie's age came in. She wore a short sundress that accented her long legs and thin arms. Her hair was pulled off her neck and fastened with a leather clasp. "You must be Connie and Eva. Welcome to Midsummer Night. I'm Dorothy." She spoke with pride and a southern accent that announced she wasn't a native Oregonian.

Connie's nerves settled with the woman's greeting. She accepted Dorothy's firm handshake. "I'm Connie."

"And I'm Eva. It's lovely in here. We've been too long on the road sleeping in cheap motels."

Dorothy glanced from Eva to Connie. "Too long? You didn't just come from Portland?"

Connie looked down at the dust on her sandals, the dirt on her shorts. "We've been driving along the coast. We stopped at the Smith River today."

"Beautiful spot. You're lucky someone canceled so I had a vacancy. Usually I'm full in August."

"A nice waiter at Huber's in Portland warned us to make a reservation."

"Huber's. Oldest restaurant in Portland. Hope you had some Spanish coffee."

Connie could still taste the drink. "Laced with rum and flamed at our table. Right now, I need food, not Spanish coffee. Do you have suggestions?"

"Omar's. Oldest restaurant in Ashland. If you're lucky, you can sit on one of their leather benches."

Connie remembered the leather seats in Boston's Eliot Lounge and felt a pang of homesickness.

Dorothy pulled up the strap to her dress that had fallen over a muscular shoulder. "You'll have to drive, just a couple of miles. The plaza in town is still finding its identity. Getting beautified for the tourists. It's nice, though, and getting nicer. Check it out tomorrow. You have a week to explore."

"Only I do. Eva's renting a car and driving to San Francisco before she flies back to Florida."

Dorothy handed them keys. "You drove from Florida, not just the Oregon coast?"

Connie felt a wave of fatigue. "Two women on a road trip. I'm staying. Do you have suggestions on how I can find an apartment?"

"Realtors. Newspapers. Word of mouth is good around here. Especially at OSF. You can ask my husband in the morning. Rodney. He'll be cooking your breakfast."

"OSF?" said Eva.

"Oregon Shakespeare Festival," said Dorothy. "Isn't that why you're here? To see the plays?"

Connie fiddled with her key, hiding her embarrassment at not knowing more about Ashland's theater than the little she had read about the town before leaving Florida. "Plays will be a bonus. I'm here looking for my uncle's daughter. Molly Anderson. Used to live in Green Springs."

"Good luck. Place is loaded with recluses and hippies. We never go up there. I don't drive the terrible road and Rodney's too busy with his performances."

"He's an actor?" said Eva.

"Playing Biff in *Death of a Salesman* this season. And the Duke in *Twelfth Night*. We've got three theaters. The Black Swan is a small one. There's a big one indoors and one outdoors that's modeled on Shakespeare's Globe. If you go before the evening performances, you can watch dancers perform Elizabethan pieces in period dress."

Connie picked up her suitcase. "We'll get tickets for tomorrow. Right now, we're ready for dinner and bed."

"I'll be here when you come down. You can give me your credit card then."

Connie followed Eva up the stairs. "We're pretty dirty. Think she wonders if we'll really pay?"

"Of course not. Don't be paranoid."

They unlocked the door to a room with two beds boasting carved wooden headboards and covered in quilts that looked handmade. She wanted to imagine Charlie staying here, but likely he stayed in some low priced boarding house. If he stayed in Ashland at all. The only evidence she had was the postmark on the envelope. She'd start her search in the morning.

They found the breakfast room just off the parlor where they'd talked with Dorothy. Five tables of varying sizes were covered in tablecloths and set with coffee cups, matching cream and sugar bowls, and silverware. They were early. Only the table for two was occupied. A young couple held hands across it. They looked like honeymooners. Connie and Eva sat at a table for four under a window that looked out on a yard in full flower.

A tall man Dorothy's age appeared with a coffee pot, said something to the couple, then approached Connie and Eva. "I'm Rodney. You must be the women from Florida." He'd be a handsome Biff with a voice that would carry to the back rows of the theater. Deep. Resonant. Clear.

Connie moved her coffee cup so he could fill it, wondering what Dorothy did in the morning while Rodney cooked.

He filled both their cups. "Dorothy said you're looking for an apartment."

"I am," said Connie. "Do you know of any?"

"No, but I can ask around. Actors come in and out. They know the unlisted places."

Eva put sugar, no cream in her coffee. "Your wife said you're in *Twelfth Night*. Is it playing today or tomorrow?"

"Tonight at the Elizabethan stage. Theater's big, so there should be tickets left."

Eva sipped her coffee and set her cup back in its saucer. "Where's the box office?"

"Just off the plaza. There's a staircase behind City Hall. Doesn't look much like a city hall. Just a light gray stucco building. Unless it's cement. I never can tell."

An older couple come into the dining room. Connie was relieved when they sat at an empty table. She and Eva needed to talk. "Where's the plaza? We need a real estate office, a bank, a newspaper."

"Go out Oak Street the way you came in. Cross the street and the plaza's to your right. You'll find everything you need there or along North Main and Siskiyou."

"Siskiyou?" Connie tasted her coffee. It was steaming and acidic on a stomach that was knotted from Omar's dinner or anxiety.

"The main street. Name keeps changing if you're in town or just outside. Best place for the paper is The Coop, off Siskiyou on Third Street. Two syllables. Like cooperative, not chicken coop like I thought when I first moved here. It's a grocery store. Great deli if you don't want to eat in restaurants every day."

"How far is it to Green Springs?"

"Half an hour. Terrible road. Broccoli omelet okay for breakfast? I can cook plain eggs if you prefer."

Eva answered for them both. "That's fine."

"Comes with a blueberry muffin and home fries. Juice is in the corner."

Eva stood up and asked Connie, "What kind?"

"Apple if there is some. I need to settle my stomach."

Eva came back with the juice. Before Connie had time to speak, she said, "We're not going to Green Springs today."

"Why not?"

"Bad use of time. You have no idea what you're looking for. Molly might no longer live there. She might have married and have a different name. She might have died."

"So you're saying we shouldn't even try? We drove all this way for nothing?"

Eva swallowed half the orange juice in her glass. "I'm saying I have today and tomorrow. I want to see the town."

Connie already felt abandoned by the woman who had been a perfect traveling companion. "So you don't want to see Green Springs at all?"

"I do. But we should spend today walking around and deciding how to research. We can go tomorrow. Molly has no phone listing, but maybe the Ashland post office has an address. We can look at tax records in the City Hall."

Rodney returned with two enormous plates of breakfast. Connie's stomach recoiled. "What time does City Hall open?"

"Not sure. Nine or ten. You hoping to find that woman Dorothy said you're looking for?"

"I am." Connie peeled the paper off her blueberry muffin.

"Good luck if she's up at Green Springs. Bunch of hippie squatters up there."

Connie bit into her muffin, wondering if Green Springs was as bad as Dorothy and Rodney thought.

They walked first to City Hall. A woman with bleached blonde hair and bright red lipstick told them they needed to go the Jackson County clerk's office in Medford.

When they left the building, Eva said, "Woman looked like

Bette Davis in *Hush, Hush, Sweet Charlotte*."

"Not that old. But brassy enough. You know Bette Davis was born in Lowell."

"Massachusetts? Home of all those nineteenth-century mills."

"Yup. And right next to Freedom. Should we go to Green Springs now?"

"Tomorrow. After we go to the country clerk's office. Today we investigate Ashland. Concentrate on finding you an apartment."

Connie wanted to argue, but she knew Eva was right. "Let's walk first, before it gets hot. I need to digest that breakfast."

"You only ate half."

"I'm too anxious. Walking will help."

They found their way into Lithia Park. They walked past a duck pond then crossed an arched bridge onto the other side of a creek that was flowing slowly in the late summer. The path led them to a fountain with two upper tiers. At the top was a statue of a boy holding some kind of bird. A duck or a goose. Water poured from the bird's mouth into a pool below. The fountain needed repair, but the water looked clean and cool. Below on the grass, half a dozen deer grazed. They did not scare when Connie and Eva followed the path through a grove of trees laid out in columns that looked more European than American. Beyond the grove was a Japanese garden where water trickled along well-placed rocks through dwarf maples and shaped bonsais. At its edge, they noticed a tree whose bark looked like a camouflage of green and red and gray.

They found another bridge near a second duck pond, crossed it, and walked along a path sheltered by trees that, except for the evergreens, Connie couldn't name. When they came to a spot where people piled small stones into miniature cairns, she and Eva each kissed a stone and balanced them together on a larger rock. The path continued to a reservoir where they dipped their hands into water icy cold from mountain snow melt. They retraced their steps, staying on the wooded side of the creek. Other people began appearing, all smiling, saying "Good morning."

"I feel better leaving you in a place like this," said Eva.

"I feel better, too." The park with its evergreen trees and sheltered paths reminded Connie of how she had developed *Secrets* around New Hampshire's Newfound Lake. She knew she had a good setting in Ashland. Now she needed to create characters, learn what they wished for when they kissed stones like the ones she and Eva had joined together.

When they reached the plaza, they stopped in front of a granite pedestal with eight drinking spigots of bubbling water inviting them to drink. Connie bent to one. She gagged on water laced with sulphur.

"What's wrong?" said Eva.

"Taste it."

Eva waited while a father picked up his toddler to let her drink from the fountain. The child took a sip and made a face. The mother watched, laughing. Neither parent drank.

"Not for me," said Eva. "I'll go find the box office. Get us some tickets so we can watch Shakespeare under the stars."

"You have enough money? I'll find a bank. I need to open an account. Stop living off a credit card and traveler's checks."

"I have plenty. Meet me here. Get a newspaper. We can find a bench and search the apartment ads."

Connie found Eva on a bench, watching tourists try the sulphur-laced water. Eva stood up and said, "One of the locals was here a few minutes ago. He says he comes by everyday to laugh. Apparently Lithia Park is named for lithium in the water. Supposed to be good for you."

"Lithium helps with depression. I should force myself to drink it."

"Just take walks in the park. It was supposed to be developed into a spa complete with mineral baths and a beer garden. Local women stepped in and said no way."

"Good choice, judging by what we just walked through. Did you get tickets?"

Eva reached into her pocket and took out the tickets. "*Twelfth Night* under the stars. Tomorrow *Death of a Salesman* at the indoor theater. We get to watch Rodney twice."

"He's easy to watch."

"Too bad he's married. Did you find a bank?"

"Right on the main street. First Interstate Bank. Seemed okay. At least they're sending for the money I have in the Florida bank. I stopped at the post office. There's no office in Green Springs and the clerk wouldn't give out any name and address. I bought a newspaper at The Coop. Rodney was right about the deli food. It looks delicious."

Eva pointed across the street at a real estate office. "No rentals. They said to look in the *Ashland Daily Tidings*."

Connie showed Eva the masthead on the newspaper she was holding. She opened to the apartment rentals and held it on her lap so Eva could see. There were only half a dozen. Three weren't furnished, one was a house with eight unfurnished rooms. One was in Green Springs. Connie pushed for going to see it.

Eva read the description. "'Rustic one room cabin ten miles beyond Green Springs on Route 66. Winter access limited.' Molly or not, it's too far and too primitive. You can't stay snowed in all winter. Unless you plan to buy a snowplow."

"You're right again. If the furnished one bedroom on Morton Street doesn't work, I'll call the others. Buy furniture."

Eva took the paper from Connie and approached a man

standing in front of a bronze statue on high pedestal to ask directions to Morton Street. He pointed up the street toward the bank Connie had found.

Eva didn't sit down when she came back to the bench. "That's the man who was here earlier. He doesn't have a wedding ring. You should come by here and watch the water-drinking tourists. You'll make a friend."

"Not interested." Connie stood up and stopped in front of the statue. She bent to read a placard. Pioneer Mike. With his gun and hat, he looked like a cavalry officer. "Can we walk?"

"Straight up North Main and Siskiyou, less than a mile."

Within just a few blocks, they found shops and a movie theater. They took a few minutes to go into the library that proudly announced itself as one funded by Andrew Carnegie. Connie imagined herself starting a new novel in some quiet corner on the second floor.

They walked a few more blocks and turned right onto Morton Street. A woman wearing an apron covered in flour answered the door to number 55. She told them the apartment was already rented and quickly closed the door.

"That was rude," said Eva.

"She probably heard my accent. Doesn't want to rent to outsiders. I'll call the unfurnished places when we get back to Midsummer Night. Too hot for much more walking right now."

They crossed Siskiyou where a church faced the road. The sign read First Congregational United Church of Christ. Connie grabbed Eva's arm. "My mother and Charlie were Congregational. We should check the church records."

"What will you look for?"

"Marriages. Births. If we can find Laura's last name, we might be able to find her family."

"Or if she's still alive."

"I doubt it. Charlie would be almost eighty. Maybe we can find Molly's name."

They tried the front door. It was locked. The side door was also locked.

Connie rubbed her hands on her shorts. It was getting hot. "Let's walk back through town. Find that church we passed coming in last night. I remember it was Methodist. Charlie might have gone there. We can come back here tomorrow."

They walked until they saw a mother and little girl stopped on the sidewalk. The mother was using her tongue to push ice cream into a cone so it wouldn't topple out. The little girl's sun dress was already dotted with chocolate. A man came out of the shop holding two cones, one vanilla and one that looked like lemon sherbet. They were half the size of the cones she and Lizzie had devoured at Kimball's six years ago when Connie was on her first book tour. He handed the sherbet to the woman and they walked away, the little girl skipping between them.

Eva read the sign. "*Sweet Shoppe Rosies*. Lunch?"

"A complete diet. Protein, calcium, carbohydrates in the cone. We can double veggies at dinner." Connie loved traveling with Eva. They used Connie's description half the days they drove cross country. A good breakfast, an early dinner, ice cream for lunch.

The inside of Rosie's looked like the drugstore Connie loved when she was in junior high. After school, she and her friends would sit at a counter drinking cherry Cokes. Only on hot summer days would they order ice cream cones and find a path to the river where they'd sit on the ground throwing bits of cone into the water. A boy who looked like Fonzie in *Happy Days* scooped peach for her and coffee for Eva.

"You changed from chocolate," said Eva as they carried their cones outside in the sunlight.

"New place. New me. I hope that church is cool inside. I feel like I'm melting as fast as this ice cream."

They crossed the street to the movie theater that was just opening for a showing of *Raiders of the Lost Ark*. Eva stopped to read the description. "Should we see it? One last movie before I leave?"

"We've got two plays, a trip to Medford tomorrow morning, and then to Green Springs."

"And an apartment to find for you. I'll see it in Florida and imagine you sitting beside me."

When they reached a car dealership just beyond the plaza and a few steps beyond that a Volkswagen repair shop, Eva said, "You need to take The Yellow Sub for service. It's had a long trip."

"She's fine for awhile. I had her checked out before we left Florida. Maybe I'll trade her for a new model."

They stopped in front of the Methodist church. Its clapboards were painted soft shades of taupe. They finished their ice cream before they looked for a door likely to be open. An unlocked one in the back led them into a large entryway. Behind it, the sanctuary was empty. A woman came out of a side room. With a tiny body and dress half-way up her thighs, she looked more like a teenager than a woman. "Can I help you?" she said in a high tinkly voice.

"I'm looking for someone named Molly Anderson. She's my cousin." Connie expected the answer she got.

"I never heard the name. And I know everyone in our congregation. I've been typing my dad's sermon. Reverend Chamberlain. I'm Cynthia."

"Could we look at some church records? Baptisms? Marriages?" Connie explained her search. How they were looking for someone named Laura who had married her uncle Charlie.

The girl thought a moment. "The books are organized by decade. Which one do you want to see?"

Connie calculated from the newspaper account of Charlie's death. "Can we see four, 1900 through 1930?"

"I'll get them. There's no place to sit in the office. Go find a pew in the sanctuary."

The sanctuary was dimly lit. "It's blessedly cool," said Eva.

"Nice word. Maybe we'll be blessedly lucky."

"Why those dates?"

"Charlie died in 1939 when Molly was a baby. So Laura was in her childbearing years. Somewhere between twenty and thirty-five. So born between 1904 and 1919. We can look for any baptism of a Laura in those years, any record of a marriage in late 1920 or in 1930, any record of Molly's birth in 1939. If we find something, I can trace Molly another day."

Cynthia came in carrying four books. "They're organized by baptisms, deaths, marriages. A bit dusty, I'm afraid. Do you need more light?"

"If you don't mind," said Connie. "And thanks. This means a lot to me."

When the light came on, Connie gave the books from the 1920s and 1930s to Eva. "Nothing before 1927 when Charlie left Massachusetts. Just the marriages until 1939."

Eva finished in a few minutes. "Nothing. What about baptisms for someone named Laura?"

"Early 1930s. Too young to have a child in 1939. I need pencil and paper."

When she came back, Eva had her finger in a page. "I found a Laura Silsbee baptized in November 1921."

"So seventeen or eighteen in 1939 when Molly was born. How do you spell Silsbee?"

"S-I-L-S-B-E-E."

Connie wrote it down. Under it she wrote Laura Nelson, baptized July 1905. Thirty-four in 1939. A little old, but possible.

Eva began paging through the record book for the 1910s. "I found another. Laura Comstock. Baptized August 1916."

"Twenty-three when Molly was born. Connie wrote it down. "She's the best possibility."

"If the Laura Charlie married was baptized in this church."

"I know. It's a reach. But it will give us something to look for in the census and tax records tomorrow."

They scooted out of the pew and returned the record books. Hot sun greeted them outside. Connie wiped hands grubby from handling the record books on her T-shirt. "We have time to call those unfurnished apartments. Whichever one is air conditioned, I'll take."

They crossed the road and followed it until they hit Oak Street and the shade of the trees.

They sat in the breakfast room at Midsummer Night, eating salads they bought at The Coop, their eyes burning from four hours in front of microfilm machines. The morning hadn't been fruitless, but it hadn't given them much. Tax records from 1970 to 1980 showed nothing for Molly or Laura Anderson. Census records might have helped more if some law hadn't been passed that they couldn't be made public for seventy-two years. Charlie's name appeared in 1930, occupation logger, residence listed as itinerant. In 1940, Laura and one year old Molly lived on Route 66, Green Springs.

Eva finished chewing a large bite of salad. "You're convinced Charlie's wife was Laura Silsbee, not Laura Comstock?"

"The census said age nineteen. Charlie would have been twice that. There's a story there that must be interesting."

Dorothy came into the room wearing a painter's smock covered in so many dabs of color she must use it to wipe her brushes.

"You're a painter?" said Eva.

"Sort of. I make wooden toys. Today I painted the ones I cut out last week. I sell them through The Coop."

"I saw them," said Connie. "Little trucks and cars in bright colors with designs for both boys and girls."

"Those are mine. Kids seem to like them. You still looking for an apartment? I have a tip."

Connie put down her fork. "Furnished? I found an unfurnished one on Grant Street yesterday. I have to let the woman know tonight."

"This one's furnished. It'll be short term. A year at the most. Ruthie's planning to sell. Finally decided she should rent her upstairs apartment. I'll call her now if you want to look."

Connie checked her watch. 2:20. She'd have to explore Green Springs after Eva left for San Francisco. It was time to sever the umbilical cord that kept them attached. She'd take a first step and go without her friend to meet this woman named Ruthie.

Chapter 25

August 1981

The house on Bushnell Street was small, a craftsman style painted in shades of tan with red trim on the upper beams. The sun was blistering, but the house spoke of coolness and comfort. A blue spruce and some kind of western pine shaded the front. A maple tree that reminded Connie of New England canopied a side deck.

She breathed heavily and wiped drops of perspiration from her forehead, whether from the heat or anxiety, she wasn't sure. She climbed half-a-dozen cement steps painted red to match the trim. The landing was shaded. Beside the door, a plaque read 1908.

Before she had a chance to ring the bell, a woman appeared at the screen. For a moment Connie thought she had come face to face with Hannah. The woman was tiny, her back curved in a dowager's hump. Her gray hair was short, her glasses wire-rimmed in the style of the 1920s. She spoke with a powerful voice that belied her body. "You must be Connie from Florida. Come in, come in. I'm Ruthie Stone."

Inside, the windows were open, but the shade from the trees kept out some of the day's heat. An open living area was furnished with mahogany curio cabinets and a sofa edged with carved mahogany. The floors had the same precise workmanship as those in Midsummer Night. Persian area carpets showed them off. Connie heard a TV through a door that opened to a side room. At the end of the living room, a mahogany table was set with a single place mat and an unlit candle in front of it. She could have been stepping into 1908.

"Dorothy said you have an apartment to rent." She'd wait to ask if it had air conditioning and water that didn't taste like sulphur.

"Short term. I plan to sell next spring, move in with my daughter down in the railroad district."

Connie stiffened at the idea of another daughter taking care of a mother.

"Just down on B Street. Actually, I'm not moving in with her. She has a cottage behind her house. Her tenant's an actor. She'll be moving on when this season's over. She's divorced. My daughter, I mean. I'll pay rent. It will help her out. I won't be a burden." Hannah used to say this before Alzheimer's destroyed her spirit.

Ruthie led Connie into the dining area. It opened from a kitchen that had thirty year old appliances that looked clean and well-used. Another open space faced a back garden ripe with vegetables and flowers. With the sun beating through the windows, the area was hot despite the fan turned on next to a small table and rocking chair.

"What a lovely yard."

"I manage it myself. Only reason I'll move to Sylvia's—that's my daughter—is she'll let me work in her garden. She's a teacher. Doesn't have much time."

Connie followed Ruthie through a door to the back yard and up a staircase to a landing where an Adirondack chair sat baking in the sun. There'd be no sitting outside in the afternoons. "The friend I'm traveling with is a teacher."

"And you?" Ruthie unlocked the door.

"I'm a writer."

A blast of cool air welcomed them. Ruthie wrapped her arms around herself. "Don't like air conditioning myself, but it gets too hot up here. Rent's three hundred dollars a month."

The moment she stepped inside, Connie knew the apartment was perfect. A sitting area furnished with a sofa whose sections could be moved into different arrangements, a bedroom with a queen-sized bed and plenty of closet space. There was room under its side window for a desk that would fit her typewriter. The kitchen's refrigerator was small and the stove half the size of the one she had in Florida, but there was enough counter space and an alcove with shelves that could serve as a pantry. The table had two chairs and from the window above it, a view of the sun-burned mountains. Even the bathroom with a shower and no tub was comforting. She hadn't been able to relax in a bath since her mother died.

"Does the water taste like the water down on the plaza?"

Ruthie laughed. "Got sucked in like the tourists, did you? Of course not. This is city water, perfectly good."

"This will be perfect, then. Can I move some things in tomorrow? Get them out of the trunk of my car?"

"Come downstairs. Have a glass of lemonade. I'd like to know something about you before I say yes."

Connie followed Ruthie down the stairs and into the house that felt sweltering after the air conditioned apartment. She wanted the rental, but she didn't want the friendship of a lonely, old woman. People who lived alone too often talked non-stop when they had company. She'd set boundaries as soon as she moved in.

Ruthie poured lemonade and led her out a double door that opened onto a deck shaded by the maple tree. It was hot, but a breeze made the dry air bearable. They sat on cushioned wrought iron chairs on either side of an matching coffee table. Ruthie's feet dangled an inch above the deck's floor until she pulled a plastic stool in front of her and propped them up. "What kind of writer are you?"

Connie tasted her lemonade. It was too sweet but pleasantly cold. "I write novels. I've been on a book tour."

"I used to listen to authors read when they came through here. Don't go out at night any more. Can't stay awake. Have to do my reading in the daytime."

Connie imagined Ruthie sitting in the recliner she noticed when she first came into the house. Her chin would be drooped on her chest, her back curved, her posture an echo of Hannah's. Connie shivered despite the heat. She relaxed when Ruthie described how she spent her days.

"You need to know that I get up early in the summer. Need to get my gardening finished before the heat. I keep busy all day. I've got my bridge group and my book club at the library and my volunteer work at the church. Nice church. Methodist. Just a block away. You a church goer?" Ruthie didn't wait for Connie to answer. "I'll take you this Sunday."

Connie needed to accept an offer that might help her solve the mystery of Laura Silsbee. "I'd like that. My friend leaves tomorrow, so I'll be feeling lonely."

"Why aren't you going back to Florida? Not that Ashland isn't a nice town. 'Least it was before the tourists took over."

"Florida never felt like home. I grew up in Massachusetts."

Ruthie stared at the hills in the distance. "Still a long way from home."

Connie studied the woman who would soon be her landlady.

She was old. Like the woman in Antelope, she resented the changes in the town. "Have you always lived in Ashland?"

"Lived right in this house since I was seven years old."

Connie risked the next question. "So you were here in 1940?"

Ruthie turned her eyes away from the horizon. "Something's on your mind."

"I had an uncle. Charlie Anderson."

Ruthie's hand shook when she put her glass on the table. Her voice quivered as she said, "He died."

"I know. I wonder if his daughter might be alive. Her name would be Molly. After my grandmother."

Ruthie stayed silent for a moment. "Molly was just a baby when he died."

"Can you tell me more?" Connie waited, listening to her own heartbeat until Ruthie answered.

"He was a handsome man. Just about my age. Lived up in Green Springs and worked with the loggers."

A squirrel ran through the yard. Connie watched it climb into an oak tree as she waited for Ruthie to continue.

"He used to come to town for groceries. This was back in the twenties." Ruthie paused again. "1927. Sylvia was just born. There was a girl in town born at the same time. Laura Silsbee. They were classmates. By the time she was twelve, Laura was playing the organ in our church. She was a brilliant musician. Had plans to go east to one of the fancy music schools."

Connie urged Ruthie to continue. "Laura. Molly's mother."

"How do you know all this?"

"I found an old newspaper article with my mother's things when she died. I know what happened. I'd like to know why."

"Laura ran off with Charlie when she was just sixteen. He was twice her age. We all thought she was pregnant, but there wasn't a baby for three more years. He still came to town for groceries.

Had a nice piano brought up to Green Springs for her. It was isolated for a woman without a child up there. Mostly men doing logging. The few wives stayed home taking care of kids."

"Didn't her parents go after her?"

"I think they were glad she was gone. They never knew what to do with her. They brought the minister up to Green Springs and saw that Charlie married her. By the time the baby was born, Laura's parents were both dead. She was an odd one, Laura. Maybe one of those savants. She played like she was channeling the gods."

"What about Charlie? What was he like?"

"He never talked much. Except he sometimes whispered to himself. He'd buy groceries and drive back up to Green Springs. Never got much mail except some kind of Chinese medicine. We all thought it was for Laura."

"How do you know that?" Connie didn't correct Ruthie. She was sure the medicine was for Charlie, not Laura. From Ing Hay at Kam Wah Chung.

"Small town then. The mail clerk talked."

"What happened to Laura and Molly after Charlie died?"

"They stayed there. Living on money Laura's parents left, I suspect. Minister used to take up groceries."

"Used to? What happened?"

"He left and Molly got old enough to drive. She went to the Pinehurst School in Green Springs. Kids get bused down here after elementary school. As soon as she turned sixteen, she got herself a driver's license."

"Laura must have dropped out of school. Did Molly finish?"

"She did. Even went to the college here in town. Don't know what she does now, but she shows up in town once a month to get their groceries. Never talks to anyone."

Connie's heart sounded as loud as the squirrel's squawking in the oak tree. "Their? They're both alive?"

"I would have heard if one of them died. My age, you read the death notices first."

Connie stood to leave. "Can you tell me how to find them?"

"Someone up in Green Springs will know. Sylvia told me there's a restaurant just opened. Taken over from a bunch of hippie bikers who called the old one Uncle Tom's Roadhouse. Creepy bunch. Lots of recluses and dropouts up there. Not sure Laura and Molly'll see you."

"At least I can try." Connie stood to leave. "Can I bring you money tomorrow?"

"Just three hundred. No deposit necessary. Sit with me sometimes and I'll tell you lots of old stories. Maybe you can use them in a novel."

"I'd like that." Maybe, Connie thought. At least Ruthie remembered the present as well as the past. She started to walk toward a gate that opened to a front yard where two deer were grazing as if they were in the forest instead of one house behind Ashland's main street. "One more thing. How do I get to Green Springs?"

"Just drive out of town past Emigrant Lake and Dead Indian Road. You'll be on Route 66. It will take you right up to Green Springs. Careful, though. It's steep and curvy. No shoulder."

Dead Indian Road. She was trading southern pride in the lost cause of the Civil War for rebels who named a place after Uncle Tom and a road that sounded like it commemorated the annihilation of Indians.

On Saturday, Connie stood with Eva at the car rental shop in Medford. They transferred Eva's luggage from The Yellow Sub into the drab blue Ford Fiesta Eva would drive to San Francisco. Eva lingered before she opened the car door. "I'm going to miss you."

Connie pushed away the urge to take the keys from Eva, tell her she changed her mind, she'd drive back to Florida with the woman whose friendship was the closest she had ever known. "Call Ruthie if there's any trouble. As soon as I get a phone, I'll call you in Florida. I want to hear how Kenny and Brian are."

"I don't know why Will made me promise to find their studio in San Francisco. I only met them a couple of times."

"He's worried about them. When they left two years ago to try their luck in a bigger place more friendly to gays, they checked in regularly. They haven't returned his calls for the last six months."

Eva looked at her watch. "If I leave now, I'll get there by mid-afternoon. Time enough to find them, return the car, and check into a hotel near the airport. I'll be back in Florida before dinner tomorrow. If you have a phone that soon, call. We'll be dying to know if you find Laura and Molly."

"Don't use that word."

"Dying? Anxious, then. Be careful on that road. The Yellow Sub's been pushed to the limits this trip."

Connie touched the hood. "She's reliable. If she made the hills at the fossil beds, she'll make the Green Springs road."

They stood facing each other for a last moment. There was nothing left to say except goodbye. They hugged and opened the doors to their separate cars.

Connie followed Eva's Fiesta until it continued down I-5 and she took the exit into Ashland. She drove through the town past Dead Indian Road and Emigrant Lake. Route 66 began to climb and wind next to a steep drop-off. At each curve, she thought of Charlie leaping to his death. She reached the building that had been Uncle Tom's Roadhouse and pulled her car into the parking area in front of it. Two men were hanging up a new sign that read Green Springs Inn. She left the car running and got out to ask directions.

The man who spoke first was her age, clean-shaven, not someone who would have been one of the hippie bikers. "Nice yellow car. Made it all the way up here from Florida?"

"She's reliable," said Connie. "I'm looking for someone. Wonder if you can help."

The other man joined them. Older, maybe in his sixties. It was hard to tell behind his full beard. His gray hair was pulled back into a pony tail. "Who you lookin' for? We like our privacy up here."

Connie thought a moment about how to answer. She'd claim kinship, hope that would get her the directions she needed. "I'm looking for Molly Anderson. She's my first cousin."

The older man went back to his work. "Don't mind Benjamin," said the younger one. "The locals leave Molly and her mother alone. Benjamin's the one who checks on them."

"You're not a local?"

"Becoming one. Name's Stuart. I just opened this restaurant for folks like you who dare to drive up here."

"Road's an adventure." Connie eased into her next question. "Are there many more steep turns before I get to Molly's?"

"She's a mile further up. First place you come to after you leave this little cluster. Road's easier." Stuart cared less about privacy than Benjamin.

"Thanks." Connie got back into her car. Before she closed the door, she said, "Is there a house number?"

Stuart laughed, in an amused not a condescending way. "No one bothers with house numbers. Just look for the mailbox tied with a bungee cord. Not sure they'll like having some cousin from Florida find them."

Connie backed out of the parking area and drove slowly so she wouldn't miss the mailbox with the bungee cord. She parked just inside a dirt path that served as a driveway. Behind the trees, she saw the edge of a log cabin. She locked her car and walked to it, her pulse sounding in her ears.

Chapter 26
August 1981

The jay quieted as Connie approached a cabin constructed of rough-hewn logs. There was no yard, only the surrounding forest. The air was cool and smelled of pine. The soft notes of a piano drifted from an open window. Mozart, Connie thought, one of his sonatas. She stepped onto a stone slab in front of the door and knocked. The piano stopped and a woman appeared, her features darkened behind the screen.

"If you're from social services, we don't need you." Her voice was strong, firm but not hostile.

Connie breathed deeply to calm her own voice. "I'm Connie Lewis. My mother was Hannah Anderson. Your father's sister."

Molly opened the door and stepped outside. They stared at each other, their likeness unmistakable. The same sturdy bodies, the same rounded face, the same brown eyes alert behind glasses.

Connie held out her hand. "We're cousins."

Molly ignored the hand. "Why are you here? I don't need a cousin."

"My mother—"

"Tell her my father's dead. I never knew him. I feel no kinship."

"My mother's dead, too. Something haunted her. I'd like to

know what."

"What does it matter if they're both dead, your mother and my father?"

Connie had no answer. A need to understand the genetics she carried in her own battle with depression? A curiosity born of her life as a writer? She had traveled this far. She wanted, at least, to see the woman who might know what had propelled Charlie to run from his home in Massachusetts, to fly off a cliff in Oregon. "I want to understand. Who I am. Who we are."

"We are who we are. I like being left alone."

"Can I talk to your mother? I want to give her this." Connie reached into her pocket and opened her hand to show Molly the garnet necklace. "Your father gave this to her. It belonged to our grandmother. Molly. You're named after her."

Molly stared at the necklace, then at Connie. "She won't know you."

"She'll recognize the necklace."

"Probably not. She's dying."

Three thousand miles to uncover the secret and to be stopped at the doorstep. Connie made a quick decision. She stepped backward and made herself stumble, scraping her knee on the stone slab. She stood and watched the blood run down her skin. "Can I come inside? Wash this off?"

Molly opened the screen door. "Okay. Then be gone."

Inside was small but uncluttered. The logs of the exterior formed the interior walls, the floor was wood and uncovered. Two windows let in some light. More came from a lamp on top of an upright piano. The piano bench was covered in a flowered needlepoint. Molly pointed her to a chair in the kitchen area then disappeared through a narrow door. She came back with a washcloth, antiseptic, and a tin of Band-Aids. She remained standing while Connie cleaned off the blood.

When she finished, Connie put the antiseptic and tin of Band-Aids on the table next to a beginner piano book. "Where should I put this cloth?"

"I'll take it."

She handed the cloth to Molly. It was covered in the blood of their shared heritage. "I heard you playing before I knocked on your door. It was lovely. I'm guessing you don't use this beginner book?"

"I give lessons. People up here are used to me. I teach them and they leave me alone."

"We're cousins, but I'll leave you alone."

"As long as you promise not to come back, you can give my mother that necklace." Molly led Connie through the narrow doorway and into a bedroom that had space for only a small bureau and a double bed. Laura lay with her hands resting outside a cotton blanket. The dim light from a tiny window made it difficult for Connie to see what she looked like. She approached the bed. "I'm Connie Lewis. Charlie's niece. From Massachusetts."

Laura's eyes were closed. Connie could see the rise and fall of her breathing under the blanket. She took the garnet out of her pocket and placed it in Laura's hand. She closed Laura's cold, dry fingers around the necklace. "This should be yours. I found it with my mother's things when she died. She was Charlie's sister." She felt unburdened, as if giving Laura the necklace released her need to know anything more about her mother's wound.

Laura dropped the necklace, her hands too weak to hold onto it. She opened her eyes and whispered. "Charlie. He was a good man." She closed her eyes again.

Molly took the necklace from the bed and put it next to a photo on the bureau. With her eyes adjusted to the dim light, Connie could make out the figure of a man standing next to the fallen trunk of an enormous tree. Molly picked it up and let Connie hold it. Charlie must have been in his thirties when the photo was taken. Connie's age with Connie's muscular build, but tall and with a face that resembled Hannah's. Molly took the photo back. "That's all I know of him. You don't need to come back."

"Thank you for letting me see her." As she left the house, she thanked Molly for the antiseptic and Band-Aid. She'd have to find another way to learn what led Charlie to jump from one of the treacherous curves on the Green Springs road.

"She's gone." Ruthie was reading the newspaper on her side deck and spoke to Connie as she came down the stairs to go for a walk in Lithia Park before someone arrived to install her telephone.

"Who's gone?"

"Laura."

Connie stopped. Her walk would have to wait. She sat on the cushioned chair and reached for the newspaper. "May I see?" The paper was opened to the obituary page. What she read was a death notice, not an obituary.

Laura Silsbee Anderson died Monday, August 10 at her home in Green Springs.

Yesterday. No cause. No funeral arrangements.

Ruthie took the paper back. "Did you see her when you went up there on Saturday?"

"You knew I went to Green Springs?"

"Not hard to figure. You were gone a long time after your friend left. Your car's dusty. I told you where to find her and I knew that you were anxious about it."

Connie studied the hills on the horizon. Somewhere among them, Charlie and Laura had made a life together. No one was left to tell her what that life had been like. "I was going to tell you. I needed time. Molly let me in to see her." Connie rubbed the cut on her knee where she had removed the Band-Aid. "She was dying. Only opened her eyes for a minute. She said Charlie was a good man."

"Maybe so. None of us knew what he was like. Just that he was mysterious. Charismatic in his silence. Such a waste of talent when Laura gave up everything for a man twice her age. Her father died of leukemia. Is that what Laura had?"

"Molly didn't say. She won't see me again. Can we find out about a funeral?"

"I expect there won't be one. Probably will just bury her next to Charlie."

"Charlie's buried here?"

"In the Ashland Cemetery on East Main Street. Drive to Litwiller Funeral Home. They should be able to tell you when Laura will be buried. Too early right now. Want coffee?" Ruthie was going to be like Jane. Always ready for a cup of coffee and a visit.

"No. I need to walk."

"You should walk now. It'll be hot later."

Connie went out the gate at the side of the house. Three deer were feasting on an entanglement of ivy that grew along the boundary to the Volkswagen repair shop that posed as Ruthie's neighbor. She walked along the main street, then into the park along the stream that cooled the air around it. It was quiet. She listened for songbirds. There were none, only the occasional squawk of blue jays in the distance. She walked as far as the reservoir where she stopped to splash water on her face. Although Ashland's park was as lovely as Florida's Gulf Coast, she missed Edgewater. She missed Will. And Eva and Jane. She missed her mother. She turned back, quickening her pace to meet whoever was scheduled to hook up her phone. She'd call Will first, then Eva, then drive to the funeral home.

Connie finished her coffee and reached for the new phone on the wall next to the kitchen table. She dialed the number she memorized when she first met Will, then pulled the cord so she could sit at her table looking beyond her window at hills that were straw color in the summer drought. "Will. It's Connie."

"Eva's here. We were hoping you'd call. Did you find her?"

"Molly and her mother both." Connie told Will about how Laura was so weak she couldn't hold the garnet necklace, how Laura had been able to whisper that Charlie was a good man. She told him how they ran off when Laura was just a teenager. She choked when she said that Laura died two days after she saw her.

When she finished, Will said, "Will you be okay? How do you feel?"

Every cavity of her body felt as empty as the coffee cup on her table. She tried to explain. "A little like the guy in a story I read in college. He spends his whole life waiting for something to happen, for some beast to jump from a jungle and overwhelm him with pain or sorrow or something that makes him know that he's lived."

"Henry James. 'The Beast in the Jungle.' I don't get the connection. You've lived. You are living."

"It's the emptiness he felt when his quest was over. I've obsessed about finding Molly for over a year. I found her and Laura. Too late for any answers. So, empty. You're there, Eva's there and I'm wondering why I'm here."

"Come back."

"Right now I'm going to find out when Laura will be buried.

Find the cemetery and Charlie's grave. Say goodbye to Charlie and his wife. See Molly one more time. She looks like me."

"Don't be like the guy in James's story and throw yourself on the grave. You have more in your life than this search."

"I know. It's not all about Charlie. I promised myself a new place to start a new novel. I signed a year's lease. Ashland's nice."

"Not as nice as Florida."

Connie imagined the glint in Will's blue eyes. "Careful how you say that. Eva's a real Floridian."

"Here she is. She's bursting to talk with you."

"Connie. I miss you." Eva's voice sounded too far away. "Tell me what happened."

Connie wanted Eva to be sitting next to her in The Yellow Sub. She wanted the search, not the futile end to the search. She twirled the phone cord around her fingers as she repeated her story. Eva kept interrupting her until she reminded her that the phone minutes were adding up. "Before I hang up, tell me about Kenny and Brian."

There was a long pause before Eva said, "I only know what they both look like from Will's photos. Kenny in person looked awful. He barely talked my whole visit. When I left, Brian told me he has Kaposi's sarcoma."

Connie tightened her fingers around the cord. "What's that?"

"A kind of cancer. It starts in the blood. There are a lot of cases in San Francisco. They're beginning to call it the gay man's disease."

Connie's emptiness filled with something else. Sadness. Worry about Will and Sid. Fear of an unnamed demon. "How's Will taking it?"

"You can ask him. Give him your phone number. We'll call you next time. Put it on our dime."

Will's voice was subdued. "When Eva told me, I called them.

Brian answered. He's spending all his time caring for Kenny. Kenny barely managed to say hello. He's dying."

"I feel surrounded by death. My mother. Laura. Now your friend."

"You're alive. Remember, another of Henry James's characters said to 'live all you can; it's a mistake not to.' Someone in *The Ambassadors*. I've forgotten who."

"I'm trying." Connie gave Will her phone number. After she hung up, she drove to the funeral home to find out when Laura would be buried. She'd say goodbye and find a way to live. Oregon would be an adventure. Maybe she'd even go back to Antelope. See how an experiment in communal living could fit into a novel.

Connie saw them as she arrived at the cemetery. They stood under an oak tree, Molly and the gray bearded man from Green Springs. Benjamin. The only other people there were the undertakers. No flowers surrounded the coffin. Connie approached quietly, carrying two roses, one for Charlie and one for Laura. She wished she had brought another to give to Molly. Beyond the grave, five deer nibbled on grass kept green with sprinklers.

Molly heard her approach. She wore the kind of black skirt that never went out of fashion. It could have been decades old or brand new. The garnet showed red against her plain white blouse. Her face that looked so much like Connie's was fatigued, drained of color.

Connie placed one of the roses on the coffin. She bent to put the other rose on the rectangular slab embedded into the earth. Charles Anderson, 1899-1940. Straightening, she reached into her pocket and handed Molly a piece of paper with her address and phone number. "If you need anything, I can help."

Molly took the paper, nodded, and walked away from the grave. Before he followed her, the bearded man said, "I look out for her. You won't be needed."

Connie watched them leave the cemetery. She stood in front of the coffin until she realized the undertakers were waiting to lower it into the grave. She walked past the deer that were still feasting. At the first noise of the lowering, they bolted. She looked one last time at the grave. She remembered what Lizzie had said so many years ago about her father and her grandfather. "They're not afraid because they're together. When it's dark, they can hold hands."

On Saturday, the note arrived in the mail. *I found something from your uncle, my father. Come on Tuesday, 10:00. Molly Anderson.*

The morning air at Green Springs was cool. The blue jays that squawked on Connie's visit ten days ago were quiet, as if they were listening to the plaintive piano notes drifting out of the window. Connie recognized the piece David played for her after George died and she was realizing that their relationship was over. She never introduced him to her family. Molly would never become family either. She had only Sarah and Lizzie, three thousand miles away.

She knocked lightly on the door. Molly finished playing the refrain before she answered. She was dressed as she had been when Connie first found her, in a T-shirt and loose-fitting pants. Her face masked any emotion she was feeling. She still wore the garnet.

"Come and sit." Molly spoke in a monotone as she gestured Connie to a kitchen chair. A pile of what looked like letters lay on the table. "I found these in my mother's drawer. I never saw them before. You can read them." Molly went back to her piano, playing like a ghost that had come in from the trees.

Connie felt how the musical chords connected them. They had mothers they cared for, mothers who died and left them to find secrets in a drawer. She picked up three pieces of folded paper, none of them put into envelopes.

> *Dear Hannah,*
> *As soon as I cut you and saw the blood, the voices*
> *stopped. I had to leave. If the voices start again, I*
> *might hurt you even more. I love you, little sister.*
> *—Charlie*

A terrible sadness flowed into her with the music. Her mother died not knowing why Charlie cut her, not knowing why he left. Her hand trembled as she picked up the next letter.

> *Dear Mum,*
> *I had to leave to outrun the voices. I took some*
> *money from your jewelry box. I knew you would*
> *give it to me if I asked. I'm finding odd jobs. If you*
> *don't hear from me again, know that I'll be okay. I*
> *also took your garnet necklace. I need something to*
> *remember you.*
>
> *It's not your fault that I'm the way I am. It was*
> *the war. We soldiers believed it was an honor to die*
> *for our country. Dying would have been easier than*
> *remembering the trenches.*
> *Your loving son,*
> *Charlie*

Molly changed her piano music to the fury of Beethoven when he was deaf and hearing music in his head. Connie picked up the last letter.

> *Dear Ing Hay,*
> *My last medicine has not arrived and I'm*
> *desperate. The voices tell me to harm my baby the*
> *way I saw too many babies die in the war. When*
> *I'm around a child, the voices come.*

There was a break in the letter, as if Charlie had stopped writing. The last line read

> *Your medicine has not come. Goodbye,*
> *—Charles Anderson*

Connie left the unmailed letters on the table and went to the piano. Molly stopped playing, turned around on the piano bench, and murmured. "Now you know."

"Now we both know. Why did he never mail the letters? The one to my mother would have comforted her."

Molly looked through the window, not at Connie. "My mother rarely talked about him. But she told me that he'd start things and forget to finish them."

"So he may have simply forgotten to mail the letters?"

"Maybe. He was haunted. By the war, she told me. That's all I know. You can go now."

Connie studied Molly's face. Her eyes were as haunted as Charlie's must have been. "May I come back? Listen to you play?"

Molly turned back to the piano. "You can try next week. Same time. If you sit quietly and ask no questions, I might say yes." She began to play, this time the sad notes of something

Connie didn't recognize.

Connie went out into air that was turning hot. Charlie had been haunted by more than the war. Charlie the schizophrenic and Laura the savant had produced in Molly something she couldn't yet name.

Chapter 27
May 1982

Through the windows, Connie saw Ruthie at the kitchen sink. She opened the door without knocking.

Ruthie looked up from the spring greens she was washing. "Why so much hurry? You're still in your pajamas?"

"I made my plane reservations. I'll be gone for two weeks in July."

"You decided to go to your sister's wedding, after all. Even though you just got back from collecting your book award. What was it again?"

"Pen New England."

Ruthie dried her hands. "Are you getting pressure to move back East? Stay a New England writer?"

"It doesn't matter where I live. New England's in my bones and keeps finding its way into my novels. I'm going to go to Florida first. Decide if I should sell my condo."

Ruthie hugged Connie the way Hannah would have. "Sell it. Buy my house."

Connie looked around the kitchen and through the window into the back gardens. It would be nice to have a home of her own. "Are you ready to sell?"

"If you're ready to buy. If you leave, I won't get another tenant. I'm used to you."

"I'm going into the park. Walk off some energy. Think about what I want to do."

"When you come home, I'll fix us something nice for lunch. I hope you're flying out of Portland again."

"I am. San Francisco would be easier for Florida, but I'd rather drive north."

"I'll call my friend in Portland. She'll let you leave your car there, same as you did when you went to Boston for that award."

Connie was glad she didn't have to ask. Her fear that she'd have to mother Ruthie the way she mothered Hannah had turned into the opposite. Ruthie was a mother woman, a guide into the life of Ashland.

She lifted a piece of lettuce from the sink and climbed the stairs to the apartment she had made into a comfortable space. A table along the living room wall overflowed with her music collection and a snapshot she had framed of her and Eva at the mouth of the Columbia River. She had bought no television and only occasionally missed watching *Columbo* with her mother. The kitchen was stocked with just one jar of peanut butter. She went into the bedroom where shelves on either side of her bed were filled with books. The desk she managed to fit under the bedroom window held neat stacks of legal pads and typing paper, evidence she'd been writing. The fern paper weight David had given her rested on top of her latest chapter. She pulled off her pajamas, pulled on a T-shirt and a pair of shorts, and laced up the sneakers she'd been walking in since she left Florida.

As she descended the stairs, she promised herself new sneakers before she left on her trip back East. She headed out the gate, past two deer in the front yard, and into Lithia Park. The park's designer, John McLaren, had brought to Ashland the philosophy he developed as Superintendent of Golden Gate Park. Nothing in Lithia had a Keep off the Grass sign and most of its hundred acres was still wooded. Often she felt like she was walking in the woods of New England.

She chose the dirt path she had been traveling for nine months. She could now tell the manzanitas from the madrones, she could identify the invasive scotch broom and find where the owl made his home on the branch of an oak tree. The creek had filled so it was no longer the trickle of August. Its flow was full and loud from snow melt on the mountains. Masses of rhododendrons had begun to bloom in colors more brilliant than the pale purple of New England, reds and yellows, and mixtures with dark centers that looked like bursting fireworks. The air was cool and dry and fresh with spring. In Florida, May would be turning to the humidity of summer. Massachusetts would be welcoming bugs along with the tulips.

She bent to pick up a stick from a fallen ponderosa pine. She plucked off a needle as if it were a daisy and she were reciting "he loves me, he loves me not." One needle for the draft of the novel she had birthed in the nine months she had been writing at a desk in the Carnegie library. One for the loneliness she felt if she wrote in the college library empty of her connection to Will. One needle for Lithia Park and the water of its creek. One for the ocean that was too absent. One for Ruthie, another for Hannah. One for Molly, who spoke little but allowed her to listen to piano playing that was so much gentler than David's had been. She had begun to stop at the restaurant in Green Springs. Stuart, the man she met the first day she went to that tiny community, had convinced Benjamin to talk with her one afternoon last September. Benjamin had little to share about Charlie. He still felt guilty that Charlie managed to jump from his car. Connie didn't press him. She rarely saw him, but Stuart was becoming a friend. Maybe more than a friend.

She ran out of needles and threw the stick away. She was calling her new novel *Twenty Years a Wanderer*, basing it on Charlie, and writing for the first time from a male point of view. But Charlie had stopped wandering, had found a home with Laura. She needed to find where she belonged.

The path opened onto the reservoir where the brave swam in water that even in summer was frigid from snow melt. She bent to splash her face.

Behind her, a voice said, "Is it cold?"

She jumped and saw a man moving next to her. He wore red running shorts and a red shirt made of light-weight cotton. A mala around his neck marked him as someone on his way to or from the community in Antelope. For nearly a year, she had been reading articles about the city being built on The Big Muddy. Oregonians resented the intrusion of the group they labeled the red people. Connie often eavesdropped on conversations among people in red clothes who passed through Ashland. They praised Rachel Carson and embraced their obligation to be stewards of the earth. They talked about communal work and equality for all. A year after his death, they invoked John Lennon's message to give peace a chance. They were well-spoken with none of the coarseness of the holdovers from the days of Uncle Tom's Roadhouse in Green Springs.

Connie tried not to stare at a man whose hair was the rust color of Everett's, but whose face was empty of Everett's freckles. She splashed more water on her own face to wash away the memory of a lover she hadn't thought about since she began her weekly trips to Green Springs and her deepening friendship with Stuart. "It's frigid," she said. "It'll stay that way all summer."

The man untied a bandana that circled his head, soaked it in the water, then tied it around his head again. "Frigid, but it feels good. I parked my car at the plaza and ran up the road.

Glad I found this spot. How about you? You live here?"

Connie heard his British accent. "I do. You're from England?"

"Not any more. I've been in Oregon for most of the last six months. I flew from London to San Francisco yesterday and drove as far as Ashland. I closed my British law office so I can stay in Oregon."

"In Antelope? Building that city that's supposed to be a model for the rest of the world?"

"It's Rajneeshpuram now. I suppose you're hearing all the rumors about it being a cult."

"Some. I was in Antelope last July. It sounded interesting."

The man held out a hand still wet from the bandana. "I'm Deepak. It means 'light.'"

She shook his hand, feeling calluses that spoke of physical labor not a lawyer's office. "I'm Connie."

"Walk back to town with me and I'll tell you about Rajneeshpuram."

She hesitated before she said, "I'm walking on the path." This lawyer turned laborer was more interesting than frightening. He could give her a side of the Antelope story she wasn't getting from the newspapers.

"All the better."

They walked side by side, past an enormous water tank where teenagers carved graffiti into the lichen that covered it. Deepak told Connie how he learned about Baghwan Shree Rajneesh at a meditation workshop in London. He was going through a divorce and was tired of working with companies that raped the environment or manufactured products for consumers who didn't need them. Connie listened until the path narrowed and she moved in front of him. They stopped when they heard a flock of turkeys foraging at the edge of the path.

"I like turkeys," said Deepak.

"When I was a kid, if someone was acting stupid, we called him a turkey."

"They're not stupid and you're not a kid anymore. They have complicated vocal patterns. They flock together. Like we do in Rajneeshpuram, but without the squabbles among turkeys fighting for dominance."

Connie shrugged off his veiled criticism. Equality or not, she suspected there was plenty of vying for dominance at The Big Muddy. She started walking again. When the path widened, Deepak moved beside her, his pace prodding her to walk faster. He stopped when they came to the place where she and Eva had kissed stones and balanced them together. Connie thought of the cairns as art in motion, miniature sculptures piled differently every time she walked by.

Deepak stepped into the area and began to build a cairn. The back of his head with his red hair falling under a bandana made Connie think of Everett sitting in front of her in the canoe on the Florida swamp. She picked up three stones and found a larger rock with an almost flat surface. She placed the small stones on it. One for Everett, one for David, one for Solomon who awakened her to the communal energy of movements for social justice before he turned his capacity for love to celibacy and God. The larger rock had too much empty space so she found four more small ones. She arranged them with a mental dedication to others she had loved and lost. Her mother. Her father. George. She placed the last one in the middle and named it Charlie for the uncle whose secret had brought her to Ashland.

She stepped back onto the path where Deepak was waiting for her. "Yours looks like a graveyard," he said.

"A memorial to my past."

Deepak pointed to his sculpture, a tower of five stones, the top one shaped almost like a spire. "Mine's a monument to the future. People should move forward, not dwell on the past."

He started walking before Connie could respond to his preachiness. She wondered if the city growing in Antelope was an escape from his past more than an embrace of the future. She thought of a line from Thoreau. How many others in Antelope were escaping lives of quiet desperation?

When they reached the plaza, Deepak stopped in front of the fountains of lithia water. He bent to drink. When he straightened, he motioned to Connie to have some. Connie gestured a "no" with her hand.

"It's good for you," he said. "Heals all wounds."

"I have none that need healing."

He drank again then held out his hand. "We all have wounds. Come to Rajneeshpuram. It's the future."

Connie took his hand, feeling the calluses that marked the new direction in his life. "Maybe. Right now, I'm enjoying the present. Have a safe journey."

He squeezed her hand. "You can't change the present, but you can shape the future. Come see what we're building."

She watched him get into what she recognized as a rental car and wondered where he'd return it before he isolated himself with thousands of others.

A group of people approached the fountain. They all wore a mala and drank as if they had tasted the water before. When everyone finished, they wrapped arms around each other and walked toward the park, their voices a joyful chorus. Connie didn't believe in utopias, but she wondered what kind of city these people were embracing. She started back to her solitary apartment, promising herself an extra day to stop in Antelope before she boarded the flight she had just reserved. Seeing what Deepak called Rajneeshpuram wouldn't decide her future, but it would point her forward.

Chapter 28
July 1982

The sign into Antelope now read City of Rajneeshpuram. Connie found her way to the café where she and Eva had eaten almost a year ago. She parked The Yellow Sub, wondering if the woman who had waited on them was still there, still resisting the people she saw as invaders. Before she went inside, she read a poster in the window advertising Rajneesh International University. Half the poster showed Rajneesh in his white knitted hat, his eyes and hands mesmeric. She read the title of the courses, all offered during a variety of three month stays. Rajneesh Breath Therapy, $2500. Rajneesh Rebalancing Therapy, $7500. Rajneesh DeHypnotherapy, $5500. Expensive, all but the first one more than she gave Ruthie for rent in a year.

Inside the café, the local who had waited on her and Eva was gone. A man in a red shirt and pants was putting a pot of tea on the table in front of the Indian woman Connie remembered. Sadhana. Connie ordered a salad at the counter and accepted the woman's invitation to join her.

"I remember you." Sadhana touched her mala, showing Connie the image of Rajneesh. "You're wearing a red T-shirt. Are you coming to join us tomorrow for our first celebration of the moon? We're expecting six thousand sannyasins. Most are already here, camped out and doing what's required to help."

Connie saw that her T-shirt was wrong. Too coarsely textured, worn over shorts that were a dull black. To fit in, she needed something light and flowing like Sadhana's robe-like dress.

"I'm on my way to Portland to catch a flight to Boston."

"Rajneeshpuram isn't on your way."

"I gave myself an extra day. I've seen some of your sannyasins in Ashland. They say that everyone is welcome."

"Stay. Baghwan will arrive tomorrow. Thousands will line the street to greet him. We have a place to take in strangers like you. After tomorrow, you can decide if you want to be one with us."

Connie's salad arrived, loaded with greens and pea pods and the kind of root vegetables that could have been stored over the winter. No imported tomatoes or cucumbers. It tasted fresh and clean.

"It's good, isn't it? We need seed money. For more than vegetables. We only ask you to pay what you can."

Connie reached for her purse. "I'd like to see what you've built. See how you transformed this vast landscape into something communal."

Sadhana watched her peel off two twenty dollar bills. Connie was sure the woman wanted more, but she accepted it without comment just as a group of red-clad people entered the café. She nodded at them, then said to Connie, "My job since the beginning has been to liaison between the ranch and the town. Easier now that we're incorporated as Rajneeshpuram."

"I imagine the people of Antelope fought that."

"Of course, but the greater good won." Sadhana gestured to the sannyasins. "Groups like this have been stopping for days. I came to check that the café has enough food."

Connie took another bite of salad. "I hope so. The food is delicious."

"Things are when they're from the earth, not processed in a factory."

Sadhana went to the counter and welcomed the group. An energy surrounding them and her memory of Deepak was seductive. She forced herself to remember that she was here for research, not to become a sannyasin. She watched Sadhana speak with the group and then the man at the counter. When she came back, she said, "Your salad's been taken care of. Follow me."

Connie got into The Yellow Sub, thinking she should rename it Surya for the Buddhist goddess of light. She drove along a dirt road, through open land that looked like it couldn't support farming, never mind a self-sufficient community. In the distance, mountains rose in dry, rocky peaks. She thought of Charlie leaping off a cliff. Here in the high open air, his flight seemed more gentle than violent.

The road was easy to navigate except for a wind so strong she could feel the car vibrate. She watched her odometer click off the miles. Five, ten, at fifteen she saw the first evidence of transformation. Fields that must be irrigated were green with vegetables and red with the people working them. Clusters of A-frame houses were painted in the colors of the sun. Men and women both were working around a huge amphitheater getting it ready, she imagined, for whatever Sadhana meant by the celebration of the moon.

Sadhana parked in front of one of the A-frame houses. Connie parked beside her and followed her inside. The house could have been a motel room with only a small space for sleeping and a bathroom. "This is where we house recru—our guests. I'll send someone to show you around."

Connie sat on the bed and waited. On a small table next to

the bed was a copy of *Walden*. These people were dedicated to living close to the land, away from the sound of trains and the machinery of industry that Thoreau despised. But Thoreau kept only three chairs in his cabin. "One for solitude, two for friendship, three for society," he wrote. He would have run from the thousands here.

A young woman came into the A-frame without knocking. "I'm Ma Kavita," she said. "It means 'poem.'" Kavita handed Connie a red dress.

Connie accepted the dress. It was as light as gossamer. "Do you write?"

"No. But I feel like I'm living in a beautiful poem. Do you? Many among us are writers and artists."

"I do."

"What's your name?"

"Constance Lewis."

"You'll be able to choose a new one." Kavita assumed Connie would stay.

Connie started toward the bathroom to change.

"You can change in front of me," said Kavita. "No one is ashamed of their bodies here. We're all equal in the eyes of Rajneesh. We're all on the same journey to spiritual enlightenment."

Connie remembered the two women on the swan boats in Boston and how they were under the thrall of Sun Myung Moon. She wondered if its critics were right, that Rajneesh had built a cult, not a utopia. Communal living seemed to require the costume that Connie slipped into, self-conscious of her extra pounds. The invasion she felt under Kavita's gaze lifted when they went outside.

The dress was cool, easy to move in through the hot sun of mid-afternoon. Everywhere she saw people working. Men and women driving tractors or working among the flourishing vegetables or hanging lights on the huge amphitheater where Kavita said Rajneesh would lead them toward spiritual enlightenment.

"What does that mean to you?" asked Connie. "Spiritual enlightenment?"

"You'll feel it. A oneness with everyone around you. A oneness with the universe."

"And with Rajneesh?"

"He's our teacher. Not our god. We don't believe in the god of any religion. We're all equal. Male and female alike."

Kavita brought her into an enormous kitchen where men and women both were preparing food. "I'll leave you here. They'll give you a job. We all work in all places on The Big Muddy."

Connie searched for Deepak and his red hair, but couldn't see him. A man with a balding head and glasses who introduced himself as Swami Harshad handed her a bucket filled with washed carrots. She stood alongside a dozen other people preparing large bowls of salad that they carried to long tables inside a dining hall set up for hundreds of people. "Rajneesh serves our souls," whispered Harshad as they set down the last bowls of salad. "The soul also needs food. We kill no animals for what we eat. Everything is natural and from the earth."

The names came at her so fast and so foreign she couldn't process them. Whatever western names most once had were transformed into Abhi, Charudutta, Diksha, Durvish, Gaman, Pavitra. A couple of times, someone looked unisex and, without the Ma or Swami that preceded it, she couldn't tell if the name was for a male or female. She talked with painters and writers, lawyers and teachers, ministers and farmers, carpenters and bankers. Whatever the skills and social status of their past lives, here they all worked together. She learned that those who wore an orange bead were banned from sex until they had seen one of the community doctors. Rajneeshpuram knew how to protect itself from the disease killing gay men in San Francisco. She thought of Kenny who died. She asked if anyone knew a Deepak who had rust-red hair. No one did, though she thought the man named Pavitra might be hiding something.

After the cleanup she was assigned to, she sat on a cushion outside her A-frame, watching the sun set. Groups of people moved in and out of the amphitheater. They seemed to float into the colors of the sky that began to darken, then lighten as it filled with stars and the nearly full moon. When the air chilled her, she went inside and fell into a sleep as deep as if she had been a child.

She woke to the sounds of a community coming alive in the natural rhythm of the dawn and the daybirds. She drew the gossamer dress over her head. Outside, the stark landscape was filled with shades of red and purple as sannyasins moved toward their jobs in the fields or the kitchen or the laundry. None of them were Deepak. The silence of meditation gave way to a refrain of "He's coming." "He's coming." "He's coming."

By noon thousands of sannyasins and a fleet of Rolls Royces lined the road leading into the compound. No one questioned the opulence of the cars. They told Connie the cars were an acknowledgment that spirituality and wealth could go together. It made some sense when she remembered that the Puritans considered wealth as a reward from God. Cheers erupted when a Rolls appeared on the horizon, slowly coming toward them. As it approached, Connie saw the driver, a bearded man wearing a white robe and white knitted cap. People began calling "Master," "Baghwan," "Teacher."

As the car passed her, Rajneesh waving a blessing.

When she could no longer see the car, she followed the line of sannyasins that threaded toward the amphitheater. On the stage, Sadhana silenced the crowd by waving her hand the way Rajneesh had from his car. "Stand or sit and breathe deep into your body."

Connie sat cross-legged next to Kavita and breathed into her belly. The sound of others' deep breathing surrounded her. It seemed to fill the entire valley. Her back began to ache, but she dared not move until a group of musicians began playing drums. Kavita leaned to her. "This is the first part of the dynamic meditation. Give yourself to your body."

Children and adults began moving to the pounding rhythm of the music. Connie stood and found her own movement, surprised as the music became louder and faster. She thought meditation was quiet, but this was different. People shouted in echolaliac voices, hands reaching skyward, bodies gyrating and writhing on the ground. The energy was contagious. She gave herself to it, wanting to tell Will that she was still capable of joy.

When the music ended, people began to jump up and down in unison, releasing their breath in a chant of "hoo." In unison, they stopped and all was silent. She looked toward the stage where Rajneesh appeared. He waved his hands slowly over the crowd in another blessing. A sense of community and purpose surrounded Connie in a way she hadn't felt since her Civil Rights and anti-war marches. But there was something more in this energy. A sense that whatever she longed for lay outside of society, fulfilled her within her own body. Kavita put her arm around her, kissing her first on the neck, then on the mouth. Connie backed away. Kavita tried to pull her closer. "Don't be afraid of the body. You felt it while you danced. Ecstasy is physical. It's a way to the divine."

Connie recoiled. She walked to the edge of the crowd and stared at a pinnacle in the distance. It rose into the sky, a silent witness to the primitive celebration she had joined.

Kavita followed her. "It's okay. We believe that sex can be an avenue to enlightenment. But no one forces it on anyone."

"Not even Rajneesh? Does he bribe women to sleep with him?"

"Of course not. He's our holy man."

Connie asked what no one had been able to answer. "Do you know someone named Deepak? I met him in Ashland when he was coming here."

Kavita flinched. "Many here are called Deepak."

"This man is about forty. He was a lawyer. Has rust-red hair."

"He's gone. Some things are best left alone." Kavita left Connie standing apart from the other celebrants, trying to understand why a man so committed to this community had disappeared. She had solved the mystery of Charlie. She didn't want another one to solve.

She went into the A-frame and changed from the gossamer light dress into pants and a shirt that felt coarse after the softness of the dress. She laid the sannyasin clothing on the bed. She was surprised to find Sadhana outside waiting next to The Yellow Sub.

Sadhana blocked the driver-side door. "Why are you leaving?" The Indian lilt in her voice was both a seduction and a challenge.

"I have a plane to catch."

"Here we need no watches. We measure time by the rhythm of the days and the months. Our biggest celebration is tomorrow night with the full moon. You should stay."

Connie glanced at her watch. Ruthie's friend expected her in time for dinner. She'd barely make it. "Perhaps I'll come back." She might, but she wouldn't stay. Right now she needed a place to escape the frenzy of the dynamic meditation she had joined.

"Do. Come back with your book award money. Rajneeshpuram needs investors like you."

The invitation felt like a bribe. "How do you know about that?"

"Kavita told me your name. I asked those in our inner circle.

Swami Mandeep knows your work. He left a professorship at Berkeley to join us. The name he took means 'lamp of mind.' He's smart, creative. One of your kind. You'll like him."

Connie wondered what "one of your kind" meant. She heard the sexual assumption in "You'll like him."

"What happened to the man Deepak who left? I met him in Ashland. I liked him."

Sadhana echoed Kavita. "He wasn't a man to like. Some things are best left alone." She still blocked the car door. "You can be one of the inner circle. Make decisions. Be a disciple. Live close to Baghwan. Hear him speak."

Connie reached out her arm to move her aside. Sadhana grabbed both her hands and stared into her eyes as if she could see the valleys of depression Connie had clawed her way through when a relationship ended or a book was completed. As if this lifestyle could shield her from the grief that came with the deaths of George, her father, her mother.

Sadhana released her. She held the mala toward her and pointed to the image of Baghwan Shree Rajneesh. "Come back. The Master will be waiting."

Connie watched Sadhana disappear into the large building that seemed to be the residence of Rajneesh and his inner circle. The building isolated them from the rest of the community. She got into her car and drove past a horde of acolytes, wondering if any of them could buy their way into the inner circle. At the end of the long dirt road out of The Big Muddy, she turned into Rajneeshpuram to look one last time at the café, the school, the community church. Antelope was gone, sacrificed to the needs of a self-absorbed Master and his fleet of Rolls Royces. Utopia had invaded with a promise as empty as the empty streets.

Chapter 29

July 1982

Connie, Eva, and Jane sat in Jane's living room, the smell of bacon lingering in the air. Jane handed Connie a copy of *Homeward Bound*. "Will you sign this for me?"

"Didn't I sign a copy before I left?"

"You did. But I want this one, too." Jane ran her finger across the cover, a photo of a New England farmhouse shaded by mature maple trees. Bold black letters beneath the title announced "winner of Pen New England Award."

Connie took a pen from her. She recognized it as a Pilot fine point she and Everett both liked. Since she landed the night before, Florida had been triggering memories of Hannah at Sunset Manor and Will at The Groaning Board. Everett felt as distant as David. She opened the cover and signed under her name. "To Jane, With loving memories. Your neighbor, Connie Lewis."

Jane looked at the inscription. "'Your neighbor'? Does that mean you're coming back?"

"I don't know. Everything feels so familiar. You're my closest friends." Connie had been ticking off comparisons the way she had the day she walked through Lithia Park plucking needles off a ponderosa pine branch. Jane and Ruthie, both mother figures, the women who would bring the chicken soup if she fell ill. One couldn't replace the other and neither could replace Hannah. She studied Eva, her blond hair and petite body making her look as youthful as when Connie arrived in Florida nearly a decade ago. Molly, whose only conversation was with her music, was no replacement for Eva.

Jane reached into her pocket and handed Connie a key. "Go check your condo. It will help you decide. Your tenants are nice, but they're not like you and your mother. I'd never invite them for breakfast."

Connie held the key. It was the same one Jane had been using since Hannah and Sam bought the condo and she checked on it during the months they lived in Massachusetts. "Aren't they home?"

"They've gone to Tallahassee to visit their daughter. I told them you were coming. Want us to go with you?"

"I should go alone." Connie left Jane and Eva and went out the front door into the smell of the star jasmine she had left a year ago. The spot where she and Hannah planted impatiens on Valentine's Day was filled in with pebbles and seashells instead of flowers. She unlocked the door and stepped inside to the familiar furniture. The same kitchen table sat under the window, the dining room table was in the same place next to the counter that opened into the kitchen. Both were spotless, as if the tenants expected her to check on whether they were keeping the condo clean. One of the blankets Hannah had knitted was folded neatly on the back of the sofa. Copies of Connie's three novels lay conspicuously on the coffee table. She sat for a moment and looked at the ficus plant in the corner. The photo of her and Sarah that she hated was gone from the stereo cabinet. The room was musty from being closed up. It made her want the openness of Rajneeshpuram.

She took the afghan from the back of the sofa. It was loaded with mistakes in the pattern, but it still held together. She put it back and went into her bedroom. The bed was covered with the same spread, another of Hannah's blankets folded at its foot, the mottled red clashing against the spread's fern pattern. The desk where she had typed her novels was empty. She had transplanted the paperweight of ferns David gave her to her desk in Ashland.

She left the room that no longer felt like hers and went into Hannah's room. She had given her tenants permission to donate her mother's recliner to Goodwill. Without it, the room looked barren. The winter/summer landscape photos were replaced with original paintings of the Florida coastline. The bureau no longer held the frayed, unframed photo of Charlie or the one of George and Sarah holding Lizzie in her Christmas hat, Hannah and Sam standing next to them. She felt like the observer she had been when she took the photo, someone invisible, outside of the life around her. The bureau was filled instead with photographs of the couple who were renting the condo, their daughter, and their grandchild. Everyone looked happy.

The bedspread was different and the last blanket Hannah had knitted was gone. She opened the closet door where the spread, blanket, and photos were stacked neatly in a corner. She touched the skirt of a black cocktail dress and brought it to her face, hoping for a smell that would remind her of her mother. A foolish move. The smell was as foreign as the design. Hannah would have been lost in the size. She had disappeared from the room along with her recliner.

She closed the door to the bedroom, feeling that she was closing the Florida chapter of her life. She paused in front of the open bathroom door. The shower curtain was all chevron angles and colors. She saw again the green trees of the curtain she had thrown out when Hannah died, saw the pill box on the counter, saw her mother beneath the water, the red of the garnet reaching toward the slash made by Charlie. She closed her eyes and held onto the wall, taking the deep breaths she used in Rajneeshpuram. Behind her eyelids, an image rose of Hannah walking among the red-clad sannyasins. She opened her eyes, shook away the image, and walked through the living room, the kitchen, the front door that she locked behind her.

Eva heard her and came out of Jane's condo. "Everything okay in there? You okay?"

"It's too full of memories."

"There were good ones. Think of all those dinners we cooked, all those games we played with your mother and Jane, all those novels you typed. I can still hear the sound of tapping keys drifting through your bedroom window."

"All I could see in there was my mother's absence. Her chair is gone, her pictures have been tucked away in the closet." Connie omitted her flashback to the shower curtain and what lay behind it.

"Want to walk? Along Edgewater? Or we could drive to Clearwater Beach."

"Maybe later. I told Will I'd come over when we finished breakfast."

"Should I come with you?"

"I'd rather go alone. I'm afraid I'll get too emotional."

"Take my car." They reached Eva's condo. Eva went inside and came quickly out again. She squeezed Connie's hands when she gave her the keys. "When you come back, we'll go for that walk."

Connie got into Eva's car. It was new, a Chevy Cavalier, white to reflect the Florida sun. The familiar clutter of Eva's old Chevy Nova was gone along with its heat-generating navy color. She drove past a new shopping mall anchored with a Piggly Wiggly, The Lobster Landing with its Early Bird Special, and Jane's church that was building a new addition. Florida's Gulf Coast was thriving. Even Will's house seemed different, the green now turned into a soft yellow.

Will was at the car before she had time to open the door. He kept his arm tight around her while they walked through the house onto his back deck. When she sat on the wicker love seat, she felt that she had never left. A year hadn't changed Will. His hair was still curling around his face, a little too long above eyes as blue as the sky. The old attraction waved through her then disappeared into the comfort of their friendship.

Will broke the silence. "Tell me about your next novel. Are you making progress?"

"I am. But I wish I could get your feedback."

"You could send me chapters as you finish them."

Connie reached into a canvas bag with an image of Ashland's outdoor theater. "I've drafted all but the ending. I brought it with me. You're still my best reader."

Will took hold of the thick pile of papers. "*Twenty Years a Wanderer.* I like the title."

"It's different from my other novels. Male point of view. I named the protagonist Cliff."

"A reference to Charlie jumping from a cliff? Is it about him?"

"Just the name. And the idea of wandering."

Will set the manuscript on the deck table and relaxed into a chair opposite Connie. "I'll read it right away. Bring you comments when I come to your sister's wedding."

"I'm glad you accepted the invitation."

"Wouldn't miss the chance to have Sarah use her matchmaking skills on us."

Connie kicked off her sandals so she could feel the familiar wood of Will's deck. "She wants me settled."

"And you want to stay twenty years a wanderer?"

"I'm deciding."

"You should come back here. But I can tell from your phone calls that you like Ashland. Are you writing in the college library?"

"Not much. It makes me think of you and I get too lonely. Mostly I walk to the public library. It's a beautiful space. And quiet."

"I did some research on Southern Oregon College. It seems to be up-and-coming."

"I told you it is. Apply there. Ashland's like New England West. In New Hampshire, people 'live free or die.' In Oregon, they live freer or die."

"Don't mock my state's motto."

"I grew up in Massachusetts. We always made fun of Cow Hampshire."

Will reached across the table and gave Connie a gentle slap on her thigh.

"Seriously, Ashland is beautiful. Summer's hot, but dry. The park in fall has colors as beautiful as the White Mountains and the Berkshires. Well, almost. There are Japanese maples that turn a soft peach color."

"What about winter? I miss skiing the most."

"There's a ski area that gets over two hundred inches of snow. The evergreen branches bow down with the weight of it. Stuart calls them praying trees."

"Stuart? A reason to stay?"

"Stay where?" Sid appeared in the doorway carrying a tray of iced tea, steamed dumplings he called momos, and chutney to dip them in. His accent reminded her of Sadhana.

Connie had never asked about his Hinduism. She thought he was secular, that he'd recoil at the idea of dynamic meditation. "In Ashland. There's a college there. I want Will to apply."

Sid put the tray onto the deck table. "And what about me?"

"You could open a restaurant. Ashland needs some of this delicious Indian food."

Will pointed Sid to the vacant chair on the deck. "I'll visit. After I go to San Francisco to check on Brian."

"How is he after losing Kenny?" Connie feared the answer.

Will reached across the table again, this time taking Connie's hand. "We wanted to wait until you got here to tell you."

"He has Kaposi's sarcoma. He'll die soon," said Sid.

"Why are so many gay men dying?" Connie held Will's hand as if holding it would keep him safe.

"No one knows why," said Will. Kenny went to a clinic the city started six months ago. They helped him while he was dying. They're helping Brian now."

"At Rajneeshpuram, some of the men had to wear an orange bead along with their mala."

"Rajneeshpuram? A mala? What are you talking about? When were you in India?" Sid's voice transported Connie back to Sadhana and her offer of buying her way into the power circle of the commune.

"A mala's a kind of medallion with a picture of Rajneesh on it. Eva didn't tell you about Antelope?"

"Now I'm really lost." Sid dipped a momo into the chutney. "American animal, Indian names."

"It's stranger than the names. Last year when we were driving in Oregon, Eva and I stopped at a café. An Indian woman there told us about the city a group of people were building on more than sixty thousand acres of land outside a tiny town called Antelope. It sounded utopian. I stopped to see the progress before I got my flight in Portland."

"Nothing's utopian," said Will.

Sid drank some of his iced tea. "Why an orange bead?"

"It's for health. If someone shows symptoms of what they call the gay man's sickness, he's marked so no one will sleep with him and spread the disease."

"So there's a lot of sleeping around in this utopia?"

Connie closed her eyes for a moment, remembering the frenzy of the dynamic mediation. The ecstatic energy had been sexual. She flinched at the memory of Kavita's kiss. "The place was amazing. Everyone working. Everyone together. Everyone wearing red. There were thousands of people when Rajneesh appeared."

"I bet he called himself Master," said Sid. "I saw men like him when I visited India as a kid. They're dangerous. They manipulate people into a cult where they brainwash them so they can't leave."

Connie remembered the way Rajneesh waved his hands over the crowd. The way people called him Master. Hypnotic hands. Away from Rajneeshpuram, she saw how the community that embraced her would have stifled her. "I won't go back." She looked at her hand that was still holding Will's.

Will released it. "After I see Brian, I'll come to Ashland to see you."

Connie watched a hummingbird in the jasmine. It fluttered as much as her heart. She stood up and pulled Will and Sid to her. "Whatever's going on in San Francisco, I need you both to stay safe."

Will looked from Connie to Sid. "Sid and I are monogamous. We won't be sharing the gay man's disease."

"I don't want to lose you. I'll be back later with Eva. She doesn't want to lose you either."

Connie left them on the deck and got into Eva's car. Despite the white color, it was broiling inside. She'd return for one of Sid's dinners, but she knew she wouldn't return to live in Florida. The few minutes she spent in her mother's condo had been enough. There were no utopias but there were places where she could find more peace than in a town where the memory of her mother was as suffocating as the communal living in the high desert of Oregon.

Chapter 30

July 1982

Connie stood with Will under a maple tree away from the others attending Sarah and Andy's wedding. Some were at tables under the tent that filled her sister's side yard. Sarah and Andy moved among them, laughing and exchanging wedding toasts. Other guests had changed into shorts and were playing a raucous game of volleyball on the make-shift court next to the backyard swimming pool. Lizzie and a good-looking boy were in the pool, splashing each other and mock wrestling. The boy, Ricky, looked like his father, who was Andy's best man. Connie remembered the father from high school. Ricky had the same dark hair and eyes, the same dimple in his right cheek, the same contagious laugh. If he wasn't Lizzie's boyfriend, their flirtation said he would be soon.

"She's glowing," said Will.

"She's fourteen. I had a crush on that boy's father when I was her age. Richard. The best man today." Connie remembered how they'd sneak away from their group of friends at the town beach and kiss in the grove of trees. The romance died at the end of the summer when Richard began dating the girl who was now his wife and Connie discovered George.

"Actually, I meant Sarah. But Lizzie's glowing, too. At her age, I would have had a crush on Ricky myself."

"Is it hard going to weddings knowing you'll never marry?"

"I don't care about the piece of paper. What bothers me is that Sid can't be on my insurance policy, can't be my automatic heir. We can't file joint taxes. If we wanted to adopt a child, it would be impossible in all but a few states."

"You'd be great parents. Do you want children?"

Will picked at the bark on the tree they were standing under. "Should I ask the same of you? Do you want marriage and children."

Connie thought of Stuart and Green Springs. She'd like a relationship, but not a marriage. "I used to think I did. Not any more. My characters become my family."

"The book is wonderful. I gave you plenty of comments." Will stopped picking at the bark. "Are you going to kill Cliff?"

"I'll know when I get to the end."

"And you? Are you ready to stop wandering?"

Connie watched Lizzie in the pool. She remembered the day in Florida when Lizzie was showing off her somersaults. Even then, she knew she'd never marry. "I'd like to be closer to Lizzie, but I won't come back here. I like Ashland, the openness of the West. You wouldn't have to hide your relationship with Sid there."

"I'm not hiding it now." Will bent down and picked a dandelion that had escaped the lawnmower. He plucked off its head. "I told my parents."

Connie took the dandelion stem away from him, letting her hand linger on his. "Did they accept it?"

"They already knew. I should have listened to you years ago and told them. They're going to come to Florida in the fall to meet Sid." Will pulled Connie to him. Over his shoulder, Connie could see Lizzie watching them. He released her and described how in the end it was easy to tell his parents. "They left a copy of *The Mayor of Castro Street* on their coffee table. Not their usual reading."

"That's the book about the politician in San Francisco murdered because he was gay."

"More complicated than that, but yes. He was a city councilman advocating for gay rights. Another councilman, Dan White, murdered him and the mayor."

"Your parents probably planned the opening," said Connie.

"I didn't ask. I was just glad they gave me one. It was easier than telling you."

"I'm glad you told me before I fell in love with you."

"Love comes in many forms." Will drew her to him again, his hug intimate. He kept hold of her hands when he said, "I need to leave to catch my flight. I promise I'll visit in Ashland."

"And think about moving there."

"It's not a bad idea." He touched his finger to her lips and walked away.

Connie leaned against the tree and watched him. He stopped at the pool, bent down, and tousled Lizzie's wet hair. When he left, Lizzie gave Connie a thumbs up before she grabbed Ricky around the waist to topple him under the water. Will stopped in front of Sarah and Andy, who had their arms around each other. Under the eave above the back deck, Connie watched a mother phoebe fly to a nest where tiny beaks cried for her. She waited until Will left and walked over to Sarah and Andy.

"You should marry that man," said Sarah.

Andy took his arm away from Sarah. "I don't think he's the marrying kind."

Sarah looked from him to Connie. "What do you mean?"

Connie steered Sarah toward the house. "Never mind. Come inside a minute. I have something for you."

Andy started to follow. "Not you," said Connie. "This is between sisters."

Inside, they walked past a table filled with wedding gifts Sarah and Andy didn't need. Next to them stood the enormous arrangement of roses and lilies that had been on the altar at the church. At the end of the table Sarah's matching bridal bouquet lay in front of a photo of her and Andy in their wedding clothes. She glanced into Lizzie's bedroom where Lizzie still kept the photo of Connie and Hannah standing near her in a rope swing. They went into the guest room where Connie stayed with Eva a year ago. The only photos were framed prints of places Sarah had visited in Europe. The manuscript of *Twenty Years a Wanderer* Will had commented on lay on the dresser next to her purse. She opened the purse and pulled out the envelope with Sarah's name scrawled in George's handwriting. "I've kept this too long."

Sarah took the suicide note out of the envelope. "Wait here." She began tearing it as she walked away. Connie heard her go into the bathroom that connected to the master bedroom. She heard the toilet flush, then flush a second time.

Sarah came back into the room. She hugged Connie to her and whispered, "Thank you."

Connie felt the soft silk of Sarah's blue wedding dress, glad that her sister hadn't tried to recreate her first wedding with a white gown and long train. Sarah looked even more beautiful today than when she married George. The blue dress drew out the color of her eyes. Two thin braids woven with flowers circled blond hair that came out of a bottle but looked natural. Connie pulled away from the hug. "My gift to you. We're different, but you're still my sister."

"Have you forgiven me for marrying George? I knew you liked him."

Connie sought understanding, not forgiveness. The last year showed her that people find happiness in different places. If she had married George, she would have stayed in Freedom, perhaps have found happiness in motherhood and maybe a job teaching English in the growing school system. She held Sarah's hands. "You're beaming today. This is a good life for you."

"And you?"

"I'm in a good place now. I like Ashland. My next novel is going well. It's the right life for me." Writing was the soil that nurtured her. It was her home more than any geographical place.

Together they left the house and went into the yard. Sarah beamed in the sunlight.

Connie knelt in front of her parents' graves planting geraniums that Sarah should have planted on Memorial Day. She wondered if her sister ever came to this cemetery or the one George was buried in. She rested her forehead on the stone. It was cool, the sun warm on her back. She tamped the soil around the flowers, stood, and brushed the dirt off her knees.

Lizzie picked up the watering can they had filled at the water spigot closest to the grave. She watered slowly, the spray blossoming from the can's head onto the flowers.

Connie ran her hand along the top of the rough-cut granite, stopping at an indentation shaped like a heart. She reached into her pocket and placed a stone from Lithia Park into the indentation. She read the inscription. Samuel Mattson Lewis, March 4, 1912 – January 24, 1973. Hannah Anderson Lewis, January 20, 1914 – May 16, 1980. She saw the graves next to her parents'. The three little girls dead in a scarlet fever epidemic. Grandmother Molly, the name on her stone empty of her husband who had disappeared and her son whose grave lay three thousand miles away.

Lizzie turned the watering can upside down to let the last drips fall onto the geraniums. "I remember Granny and Grampy better than my own father. What was he like?"

"Funny. Smart. Good-looking. What matters is how much he loved you." Connie would never tell Lizzie that George returned from Vietnam so damaged he chose death over fatherhood.

Beyond a plot of older lichen-covered stones, a hole gaped where someone would soon be buried. Memories rose from the earth. George sitting across from her at a school table arguing about the lead into some story for *The Lion's Pride*. Dancing with him at his and Sarah's wedding reception, feeling the warmth of his body against hers. Holding the newborn Lizzie in his arms.

Lizzie touched the stone in the granite's indentation. "It's sad. I don't even remember Granny very well. When I'm dead, there'll be no one to remember her or Grampy or my father."

"That's why we have stories. Individuals might die, but we keep the world they lived in alive in the stories we tell."

"Tell me some about my father. Mum never talks about him."

Connie picked up the trowel and empty geranium containers. "You get the watering can. I'll tell you stories while we drive to his cemetery."

"I like this cemetery better."

"So do I."

They slowly walked to the car. Around them, trees shaded graves three centuries old. They passed a woman crouched alone in front of a new headstone. A little girl skipped from stone to stone chasing a robin. Watching, Connie knew that no matter how far she wandered, New England was her home soil. She believed it lived in Charlie even as he flew to his death. It lived in her novels. The robin flew into the branch of a maple tree to feed its young. Connie imagined a scene for another novel. No matter where she set it, what the plot, it would begin with a little girl in a cemetery chasing a robin.

Acknowledgments

If I'm asked "Are you a plotter or a pantser?" I reply that I'm a bit of both. I began writing *Leaving Freedom* with a clear idea in mind and a plan for where the plot would take Connie Lewis. I imagined her journey toward becoming a writer much like the journey of Constance Fenimore Woolson. After all, I had spent years editing the letters of this nineteenth-century writer. I knew that Woolson followed her mother to Florida and that after her mother's death she moved to Europe, never returning to the United States. In the letters, I could hear the tension between Woolson and her wealthy sister and her love for her sister's daughter. I had the outline. But I hadn't written more than a few chapters before I knew I couldn't have my Connie, like Woolson, jump to her death next to Venice's Grand Canal. I wasn't exactly writing by the seat of my pants, but my character was leading me. She needed to leave Massachusetts and Florida, both states I know well, and end up in Oregon, a state I've been discovering for the last fifteen years.

I fictionalized and renamed towns in the Massachusetts and Florida sections of the novel. Although I felt free to alter details, I kept the real names for places in Oregon and enjoyed uncovering what they would have been like in the mid-twentieth century. I discovered the town of John Day where the Chinese herbalist Ing Hay practiced. The state heritage site Kam Wah Chung contains a wealth of information on Chinese medicine.

Ruby Whalley, her son Michael, Colleen Curran, and Jean Taylor filled me with valuable historical information about the city of Ashland. A college friend from the University of New Hampshire, Betty/Surja Jessup, shared her experience with the Rajneesh community that took over the small town of Antelope, Oregon, from 1981 to 1985. I am indebted to her for a more personal view of Rajneeshpuram than I got from reading various newspaper articles and from the book *A Place Called Antelope: The Rajneesh Story* by Donna Quick (August Press, 1995). I had completed and revised the chapters that include Connie's time in Antelope and Rajneeshpuram when the documentary *Wild Wild Country* began airing on Netflix (Directors Chapman and Maclain Way, 2018). I call it serendipity and am happy to see the fraught history of Baghwan Shree Rajneesh and his followers come back into the public view.

I am indebted, as always, to the members of my Monday Mayhem writers group, Carole Beers (Pepper Kane mysteries), Michael Niemann (Valentin Vermeulen thrillers), Clive Rosengren (Eddie Collins mysteries), the late Tim Wohlforth (Jim Wolf mysteries), and Jenn Ashton (first mystery in progress). They are never afraid to tell me when I'm drifting into an academic voice. Their lively discussion of my search for a title led me, at the eleventh hour, to one we all like. Arzani Burman, now sadly deceased, gave valuable feedback on my nearly completed manuscript, particularly on what Alzheimer's would be called in 1973. I am grateful for the support of my first publisher, W&B Publications, and to Encircle Publications for reissuing *Leaving Freedom* along with its sequel, *Finding Freedom*, in 2023.

I am most grateful to my family and their unwavering support, especially my husband Ron, who lived to see this novel and the two I wrote after this one. He and my brother, Rod, gave feedback on the final draft. My sister, Sheila, and my cousin, Carolyn, remain living in Massachusetts and keep me connected to my roots. My son Michael and his children, Juliana and Ryan, have shown me parts of the world I would never have seen had they not been ex-pats during the time I wrote this book. My daughter Emily, her husband Peter, and their son Jasper have taught me how to feel at home in Ashland. All have taught me the importance of family that Connie comes to recognize.

About the Author

Sharon L. Dean grew up in Massachusetts where she was immersed in the literature of New England. She earned undergraduate and graduate degrees at the University of New Hampshire, a state she lived and taught in before moving to Oregon. Although she has given up writing scholarly books that require footnotes, she incorporates much of her academic research as background in her mysteries, and continues to write and research in the landscape she's still discovering in the Northwest.

She is also the author of the sequel to *Leaving Freedom* which is entitled *Finding Freedom*, published by Encircle Publications in June 2023. Sharon's mystery series featuring librarian and reluctant sleuth Deborah Strong includes *The Barn* (Encircle, 2020), *The Wicked Bible* (Encircle, 2021), and *Calderwood Cove* (Encircle, 2022). Her highly-acclaimed collection, *Six Old Women and Other Stories*, was published by Encircle in December of 2022. You can learn more at sharonldean.com, and follow Sharon L. Dean, Author, on Facebook, and @sharonldean3 on Instagram.